A STOLEN KISS

"Elizabeth—" Nicholas's fingers slid across her cheek to curl around the nape of her neck.

He had few inhibitions about the satisfaction of his appetites and he was no stranger to sexual passion. But his upbringing had been scrupulously correct about the differences between ladies and the women to whom a man might properly make love. He knew it was wrong to want to make love to Elizabeth, but he did— badly enough to risk everything to have her.

Nicholas didn't know if Elizabeth took a step nearer or if he pulled her to him, but they were suddenly so close it was a simple matter to tip her head so their lips would meet. She didn't pull away from him as he was afraid she might. Instead, her arms went around his neck and she melted against him.

It wasn't a chaste kiss. He could never get enough of her. Just kissing her would never— could never—be enough.

Stolen Love

Carolyn Jewel

HarperPaperbacks
A Division of HarperCollinsPublishers

This is a work of fiction. The characters, incidents, and dialogues are products of the author's imagination and are not to be construed as real. Any resemblance to actual events or persons, living or dead, is entirely coincidental.

HarperPaperbacks   *A Division of* HarperCollins*Publishers*
                    10 East 53rd Street, New York, N.Y. 10022

Copyright © 1991 by Carolyn Jewel
All rights reserved. No part of this book may be used or reproduced in any manner whatsoever without written permission of the publisher, except in the case of brief quotations embodied in critical articles and reviews. For information address HarperCollins*Publishers*,
10 East 53rd Street, New York, N.Y. 10022.

Cover illustration by Bob Berran

First printing: March 1991

Printed in the United States of America

HarperPaperbacks, HarperMonogram, and colophon are trademarks of HarperCollins*Publishers*

10 9 8 7 6 5 4 3 2

CHAPTER
1
❈

WHEN GEOFFREY VILLINES DIED IN 1836, HE LEFT BE-
hind him a twenty-two-year-old son ill prepared for anything but a life as a gentleman of
leisure. There were so many things for Nicholas
to attend to, he hardly knew how he found time
to see the family solicitor. What he learned was
no less shocking than his father's sudden death.

Very little remained of a once sizable fortune.
Money that should have been spent paying off
mortgages had instead been invested in creating
the appearance of abundant wealth. To make
matters worse, in the year or two before his
death, Mr. Villines had made several attempts
to regain his declining fortunes by dipping into
the capital of what remained and speculating
with the sums. The afternoon Nicholas spent
with the solicitor gave ample evidence that his
father's talent for business had been close to
nonexistent.

For a young man brought up to believe he

1

would never have to work for a living, Nicholas Villines was in a trying situation, to say the least.

It did not occur to him to ask for help from his family, though any one of them would have been more than happy to do so. Indeed, he was shocked when his solicitor advised him to borrow from his relatives or to leave the country for a prudent period of time. Either course was inconceivable to him. Nicholas intended to restore his ruined inheritance, no matter the personal cost. He set himself to the task with all the optimism of his twenty-two years; he resigned his memberships in clubs that cost him money, sold his horses and his carriage, gave all his servants notice (with the single exception of his valet), and moved from his spacious quarters in the Albany to two small rooms on Pycham Street. His resolve hardly wavered at all when he calculated that notwithstanding his severe reductions in expenses, he would be approaching seventy years of age before any significant amount of the interest paid on the remaining capital might be applied to his pocket rather than to mortgages and the like.

It was several weeks after his removal to Pycham Street that Nicholas sat in his room, trying to reconcile himself to the necessity of letting Mr. Chester go. His valet, who was repairing a shirtsleeve at the time, seemed oblivious of their cramped surroundings, but Nicholas was unable to believe Mr. Chester did not feel the reduction in circumstances just as keenly as he did himself. He cleared his throat, meaning to tell Mr. Chester that he was sorry, but if he wanted his wages, he had better find an employer who did not need to have his shirt-sleeves mended. What came out was, "It is a pity, Chester, that I cannot discover some way to make a few pounds without any risk."

"You might apply for a position in a bank, Mr. Villines," said Mr. Chester, never taking his eyes off the shirtsleeve.

"In a bank!" It was testimony to his present difficulties that Nicholas's first thought was that engaging in commerce on such an intimate level was not entirely out of the question. But he knew his family would not stand for it, and more important, he did not wish to be forced to explain that his father had left him in straits. If the truth were known, he felt lucky to have so far succeeded in preventing them from learning where he now lived.

"There is a great deal of money in banks," Mr. Chester added.

This was just the sort of observation Mr. Chester was prone to make and that had once been a source of great amusement to Nicholas. Mr. Chester's pronouncements were invariably accurate and, as a practical matter, generally useless.

"There certainly is," Nicholas agreed with a sigh.

"It seems to me, sir, that people are inexplicably anxious to give their money to thieves." Mr. Chester shook his head sadly.

"What has that to do with banks?" asked Nicholas.

"It is my opinion that bankers are thieves."

Nicholas began to laugh but stopped when he saw Mr. Chester's offended expression.

"I fail to see the humor in the subject," the valet said huffily.

"You are perfectly right. It is a very serious subject indeed. One should never laugh at another's livelihood."

"The difference between a thief and a banker," Mr. Chester continued, warming to his subject, "is that one may call in the aid of the police when robbed by the former. With the latter one hasn't any recourse."

Nicholas felt compelled to respond. "At least one consents to be robbed by a banker, Chester."

"If you will forgive my impertinence, Mr. Villines, I should rather be robbed by a thief than a banker! I've insurance on everything of value and wouldn't be out so much as a shilling if I were to be robbed by a thief."

"Indeed?" There ensued a silence during which Nicholas gazed thoughtfully at his servant.

"Give me an honest thief, I say, sir. There's no pretense with him. One knows where one stands with a thief."

"Mr. Chester, you've given me an idea," said Nicholas.

"You're very welcome, sir."

Nicholas's reentry into Society was gradual. He began by attending dinner parties. Then he had tea at Lady Lewesfield's, was occasionally present in his grandfather's box at the opera, and now and then took a walk in Regent's Park. The following year he was seen riding in the Park, and only a few months later he had acquired a rather dashing cabriolet. The very next year he'd hired a groom and by Christmas had purchased a large house overlooking the Park. Though he sometimes disappeared for lengthy periods (to look after some property in Derbyshire, it was said), he was much in demand at social events requiring the presence of handsome young gentlemen. Nor was it long before he had obtained a reputation for gallantry. Several broken hearts were directly attributed to the fact that Nicholas Villines preferred brunettes over blondes.

Society welcomed him back; he had absolutely sterling connections, after all. His paternal grandfather was Viscount Eversleigh, and though Nicholas's father had been the youngest of the viscount's three sons, by the start of 1840 Nicholas was third in line to the title. Lord Eversleigh's eldest son had died in 1838, leaving behind him only a son. This scion of the family honor soon found himself twenty-one years old and in control of a considerable income. Having been turned loose upon London at last, he appeared to be making the most of his freedom. It was said Henry took after his father, and there was speculation in some circles that it would be a miracle something on the level of the Second Coming if the health of Nicholas's cousin did not go into a serious and fatal decline as the result of his profligate ways. The current odds were three to one the Honorable Henry Villines would not live to see thirty and five to one his demise would occur before he had got a legitimate son.

The viscount's middle son, Russell, was second in line. Russell had no children, and he was now expected to leave his own fortune to his nephew Nicholas. Nicholas was, perhaps, the only person in all of England who paid no attention to distasteful speculations regarding whose death would make him rich, and he did not scruple to let it be known in what light he saw the matter. *His* hopes for the future, said he, were based solely on the balance shown in his bank book.

Nicholas's past hardships had taught him that in adversity one might learn a great deal about human nature. Consequently he had few friends, but the few acquaintances he did cultivate were deep ones. He was a generous man since he could now afford the luxury and a thoughtful one; he was quick to return kindness for kindness. Though it was not entirely intentional, he kept quite a bit to himself. He had little patience for fools, and it seemed to him London had more than its share of them.

There was something about Nicholas that set him apart from other wealthy young men of society. First, he was intelligent. Second, he had a great deal of presence; one always noticed when he came into a room. And third, though not precisely handsome, his features were strong, regular, and interesting—commanding, even. If not for a certain gentleness about the set of his mouth, he would surely have seemed forbidding. His eyes were a piercing and unfathomable black. He was tall, broadshouldered, and long-legged. If he had chosen to have his clothing made by someone other than Mr. Henry Poole (which he did not), he would still have looked good in them. His black hair had a hint of curl in it, and it was worn just long enough to make him seem daring, though he did not know that was the effect it had. There was a small scar on his cheek near his right ear he had once jokingly said was the result of a duel over a woman in Paris. To his chagrin, the tale was quickly repeated all over London and generally credited as true. The more he denied it, the more credence it seemed to gather, so he took to snorting derisively whenever the subject came up. He was almost completely unaware of the influence he had with women on the strength of his smile alone.

Doubtless he would have smiled more if he had known it.

Though Nicholas became passionately attached to a suitable young lady, the attachment was not quite deep enough since toward the end of 1839 she married a baronet. On the advice of Mr. Chester, Nicholas distracted himself from his admittedly mild disappointment by building a conservatory. Upon its completion he filled it with orchids and was soon thoroughly enamored of the hobby. The pastime enthralled him. He spent hours caring for the delicate flowers, and he quickly discovered he was able to concentrate his thoughts most efficiently while working in the carefully controlled environment, pruning, cutting, grafting, or cataloging his precious orchids. In the confines of his conservatory, Nicholas was utterly free to construct, test, analyze, and refine his plans for the future until he was certain they were foolproof.

CHAPTER
2
➤➤✕❅❅

Mrs. Russell Villines
Fitzroy Square, London

August 18, 1840
Breakley House
Dartford, Kent

My Dearest Winifred,

I hope this letter finds both you and Mr. Villines in good health—you are always in our thoughts and prayers. We are well here in Dartford. Mr. Willard is just over a complaint of the chest, but he is as fit as ever now, no thanks to Mrs. Wilson, who upon my soul, Winifred, spent so little time in my relief that it will be a miracle if I do not myself come down with a fever from the time I spent nursing him back to health! Amelia was never in any danger, thank the Lord! I shall tell you honestly, my dear, she has, if you will make allowances for a mother's pride, grown even more lovely since last you saw her.

I write to inform you we expect to be in London within the fortnight. My husband has found us a house to let on Tavistock Square. It is not far from you, so we shall be able to see each other quite often, I think. Would you be kind enough to send us your recommendations about servants etcetera? It would be a comfort to know they came from so reliable a source. We are so very much looking forward to seeing you again!

Beth has just now seen that I am writing to you and has given me strict instructions to tell you good evening (it is evening as I write), and I am also to tell you she wishes to hear you are well. She is home from school now, and Mr. Willard insists on bringing her to London with Amelia. Your "dear little Elizabeth," as you persist in calling her, is, I fear, somewhat awkward. However, it is not *absolutely* impossible to think London Society may cure her of some part of it.

We have a new curate here in Dartford, and I daresay he might do very well for Beth; he is not yet 50 years, or so I imagine. But, alas, this past Sunday I happened to perceive he looked quite often in the direction of our seats. No doubt he has his heart set on Amelia, but *she* cannot marry a curate! Someone more noble than he awaits my Amelia. Dearest Winifred, if you know of some clerk, a gentleman, of course, of your acquaintance who would do for Beth, might not the two of us contrive for them to meet? It would be a good thing if she were to find a husband. She has no fortune from her father, the poor thing, though I do not think my husband would let her go with nothing—he loves her too dearly for that.

Just as soon as we arrive and are settled, my dear Winifred, we shall call on you. I long to see you again! I remain—

Your Greatest Friend,
Mrs. Havoc Willard, and
Your own Mary

CHAPTER
3
※※※

"Mama!" The boy tugged on his mother's skirt. He was six years old, with a pinched expression and eyes that seemed unnaturally large. He was more than a trifle dirty, but his shabby clothes were neat. He wore trousers made from an old coat that had once belonged to his father. "Mama!"

"What is it, Johnny? I'm trying to get your sister settled!" She squinted down at the boy and with her free hand reached to wipe at a smudge of dirt on his face. "Really, can't you even try to keep clean?" she asked, sounding as though she knew he could not.

"Here." Johnny thrust something into her hand and retreated to the far side of the room to stare into the empty fireplace.

She looked at the paper only briefly before letting it fall to the table. Another bill she could not afford to pay was the least of her worries.

The infant in her arms coughed, a soft hacking sound that brought a crease to her forehead.

"Mama?" Johnny turned from his position at the fireplace to look at his mother.

"What is it?" She blinked eyes red from long evenings spent bending over the piecework that earned her three shillings an item.

"The man said give it to you and tell you it's not no bill."

The woman looked at the packet before reaching for it. She could read just well enough to recognize her name written on the outside. Her first thought was it must be from her husband. She had not seen him since shortly after telling him of the impending birth of the child she now held in one arm. Judging by the quality of the paper, he'd done well for himself. It would be heaven to be able to afford such paper as this! She rose, tucking it into a pocket of her skirt, and put the baby down on the bed. The door was always shut against the noise and stench of St. Giles, but now she opened it, leaning back to keep it from closing. She took the letter from her pocket and tore the paper, standing at a peculiar angle in order to see in what light managed to penetrate the alley.

"Johnny!" she gasped. She clutched five crisp one-hundred-pound notes in her reddened hands. "Where did you get this? Who gave this to you?"

"I told you, Mama. A gentleman gave it to me. He said, 'Are you Mrs. Dwight's boy?' and

I said, 'Yes, sir, I am, sir,' and he said, 'Then give this to your mother, it's not no bill.' And I did." He bit his lower lip, anxiously watching her rapidly blinking eyes as she stared at her hands.

She shut the door and sat down on the chair. "Come here, Johnny." She held out her arms, and when he came to her, she gave a hiccuping sob.

"Mama, don't cry."

Mrs. Dwight wiped her eyes and carefully re-wrapped the letter and money before putting it back into the pocket of her skirt. "Come with me." She put a careworn shawl around her shoulders, picked up the infant, and waited for her son to take her hand before going out into the narrow alleys of St. Giles. She walked rapidly, keeping her eyes fixed on the ground until she reached the police station on George Street. She stood outside for several uncertain moments before finally starting up the stairs.

"May I help you?" The words were kind, but the voice was not.

"I don't know, sir." She clutched her infant.

"Have you come to report a crime, then?"

"I don't know, sir."

"I suggest you come back when you're certain," the officer said.

"Please, sir, is there somewhere I can show you something?"

The officer's eyes narrowed. "And what might that be?"

Mrs. Dwight took out the packet and let go

of Johnny's hand long enough to extract the letter. "This." She held it out. "I think it's from my husband, and I need to know if I can keep it." She waited until he looked up from the page. "There was money with it," she said, "but if it was stolen, I want no part of it!"

"How much money?" He regarded her intently.

"A fortune, sir," the woman whispered.

The officer looked at her, the child in her arms, the boy by her side shifting on nervous feet. "When did you last see your husband?"

"Last was over a year ago, and not a word since."

He shook his head. "Ma'am, this isn't from your husband." His fingers smoothed the expensive paper. "The letter says you are to keep the money, spend it however you like."

She took the paper back. "Who? Who is it from?" she asked.

"He wishes to remain anonymous, ma'am. But if you want my advice, you take that money and move as far away from St. Giles as you can get."

CHAPTER
4
→≫≫⊁⊀←

"Bon soir, Monsieur Villines!" The clerk at the Hôtel des Fleurs smiled as Nicholas approached the desk.

"Bon soir, Jean-Marc. Comment vas-tu ce soir?" Nicholas's French was flawless, and that, combined with his tendency to overtip, made him Jean-Marc's favorite Englishman.

"Ça va bien," he said, handing over the key to Nicholas's suite along with a letter that had arrived earlier in the day. Jean-Marc had arranged to work past his usual time in order to deliver the letter personally. Mr. Villines tipped extra when he had a letter from this woman. He was not disappointed: five francs this time.

The first thing Nicholas did when he reached his rooms and had given Mr. Chester his coat was sit down and read the letter. It had taken nearly six weeks to reach him. He'd been traveling for almost that long, and the letter had been sent first to Rome, then Naples and Pompeii before finally arriving in Paris. He smiled while he read, then sat back and read the letter again. "Elizabeth is in London," he said, taking the glass of brandy from the salver Mr. Chester presented to him.

"With Mrs. Villines, sir?" asked Mr. Chester, meaning Nicholas's aunt Winifred.

"No. The Willards are staying in London for the season, it seems."

The friendship between the Willards and the Villineses was long-standing, Mary Willard and Winifred Villines having gone to school together. The Willards had only one child, Amelia, who had been an immensely pretty girl the last time Nicholas had seen her some three or four years ago. No doubt the Willards were in London to find her a husband. Elizabeth Willard was their niece. Though her father was alive, he'd sent her off to live with his brother soon after she was born and had, so far as anyone knew, made no effort to see her since.

Though Nicholas was almost seven years older than Elizabeth, the difference in their ages had not prevented them from becoming friends. When he first met the Willards the year after his mother's death, he and Elizabeth had been constant companions during the summers and holidays the families spent together. He had a special fondness for Elizabeth. She was fearless (unlike her cousin) and clever (very unlike her cousin), hardly like a girl at all, as it seemed to him then. It was flattering how she adored him, and even when he was too old to play games with her, he would still take her on his knee to tell her stories and to do the magic tricks she begged him to perform for her. Mrs. Willard had discouraged Elizabeth's tomboyish streak while Nicholas had done his best to encourage it because he could not bear to think of her simpering about like Amelia.

When he moved to Cambridge to attend university, he continued his subversion of her via the post. He had become committed to saving Elizabeth from her aunt after he took her to an afternoon concert for her thirteenth birthday. The orchestra had performed a selection of Haydn and van Beethoven. Elizabeth had sat very quietly through the Haydn, never moving her gloved hands from her lap. The van Beethoven was last, and it touched her as the Haydn had not. He had known it would because he'd felt the same way the first time he'd heard it. She had grasped his hand and not let go until the last movement was over. That afternoon had convinced him Elizabeth was different. The two of them were alike, he thought, a little apart, a little lonely, perhaps. It was comforting to think there was at least one other person even a little like him.

Although his letters to her never mentioned his difficulties after the death of his father, not long after his move to Pycham Street he'd received a letter from her enclosing a five-pound note—more than half her allowance for the year, he later found out. Her letter did not explain the money; there was no need to, so much between them went unspoken. And, damn it all, it had come in handy.

Now Nicholas wondered if she had changed much since the last time he'd seen her. Elizabeth was now twenty—he had sent her an edition of Voltaire's letters for her birthday this past May—but he would always think of her as the thirteen-year-old he had introduced to van Beethoven.

Nicholas read the letter a third time before folding it carefully and placing it in an inside pocket of his waistcoat.

"We will be returning to London on Friday, Chester," he said.

CHAPTER
5
❯❯❳❴❴

AT FORTY-NINE HAVOC WILLARD WAS STILL A HANDsome man. His brown hair was just beginning to go silver at the temples, and in his gray eyes was reflected the quiet demeanor that had so often caused his business partners to have confidence in schemes that might not have succeeded had they been attempted by another man. He was the middle son of eleven children and one of only two boys to survive into adulthood. Being the eldest son, Havoc inherited his father's business, which he had turned into one of the richest, if not strictly the largest, trading houses in London. Havoc was a lucky man, and he was wise enough to appreciate the fact.

At present he was waiting for his wife, daughter, and niece to arrive from Dartford. He firmly believed that London was the place to bring one's daughter to get her married. Not that he worried a great deal about her making a good marriage. It was his niece who worried him. Havoc sometimes thought she was more like a daughter to him than his own. Elizabeth tended to be a little too solemn; even as a child she had been grave, but she had a quick mind and sound judgment. Mrs. Willard called her stubborn, and though Havoc had to agree, he admired her for it. Stubborn she was, but it was a subdued obstinacy, rarely seen by strangers, and disconcerting to those who expected a shy young girl to be easily led. She was also thoughtful and kind, which was a surprise to no one because it was in keeping with her looks.

In the interest of fairness, Havoc had sent both girls away to school when they were sixteen despite his private conviction that Elizabeth was much too intelligent for a girl's school. Now they were back and ready to be found husbands. He was not sure Miss Langford's School had benefited either of them. Elizabeth's mind was already superior and not in much need of improvement, and Amelia simply did not care to know anything much over what might be necessary to attract a man. Amelia, who had been beautiful her whole life, now had a taste for ruinously expensive gowns, while Elizabeth, who had gone through a painfully long awkward stage, was as unassuming and artless as ever.

The contrast between the two girls could not be greater. Amelia was light-hearted, always smiling and laughing at the simplest of jokes, if a man told them. She played the piano with skill and feeling, sang with a pure voice that delighted the ear, and she could read French with an impeccable accent. She was spoiled, of course, but it was a part of her charm. One would be hard-pressed not to think Amelia deserved to be spoiled. Amelia could easily fascinate a man, a good deal of the reason for it being her unshakable belief that she was fascinating. With such beauty as was hers, and a fortune to be had from her father, there was no doubt that she would marry well.

Elizabeth did not have the sublime attraction of a fortune. Havoc prayed that in all of London there would be at least one man capable of seeing his niece for the prize she was. To that man he would gladly give a fortune—if that was what it took—to secure the match. In his most private moments Havoc wondered if he did not love Elizabeth better than Amelia. The suspicion that it was true tortured him, and he had always indulged Amelia's many whims to atone for it.

The sound of a carriage outside interrupted Havoc's thoughts, and soon the unmistakable sound of Amelia's laughter could be heard. He sighed, put out his cigar, and rose to his feet when he heard Mr. Poyne, the butler, pulling open the front door.

"Good afternoon, Father," Amelia Willard said a few minutes later as she glided into the room in her characteristically regal fashion. She stopped just short of Havoc to take off her hat and survey the room. The top of her perfectly coiffed head was barely level with the middle of his chest.

Every time Havoc looked at Amelia, he was struck by how much she resembled his wife. Mary Willard had been an acknowledged beauty in her day, and their daughter had the same delicate looks. She was nineteen years old, with a plump but well-proportioned figure, jet black hair, startlingly blue eyes in a heart-shaped face, and a perfect, pink-tinted complexion.

"Why, this is simply too lovely!" She faced her father again. Not one bow on her dress looked the slightest bit affected by the journey to London. "Isn't this room lovely, Beth?" Her smile revealed two dimples in either cheek.

Elizabeth was just coming in as Amelia spoke. Taking off her hat, she gazed at their surroundings. Her simple blue dress and plainly braided hair would have instantly told even a stranger that she was a schoolgirl new to London. She pushed a lock of chestnut hair from her face and then stooped to pick up her hat when it dropped to the floor. She was taller than Amelia, and her slender figure added to the impression of height. Elizabeth Willard was not the sort of woman who immediately struck one as beautiful. She was certainly not beautiful in the same way her cousin Amelia was, but still there was something about her that eventually made a man wonder how it was that he had not noticed her sooner.

"Uncle Havoc, you've been smoking one of those vile cigars!" Her hat fell to the floor again as she stepped into Havoc's outstretched arms. "The house couldn't be lovelier," she said, looking up into eyes that were the same quiet gray as her own.

Havoc briefly rested his chin on Elizabeth's head. "Welcome to London." He released her to ask, "Where's your aunt? You didn't leave her at the station, did you?"

"Oh, Father!" Amelia said. "Don't be silly! She's making sure the servants don't mix up our trunks."

"There you are, Mr. Willard!" Mrs. Willard stepped into the room after Mr. Poyne and his wife, the housekeeper. "What a lovely house you've found us!" The silk of her skirts rustled as she crossed the room to her husband's side, where she put a hand on his arm. Her hair was lightly streaked with gray, but she stood as straight as Amelia. She was still a striking woman. "Please show us the house, Mr. Willard."

After he had left his wife to meet the servants and had shown Amelia to her room, Havoc took Elizabeth's arm to guide her to the room he had reserved specially for her. It was not as large as Amelia's and perhaps not as conveniently situated, being located at the very end of the hall, but he had reason to believe Elizabeth would prefer this one. He opened the door and waited for his niece to enter. The walls of the L-shaped room were covered with a green striped paper, and on the floor were thick wool rugs from one of Havoc's London warehouses. The bed, a bulky, overcarved mahogany, was in the section farthest from the door, immediately around the corner and thus hidden from view upon first stepping inside.

"I expect you to have the garden looking worthy of the name, Elizabeth," he said, leading her to one of the windows overlooking the sizable gardens at the back of the house.

"You knew I'd love to have this room, didn't you?" Unlike Amelia, Elizabeth did not have dimples, but her smile at Havoc was becoming all the same.

"I had an idea," he said. "While you were away at school we sorely missed your touch with the garden at Breakley House. The roses just weren't the same while you were gone."

She threw her arms around him. "I must be the luckiest girl in the world to have an uncle such as you!"

"Well, now, Elizabeth, I daresay you are."

When Havoc was gone, Elizabeth went back to her place at the window. A wrinkle appeared on her forehead, and she sighed. Just before they left Dartford for London Mary Willard had taken Elizabeth aside and told her that as she had no fortune and no marriage settlement to speak of, she was likely to find that her experiences of London Society would be markedly different from Amelia's.

"Amelia is a beauty," her aunt Mary had said, "and she will have her pick of the gentlemen who, you may rely on it, will surround her when we are in London. It isn't likely you will receive many offers, Beth, and you would be foolish indeed to refuse one honorably offered." Mrs. Willard had then warned her that if she found a gentleman was paying her particular attention, it was important to understand marriage might not be uppermost in his mind. Men, she had said in an ominous tone, would not take much serious interest in a poor relation.

As Mrs. Willard had known she would, Elizabeth took the advice to heart. Though she had once or twice looked in the mirror and thought it might be possible for a man to think her pretty, she now knew how ridiculous such thoughts were. Never had it occurred to her that her fortune was more important. Her aunt, whom she had no reason to doubt on the subject, had as much as told her no gentleman would be interested in her. She suddenly had a whole new set of worries; in the unlikely event that a gentleman did notice her, how was she to know if his interest was an honorable one or a dishonorable one? The more she thought about it, the more inclined she was to think it was for the best she was not beautiful like Amelia. She had once looked forward to coming to London, but now she was not so sure it would be the adventure she had imagined.

Elizabeth continued to stare out the window. Would Nicholas fall in love with Amelia? she wondered.

CHAPTER
6
>≍×≍<

RUSSELL AND WINIFRED VILLINES LIVED ON FITZROY Square in a gray building surrounded by an iron fence separating the house from the walkway. The gate was identical with the one at the house the Willards were letting on Tavistock Square, except the brass spikes of the Villineses' gate looked as though someone polished them on a regular basis.

"Beth! Do come along!" Mrs. Willard's impatient command interrupted Elizabeth's examination of the gleaming brass.

"I'm sorry, Aunt Mary."

The Villineses' butler opened the door just as she reached the steps.

"Mr. and Mrs. Villines are in the drawing room," the butler said when Mrs. Willard presented her card. "If you will be so kind . . ." Obediently they followed him down the hall and waited while he threw open the doors to the room.

When the Willards were announced, Mrs. Villines put down the book she had been reading and rose to greet them. She was a stately woman of about forty-five who wore only two pieces of jewelry; her wedding ring and a small cameo pinned to the collar of her blue crepe dress. Everyone waited while Mrs. Villines and Mrs. Willard embraced and exclaimed that the other looked even younger than the last time they'd seen each other. Finally Mrs. Villines stepped back and offered her hand to Mr. Willard.

"You must sit down, all of you," she said when her husband had also greeted the Willards. "But first let me look at you, my dear little Elizabeth!" She took both of Elizabeth's hands in hers and, cocking her head, assumed a critical expression. "I see I shall have to stop calling you 'little'!" She smiled when Elizabeth blushed. "Now, you must sit next to me. And you, Amelia," Mrs. Villines said when she had established Elizabeth in the chair next to hers. "Why, you are the very image of your mother when she was your age!"

Mr. Villines had retaken his seat and was sitting with his legs crossed at the ankle, one hand resting lightly on the arm of his chair, smiling at Amelia while she thanked his wife. He held a cup and saucer in his other hand, lifting his arm occasionally to take a sip of tea. His dark hair was almost completely gray now, and though Elizabeth tried to remember what he had been like the last time she had seen him, she could only recall that he had, as now, seemed stern.

She accepted a cup of tea and looked around, thinking the room had changed very little. The furniture was still dark and heavy looking, all of it ornately carved and uncomfortable to sit on. Red-and-cream India rugs of varying sizes still covered the floor, and the wallpaper was still the same red-and-gray-flowered pattern. The curtains, a deep red, were drawn back from the windows to take advantage of the view of the gardens.

One thing was different, she noticed: the portrait hanging over the fireplace. The painting of Mrs. Villines's father had been replaced by another portrait. Every feature was almost exactly as Elizabeth remembered. Nicholas was seated at a desk, turned half to one side to face the painter. He was leaning back, one hand holding a book open on the desk, the other dangling over the side of his chair. He was clean-shaven, with his black hair curling over his forehead and down to the collar of his coat. The portraitist had captured in his subject's smile the same look of amusement Elizabeth had seen on Mr. Villines's face just a few moments ago. The eyes were extremely dark, but they were sober, cold even; not so much as a trace of amusement was in them. It surprised her because she remembered how he loved to tease her.

"That is Nicholas, is it not?" she asked suddenly, blushing when she realized her abrupt question had interrupted something Amelia was saying.

"Yes, it is," answered Mr. Villines, looking up at the portrait of his nephew. Everyone's attention was now focused on the painting.

"He's become very handsome," Elizabeth said after a moment. She had always thought so.

"He certainly is handsome," Amelia agreed.

"Nicholas is a most remarkable young man," said Mr. Villines. "We were quite surprised to learn the extent of the debts my unfortunate brother left him. He did not breathe a word of it until there was no need for anyone to help him."

"Surely he didn't go bankrupt?" Havoc exclaimed.

"It's a wonder he did not," Mr. Villines replied. "No, Nicholas paid off the debts without once asking for help."

Havoc made a small noise of approval and sat back in his chair.

Mr. Villines glanced mischievously at the two girls. "I'll wager you think him even handsomer than this painting when you meet him."

"Is he in London?" asked Mrs. Willard, looking from the portrait to Amelia and then back.

"No, he's in Europe at the moment," Mrs. Villines answered. "He's fond of traveling, so he does quite frequently, now that he can af-

31

ford to." Mrs. Villines looked from the portrait of her nephew to Elizabeth.

"He deserves to enjoy the fruits of his labors," said Havoc.

"How simply wonderful that he is able to indulge his taste for travel," said Amelia.

Mrs. Villines glanced at Amelia. "We expect him back within a fortnight or so. But it won't do to have you pine away in the meantime. We are having guests for supper next Wednesday, and Mr. Villines and I shall be very unhappy if you do not come. Sir Jaspar Charles and his wife have just come back from a tour of Europe, and I'm sure he will have a great many tales. Sir Jaspar is a great one for tales, is he not, Russell?"

"Oh, indeed he is!"

Elizabeth continued to look at the painting even after the subject was changed. The Nicholas in the portrait was older, his expression more reserved, wiser perhaps. It should be no surprise, she thought, they had both changed since they'd last seen each other. In two weeks she would find out how much he'd changed. And surely Nicholas would see that his childhood friend had also grown up.

CHAPTER
7
❖❖❖

"BUT I DON'T NEED A NEW GOWN, UNCLE HAVOC!"
Elizabeth said when the subject of what the
girls would wear to their engagement at the Villineses came up. Elizabeth's frown disappeared
magically. "No one in London has seen my
clothes, so my green silk will seem new to
them."

"I won't have you seen in last year's fash-
ions," cried Mr. Willard. "I'll not have people
thinking I can't afford to properly dress my
family."

Even Mrs. Willard had to admit the justice
of her husband's sentiment. "We can take her
to Amelia's dressmaker, I suppose," she said
with only a little reluctance.

"I suppose we can, Mary!"

Because her aunt insisted she pay all her expenses from her allowance, Elizabeth protested.
"Uncle Havoc, I could never afford her dress-

maker. If Amelia will help me choose a pattern, all I really need is the fabric."

"Pshaw, Elizabeth! There isn't time to make a gown."

"Of course there is."

"And will you wear the same gown every time you go out?" Mr. Willard demanded.

"I think the clothes I already have are quite suitable, don't you agree, Aunt Mary?"

Havoc knew he was defeated when Elizabeth resorted to asking his wife's opinion. He sighed; maybe she knew what she was doing. "Very well, then. Disgrace me if you must."

"Beth has very sensible taste, Mr. Willard. I'm sure she won't disgrace us," said Mrs. Willard. "Especially with Amelia to help her."

"Amelia, do you hear?"

"Yes, Father."

That afternoon Elizabeth, Amelia, and Mrs. Willard took the carriage to the Regent Street dressmaker Amelia patronized, where they were soon flipping through pattern books. Elizabeth, seeing Amelia was occupied with an examination of notions, passed over several patterns without even a second glance before finding the one she had in mind. It was the sort of dress she dreamed of wearing; shown sketched from the front and back, it had a rounded collar folded over itself with a generous amount of lace trimming the edge. Just low enough to be daring, she thought, without quite seeming scandalous, though it was one of her secret desires to one day wear a scandalous dress. The sleeves of this gown were wide and also lace-trimmed, and the skirt, with six flounces at the bottom, would be nothing short of perfect with the addition of bows. Such a dress would surely turn a few heads. She was already settling on the color when she showed it to her aunt.

Mrs. Willard gazed at it and shook her head. "The fabric could be purchased for a decent sum, but the trimming!" She clicked her tongue. "Do you think you can afford the extra cost of the flounces? And look here." She pointed to the neckline. "Why, it would take weeks just to sew the collar."

It was a moment before Elizabeth could bring herself to answer. "I suppose so, Aunt Mary," she said, turning the page at last. The next dress she showed her aunt had a simpler collar and fewer flounces by half, but it was disapproved of because the shape of the sleeves was expressly designed to waste fabric, surely not something Elizabeth could afford to do. Her next choice was disapproved of on similar grounds.

"Now, this one, Beth. This will suit you." Mrs. Willard put a hand on the page and turned back to a pattern Elizabeth had passed over because it was so plain.

"I don't think so, Aunt Mary." She wanted a dress with flounces and bows, and this one had none. "It isn't even an evening gown."

"Nonsense! It's perfectly suitable. And I saw the most wonderful silk when we came in. It wasn't more than three or four shillings, I'm sure."

"Yes, Aunt Mary," Elizabeth answered dutifully.

So it was that the dress Elizabeth wore to the Villineses was a high-collared gold silk with a plain skirt and bodice without any of the lace, pleats, or braid trim she would have liked. She had saved enough of the dull gold fabric to fashion two tiny bows which she affixed at the sleeves, but except for the ribbon she had carefully sewn around the collar, the dress was exclusive of decoration.

As usual, that evening Mrs. Willard insisted only Elizabeth could help her dress. By the time she was done helping her aunt, she had less than an hour to get ready herself. A young woman had been hired as ladies' maid to the two girls, but it was clear that Miss Lincoln's first duty was to Amelia. When she finally came in, Elizabeth had already put on her dress, and all Miss Lincoln had to do was fasten the last few buttons while Elizabeth secured her hair with a comb. She fastened around her neck a gold chain that had been a birthday present from Mr. Willard. Her mother's wedding ring hung from the chain, and she fingered it as she stood in front of the mirror looking at her reflection. She wished there had been enough of the gold silk left to make a bow for her hair.

"Hurry, Miss Elizabeth," said Miss Lincoln, handing her a pair of gloves to put on. "It's past eight o'clock."

Elizabeth sighed when she saw Amelia's dress, a blue silk that perfectly matched her eyes and was decorated with more than enough bows to have kept several women sewing for a week. When she stood next to her cousin while they waited for the carriage that would take them to Fitzroy Square, Elizabeth sadly thought that she looked all of sixteen years old, and so plain she might as well be wearing a sign that read "Poor Relation."

The Willards were the last to arrive at Fitzroy Square. They followed the butler into the drawing room, where Mr. Villines rose to introduce them to the other guests. Elizabeth curtsied to the gentlemen (who merely glanced at her and immediately returned their attention to Amelia), nodded to the ladies, and felt decidedly insignificant. The elegant attire of the other women made her wish even more acutely that she had been able to manage a bow for her hair. She took a seat near Mrs. Villines and doubted anyone would even notice her.

There were ten guests besides the Willards. There was Mr. R. Robert Smithwayne, who, like a true gentleman, did nothing in particular, and his wife, Annabelle, who devoted her energies to the Smithwayne Foundation for Abandoned Children. The Smithwaynes' two children were Frederick, twenty-three years old and the image of his father, and Jane, and Elizabeth's age and very pretty. The guest of honor was Sir Jaspar Charles, Baronet. He was in his late thirties, and what little remained of his red hair was mostly directly under his nose. His wife, Lady Charles, was wearing red silk and a necklace of blood red rubies to match. Her dark hair was worn in a sweep of curls held up by combs set with rubies to match the necklace. She was still beautiful, and Elizabeth was certain that, had she been so inclined, she might have distracted everyone's attention from Amelia.

The other two guests were unmarried gentlemen. Mr. Beaufort Latchley was a wealthy banker of some thirty-five years who had just come out of mourning for his wife. His hair was a light brown, his eyes about the same color. He smiled often, but the fascinating thing was that he utterly failed to seem cheerful. Several times he leaned back to listen to the conversation with an expression of contempt of his sharp features, particularly when the other unmarried male guest was speaking.

The Honorable Ripton Rutherford was twenty-five, and he had first provoked Mr. Latchley's scorn just after the Willards' arrival when he commented it had taken his valet nearly a hour to tie his cravat to his satisfaction. In spite of his professed difficulty, Ripton was the picture of sartorial perfection. It had to be allowed he was quite the best dressed man present and no doubt the handsomest one. His blond hair, which he had in great abundance, was brushed away from his forehead, and he was the possessor of the bluest eyes Elizabeth had ever seen in anyone besides her cousin. Ripton Rutherford was Nicholas's best friend, and on that account alone Elizabeth was prepared to like him.

When the meal was announced, it was Frederick Smithwayne who took Elizabeth to the table. "Goodness, you're tall!" he exclaimed when she stood beside him, eyes level with the top of his head.

"I'm sorry." She shrugged. Her aunt's prophecy was coming painfully true.

"Nothing to be sorry for. It isn't your fault. Mr. Rutherford"—Frederick nodded at him— "ought to have been the one to take you in. He's tall enough for you."

Elizabeth was not surprised when Frederick turned his attention to Amelia after he had shown her safely to her seat. She sighed, looked down at the table, and was pleasantly surprised to learn the dreadful years spent at Miss Langford's School had at last proven not to have been a complete waste of time. She knew what to do with every utensil in front of her.

Sir Jaspar sat to Mr. Villines's left, and as the first course was brought in Mr. Villines signaled to the butler that the dishes should first be presented to Sir Jaspar, who seemed to relish slowly uncovering them as each arrived. He took a small bite of each, chewed reflectively, and, since the Villineses's cook was French, nodded to indicate he should be given a larger portion. By the time the food was on Elizabeth's plate, it was considerably cooler than it had been when Sir Jasper sampled it. Not until one of the soup courses did the baronet finally begin to talk about something besides the food.

"Lady Charles and I have just returned from a tour of Europe," he said. "And I must say, I am glad to be back in England."

To hear him tell it, the whole of the Continent was nothing but inadequate service and dunderheads who would not understand the queen's English.

After all of Mrs. Willard's exclamations about the consequences of meeting someone with a title, the baronet was a decided disappointment. Even considering the man in the best possible light, Elizabeth was convinced boredom was the most likely consequence of meeting Sir Jaspar Charles. It was hard to understand why an elegant woman like Lady Charles had married him.

Lady Charles smiled indulgently when Sir Jaspar began telling of their adventure during a tour of a winery somewhere in France. He had very nearly been attacked by a rat the size of which was beyond description in mixed company. "Put me off French wines for nearly a week!" he marveled.

It was, all in all, a well-balanced group. Jane Smithwayne was almost as quiet as Elizabeth, speaking mostly to her brother and once or twice with Mr. Latchley. Though she did not often join in the conversation, she listened earnestly, a habit Elizabeth found flattering and soon resolved to cultivate herself.

As the meal progressed, Elizabeth kept a careful eye on Mr. Rutherford. Besides impressing Amelia, his aim seemed to be to infuriate Mr. Beaufort Latchley—probably because Mr. Latchley seemed equally intent on attracting Amelia's notice.

It was sometime between the vegetables and a mutton that managed to reach Elizabeth before it was cold that Mrs. Smithwayne took advantage of a brief silence to bring up her favorite subject. "A solid foundation in religion would prevent poverty, I am convinced of it," she said. "A true Christian is never poor. Parents who refuse to instruct their children in the proper moral grounds are truly the greatest evil in the world."

"My dear woman," drawled Ripton Rutherford, "the greatest evil in this world is a valet who takes an hour to properly tie one's cravat."

Mr. Latchley snorted and scornfully lifted the corner of his mouth.

"Mr. Latchley—" Ripton glanced in his direction. "I've no idea how long it took to tie your cravat, but evidently it was not nearly long enough."

"I am quite satisfied with my appearance, Mr. Rutherford."

"Yes, quite. I might have guessed."

"I submit to you, ladies," said Mr. Latchley, looking directly at Amelia, "that we have before us an example of the greatest evil in the world. A gentleman whose first concern is the state of his clothes."

"Well, now, Mr. Latchley, do you mean to say one ought not be concerned with one's appearance?" asked Sir Jaspar, who spent upward of eight hundred pounds a year on his wardrobe.

"No, Sir Jaspar," answered Mr. Latchley. "Only that one should not be concerned with it above all else."

Lady Charles interrupted just as her husband was taking a breath to answer Mr. Latchley. "I understand that while we were gone there was another robbery. The Mayfair Thief, I believe they are calling whoever is responsible?"

"Yes, Lady Charles," said Frederick Smithwayne, eager to show off his knowledge. "It happened at Lady Stinforth's ball."

"The Mayfair Thief?" repeated Amelia.

"Yes, Miss Willard." Beaufort Latchley turned to look at her. "The name is of fairly recent coinage."

"The police have only now come to the conclusion that the same man must be responsible for several daring thefts," Ripton added. "There were three or four robberies last year. And, it is suspected, quite a number before then."

"Do you know," said Lady Charles, "a very peculiar thing happened when we were in Paris. Madame de Nouillier lost a very valuable sapphire brooch at a masquerade ball." Mr. Willard and Mr. Villines interrupted their discussion of agriculture in the shires in order to listen. "She claimed it was stolen by a mysterious gentleman whom she was unable to identify, his features having been covered with a black mask. She gave us to understand he lured her onto a secluded balcony and there relieved her of her brooch."

"Lured her my eye!" said Sir Jaspar. "What's a respectable married woman doing following someone out onto a balcony, I should like to know."

"You forget, she is French, Jaspar, and she had argued with the count not ten minutes before."

"And what difference does that make?"

"Well, no matter." She waved a hand. "Madame de Nouillier was overheard to say she would have cried the alarm much sooner had he not kissed her quite so skillfully just before disappearing with twenty thousand francs' worth of her jewelry."

"Is that what the Mayfair Thief steals? Jewels, I mean?" Elizabeth asked.

"Yes, but only the most expensive ones," said

Ripton. For some reason Elizabeth immediately conjured up images of caskets filled with precious stones hidden away someplace, most likely in the secret room of a moldering castle tower. "He is a thief of the most discriminating taste. Ladies are said to be mortified if their jewels are not stolen by the Mayfair Thief."

"Whom did he so honor this time?" asked Lady Charles.

"Lady Stinforth herself," Mr. Latchley replied.

"She had her hair arranged in a most dramatic fashion," Ripton broke in. "Unfortunately it also prevented her from feeling her tiara being removed until it was too late."

"Fifty thousand pounds, gone in a flash," said Frederick Smithwayne.

"How simply horrible!" Amelia looked appropriately frightened.

"Did she not see who took her tiara?" Elizabeth asked.

"She claims she saw only a glimpse of him as he melted into the shadows."

Mr. Smithwayne bristled. "You romanticize a common criminal, Mr. Rutherford."

"Surely he is no common criminal, Mr. Smithwayne. He is a gentleman criminal. Perhaps even a noble one."

"A gentleman does not go about snatching other people's property, I can assure you of that," said Sir Jaspar. "And as for a nobleman . . ." He sniffed. "Why, the very idea is preposterous!"

"The Metropolitan Police believe the man must be a gentleman. He seems to move about society easily enough."

"You know quite a lot about him, Mr. Rutherford," said Beaufort Latchley.

"I admit I follow his career rather closely." He lifted one shoulder.

"Is there some particular reason for that?" Mrs. Willard asked.

He shrugged again. "I admire the man."

"Admire him!" exclaimed Sir Jaspar, Mr. Smithwayne, and Mr. Willard all at the same time.

"I admire his courage and his cunning."

"His misplaced courage and his low cunning, you mean," Mr. Villines put in.

"La!" cried Lady Charles. "I wish I had not brought up the subject."

"Surely it is time to change it," Mrs. Villines said.

"I expect the ladies are wondering whether they will mysteriously lose their jewels before the night is over."

Lady Charles looked at Ripton reproachfully. "Tell us," she said to her husband, "about the Van Dyck you found in Geneva."

Elizabeth was sorry to have the subject changed. She wanted to hear more about the Mayfair Thief. It was certainly a more interesting topic than the painting Sir Jaspar had bought while touring Switzerland.

The rest of the evening passed pleasantly enough, even without further discussion of the Mayfair Thief, and when the men rejoined the women after the ladies had left them to their cigars, Amelia entertained them by singing six of the seven French songs she knew. She would have sung the seventh had not Mrs. Villines then suggested a game of cards. Mr. Rutherford was Elizabeth's partner, and the two easily defeated Mr. Smithwayne and Mrs. Villines. The evening ended with everyone feeling his time had been well spent. Even Elizabeth was inclined to think London might be much more pleasant than she'd a right to expect.

At two o'clock the Willards arrived back at Tavistock Square, and Elizabeth fell exhausted into bed. The ladies had managed to leave without losing their jewelry, but still she dreamed of a mysterious gentleman who could steal a tiara and disappear as though he had never been there.

CHAPTER
8
❖❖❖❖

AMELIA STOOD IN THE DOORWAY OF HER COUSIN'S
room looking impatient. "Hurry up, Beth, or we
shall be late."

"Late for what, Amelia?" Elizabeth continued searching for her gloves.

"What difference does it make? I want to go.
Why are you always so slow?"

She found her gloves and pulled them on
hastily. "I'm ready now. Where's Miss Lincoln?"

"She's waiting downstairs."

Amelia set a quick pace toward Regent's Park
after the three women stepped into the cool afternoon air. The reason for Amelia's haste became apparent when they reached the Park
Crescent. Lady Charles was there, standing at
the edge of a group of some fifteen people, Ripton Rutherford and Beaufort Latchley among
them.

"Lady Charles," Amelia said, extending her

hand and looking for all the world as though she was astonished to see her. "Good afternoon. We must have had the same idea—to walk in Regent's Park, you know."

"Good afternoon, Miss Willard, Miss Elizabeth Willard." Lady Charles looked pleased to see them, and Elizabeth breathed a sigh of relief that Amelia's brash greeting had not offended such an elegant and refined woman. "I am pleased to see you do not neglect exercise," she said.

"Oh my, no. We walk almost every day, don't we, Beth?" Amelia did not wait for an answer. "And how is Sir Jaspar, Lady Charles? He was so amusing at the Villineses the other night," she giggled. "It was a pleasure to meet him and yourself."

"He is very well, thank you, Miss Willard." Apparently Lady Charles had decided the Willard girls were interesting enough to merit an invitation to join her, for she asked, "Will you walk with us? We are just taking a stroll to the zoo."

"Why, thank you," Amelia said. "You are just too kind to invite us." She dimpled and glanced around to see who had noticed her.

Ripton and Beaufort Latchley saw Amelia at about the same time, but Ripton reached Lady Charles first. He fell into step with them.

Lady Charles glanced at Amelia before speaking to Ripton. "Sir Jaspar and I missed you at tea yesterday, Mr. Rutherford." She reached over to tap the middle of his chest with her fan.

"I was upset at being unable to attend, naturally, but I had a prior engagement, and it was impossible for me to break it."

"My husband is planning a rather grand celebration to show his painting, Mr. Rutherford. The date is not yet fixed, but might I extract from you a promise to attend?" Lady Charles's smile was just short of flirtatious.

"You have my most solemn promise. And will you do me a favor in return?"

"If it is within my power, Mr. Rutherford."

"I assure you, it is. Would you be too desolate if I took Miss Amelia Willard away to walk with me?" He looked hopefully at Amelia.

"I certainly would be, Mr. Rutherford, but go along anyway."

"I would be honored, Miss Willard," Ripton said, offering his arm to Amelia.

"Come, Miss Willard," said Lady Charles after Ripton and Amelia left, with Miss Lincoln following behind them. "I want you to stay by me." She drew her arm through Elizabeth's. "Tell me, how long have you been in London?"

"Hardly two weeks." Next to Lady Charles's silk gown, Elizabeth's blue dress looked positively drab, and she wished enough of her allowance was left so she might have a dress even a little like Lady Charles's.

"Is this your first time visiting London?"

"We used to live here when I was a girl. We

moved to Dartford when I was eight, and this is the first time in four years that I have been to London."

"Then it may as well be your first time. One's first time in London as a young lady is a vastly different thing. How do you find it so far?"

"I like it a great deal." Lady Charles's interest in her impressions of London went a long way toward making Elizabeth relax, and she smiled for the first time since reaching Regent's Park. "I have been with my uncle to the British Museum and to St. Martin-in-the-Fields. I have also been shopping with my aunt Mary and my cousin Amelia at Regent Street. And I have found a bookstore where the proprietor does not mind if I spend more time than money. There is so much to do here that I am afraid to stay at home. I do not want to miss anything."

"Have you been to any balls?"

"No, not yet."

"Good heavens! You sound relieved." Lady Charles shook her head. "I can remember my coming-out. I was dreadfully nervous myself. I soon got over it, though, just as you will, you may depend on it."

"But I don't know anyone in London. Except Mr. and Mrs. Villines, that is. And I do not enjoy meeting strangers, Lady Charles."

"It would not matter if you did not know a soul. In London a pretty girl does not lack acquaintances for long. Soon you won't even want to walk with me, there will be so many gentlemen waiting for the pleasure."

"It isn't true, Lady Charles!"

"Of course it is. And that's as it should be."

"I pray I shall never treat a friend as badly as that." Elizabeth hesitated. "I hope I am not presuming too much in hoping I might call you a friend one day, Lady Charles?"

"No, Miss Willard, you are not, but I would think you a peculiar young lady if you were to persist in being so disinterested in gentlemen."

"I think they won't be much interested in me, Lady Charles," Elizabeth said after a reluctant pause.

"Nonsense! If I were to ask you about London two weeks from now, you would talk of nothing but balls and the handsome men you have danced with."

"I think I had best leave the gentlemen to my cousin." Elizabeth was tempted to believe Lady Charles, but she knew what disappointment was like. Far better never to have one's hopes raised in the first place.

"Mrs. Villines is quite certain you will be married this season." Lady Charles laughed at Elizabeth's expression. "Mrs. Villines and I are great friends. We've talked about you at some length, Miss Willard. She speaks very highly of you, you know." She tapped Elizabeth's arm with her fan.

"You seem to think I might be married any minute, Lady Charles." Elizabeth laughed.

"I think you will be astonished at how soon you are proposed to. I expect you might marry any gentleman you choose."

"My cousin may marry any gentleman she chooses, not I."

"You underestimate yourself."

"I think not." Even to her ears, the words came out sounding sorrowful. "I haven't any fortune," she explained.

Lady Charles smiled. "Time will show which of us is in error." Elizabeth felt the woman's fingers gently squeezing her arm. "Dear Miss Willard," she said softly, "I am in full agreement with Mrs. Villines. I therefore hope you will allow me to give you a piece of advice. Reflect carefully before you choose a husband. If you make a bad marriage, you will be miserable your whole life. Too many women accept the first man who offers."

Elizabeth was touched by her kindness and flattered at the implied compliment. Because she could think of nothing to say, she made a pretext of looking at the park grounds. Lady Charles chose not to interrupt her silence, and in the quiet that followed, the conversation of the men directly in front of them caught Elizabeth's attention. It was the name that riveted her.

"I hear Nicholas Villines is in London again," one of the men was saying.

"Indeed?" His companion snorted.

"I understand he's brought back another orchid. A rare violet cymbidium. It's said he carried away the only specimen to arrive here still alive."

"Stole it, more like!" exclaimed the second.

"Now, now," the other said.

"Well, that's what it amounts to."

"If you had his connections, you'd do the same," said the first.

"You're probably right about that. Only I'm convinced it would take more than his connections to explain how he came to be so bloody rich after the mess his father left him in."

"Well, whatever the explanation, I expect you shall soon have yet another reason to envy him."

"So?" said the other sourly, not sounding very interested at all.

"Lord Eversleigh is said to be encouraging him to take a wife, and I'll give you odds the woman he'll marry is right here among us."

"Eh, what?"

His companion answered him by pointing a finger.

Both Lady Charles and Elizabeth looked in the direction he was pointing and saw Amelia walking with Ripton Rutherford on one side and Beaufort Latchley on the other.

"That, my friend, is Miss Amelia Willard. Eighty thousand pounds, so I hear, and the daughter of close friends of Mr. Russell Villines."

"Who is her family?" He sounded distinctly interested now.

"The father is Mr. Havoc Willard, a wealthy merchant. He married the former Miss Mary Redingwood, of the Harford Redingwoods. The former Miss Redingwood and Mrs. Russell Villines were at school together. The Willards hope to have their daughter married this season. Who better than to Nicholas Villines, I ask you? I don't imagine but that the two families have planned it for some time."

"You don't suppose she has a sister?"

"There is a cousin about the same age, but she is nowhere near as pretty as the daughter. In fact, I'm told she's rather plain."

Lady Charles, who had been listening up to that point with evident amusement, cleared her throat.

The two men turned around. "Ah, Lady Charles!" said the first gentleman, sending a penetrating look in Elizabeth's direction when he had straightened from a polite bow.

Elizabeth could feel her cheeks burning with mortification, and she was doubly mortified to see that Lady Charles intended to introduce the men to her. "Excuse me," she said quickly. "Do forgive me, but I believe I hear someone calling me." She was gone before Lady Charles could stop her.

"Who was that pretty creature?" asked the second gentleman as he watched Elizabeth walk quickly away.

"That, my dear gentlemen, was Miss Elizabeth Willard. Miss Amelia Willard's cousin."

Plain! People were talking about her and calling her plain! Elizabeth did not stop walking until she had left Lady Charles's group behind. What she had overheard only confirmed what her aunt had already told her. It must be her vanity that made the truth hurt so much. She was staring at the skirt of her dress, absorbed in self-pity, when a shadow fell across her face. She looked up and was surprised to see Ripton Rutherford standing before her.

"Miss Willard. I thought you were with Lady Charles." He was obviously waiting for her to take his arm.

"And I thought you were with my cousin, Mr. Rutherford," she said when she had.

"As you can see, I am not." He smiled slightly.

"So I perceive." She managed a smile in return.

He began walking but made no effort to catch up to Lady Charles. "You were not in London last year, Miss Willard?" he asked after they had been strolling for a time.

"I was not." She almost succeeded in putting her misery from her mind.

"I suppose everyone asks you how you like London."

"Yes."

"And what do you tell them?"

"That I find it very interesting, that there is much to do here, and that I find the prices shockingly dear." Ripton smiled encouragingly, so she added, "My uncle gives me a generous allowance, or so it seemed until we came here. I am daily tempted to spend more."

"I daresay when, or if, you leave London, it will be with an empty purse and full trunks." He smiled as he said this.

"I daresay you are right. I shall have to throw out all my clothes to make room, for I know I'll be too poor to buy another trunk."

"On what do you spend your pounds and pence?" He looked surprised that it was evidently not clothing.

"Books, Mr. Rutherford. I love nothing more than to spend an afternoon in a bookstore. I try to leave my money at home when I visit one, for it is certain I should leave there without it."

"Nicholas told me you like to read," he commented.

"Oh, yes! He sends me his recommendations quite often."

"And do you always approve of them?"

"Of course I always approve, Mr. Rutherford. Nicholas would never send me something unsuitable. I do not, however, always agree with his thoughts on them."

Although they'd continued to walk slowly, they were now almost even with Lady Charles's group. Ripton did not seem much disposed to join them, and slowing so they would remain behind the others, he stared intently toward Amelia, who was walking with Beaufort Latchley still at her side.

"Have you ever remarked, Miss Willard, upon the importance of one's name?" he asked with a wry grin when he saw she was following his gaze. "Have you, for example, ever read a novel in which the hero had an inadequate name?"

"I've always thought the greater the writer's skill, the less important the hero's name."

"I must disagree. The name is all important. Take my name, for instance. It's a good English name. Dashing, heroic even, if you will pardon my immodesty."

"To be sure, Mr. Rutherford." She smiled.

"Other names are only pretentious." He shot a poisonous look just ahead of them.

"Such as 'Beaufort,' Mr. Rutherford?"

"The very name I was thinking of, Miss Willard. What right-minded fellow would have a name like that?"

"I'm sure if your parents had named you Beaufort, you would think it a fine name."

"On the contrary, *I* should have changed it immediately upon my majority."

"I suppose you think 'Amelia' to be another fine name."

"It is, Miss Willard. It is a wholesome name deserving to be linked only with an equally fine one."

"Well, you needn't worry about Mr. Latchley," she responded. "I overheard a gentleman saying that Nicholas will marry Amelia."

"Nicholas? An interesting thought. He would find that rather amusing, I think."

"Would he? Why?"

"Ah! Then you don't know everything about him after all. Do you know how many lovely women have wanted to marry Nicholas? He will encourage her to a point, and then—" He snapped his fingers. "She finds another woman has supplanted her in his favor. He's quite without scruples when it comes to women."

"I don't believe that," Elizabeth said. "And anyway, Mr. Rutherford, whom Nicholas falls in love with is none of our business."

"True enough."

"And," she added, "if Amelia is lovely enough to attract your notice, do you not think she might attract his?"

Ripton sighed. "A point, Miss Willard. A point."

"May I give you a piece of advice, Mr. Rutherford?"

"You may."

"You should think less about Mr. Latchley's name and more about Amelia. A woman notices what a man does more than what he says."

"Wise advice, Miss Willard. And like most advice, difficult to practice."

"Amelia, more than anything, craves attention. You should not ignore her, Mr. Rutherford."

"Now, here is something of practical use."

They were close enough to their party that Elizabeth could see Lady Charles strolling with another woman. She felt a pang of remorse at her hasty departure. "Will you excuse me, Mr. Rutherford?" she asked. "I must speak to Lady Charles. I'm afraid I owe her an apology." She ought to face up to the unpleasant, or she would never be deserving of Lady Charles's friendship.

"You are excused," he said, nodding his blond head. He watched her for a moment before rejoining Amelia and Mr. Latchley.

CHAPTER
9
❧❂❧

Nicholas was sitting in the drawing room at Fitzroy Square enjoying the fuss his aunt always made over him when he was back in London after an absence. He was, therefore, mildly disappointed when the butler came in to announce the arrival of visitors.

Mrs. Villines stood up. "Mary, how wonderful that you've come today." She held out her hands to Mrs. Willard. "Do make yourselves comfortable," she said. "Nicholas is here." She turned to make sure he was coming. "Nicholas!"

He rose. "A pleasure to see you again, Mrs. Willard." He took her hand and pressed it briefly. Upon seeing Amelia, he paused for a beat before lifting her hand to his lips. "A true pleasure, Miss Willard, to see you again." He could not help putting just a small emphasis on the "you." Since he had last seen her, she had gone from pretty to strikingly lovely.

"Thank you, Mr. Villines," she said as she curtsied. "I was so terribly sorry to learn you were not in London when we arrived. I am sure it will be grandly amusing now that you are." She ended the sentence with a small giggle.

The corner of Nicholas's mouth lifted when Amelia laughed, and he acknowledged the compliment with a slight nod of his head. He turned to follow Mrs. Willard and Amelia into the center of the room, thinking as he did so that Amelia Willard was far lovelier than any woman had a right to be. Mrs. Villines put a hand on his arm to stop him, and from the corner of his eye he saw that someone else had come in. He turned. The girl was plainly dressed and at first glance not at all stunning. An oval face, chin slightly pointed, eyes of an unremarkable color. Her full lips parted in a hesitant smile. Yet her every feature was so perfectly and delicately drawn, she might have been a statue come to life. He did not look away. Her dark hair, pulled back from her face and fastened at the nape of her neck, only emphasized pale, flawless skin. She was tall and quite slender, but then, he liked slender women. Even as he wondered who she was, he thought that if she was half as innocent as she looked, she would likely drive him to distraction. That shy smile was entrancing.

"I thought for a moment you hadn't come, Elizabeth," he heard his aunt say.

He recovered himself quickly. "Elizabeth!"

He took the hand she extended to him and held it. "How are you? I've missed you, you know." He hardly knew what he was saying in his struggle to see the Elizabeth he remembered. "We've a great deal to talk about." His Elizabeth was a girl still in pigtails!

"Good afternoon, Nicholas," she said. Her smile was no longer hesitant. "I've missed you, too."

The voice, though a little deeper now, was the same.

"She's hardly changed at all, has she, Mr. Villines?" Amelia said. "Except she's immensely tall." He glanced down at Amelia when she put a hand on his arm.

"Allow me to show you to a seat, Miss Willard," he said, almost relieved to have an excuse to look away from Elizabeth. It was unthinkable that he could have such a visceral response to a girl he thought of as a sister.

"Your aunt tells us you have been traveling," Amelia said when he had helped her to a seat near his. "I hope you will tell us of your adventures, Mr. Villines."

"I should be delighted to." He sat down and discovered Elizabeth was sitting directly across him on a chair next to his aunt.

"Nicholas," Mrs. Villines said, "was just telling me about his sojourn in Italy. He has been to the excavations at Herculaneum."

"How interesting!" Amelia cried.

"I have always longed to go there," Elizabeth said.

"Did you see any skeletons?" Amelia broke in. "It would be simply too horrid to see a skeleton. I cannot imagine anything more frightening."

"Not precisely skeletons, Miss Willard." He was rewarded with a small screech of horror.

"How terrible!" she said, raising a hand to her lips. "How could you stand to look at something so terrible?"

He deliberately devoted himself to making Amelia screech, and his attention was not significantly distracted from the endeavor until one of the maids came in with more cakes. He watched Elizabeth accept a plate. Because his aunt was between her and the table, there was nowhere for her to place it except on her lap. She actually managed it quite well, back erect, knees pressed tightly together, plate balanced, all the while holding her cup and saucer. She had been keeping those big gray eyes of hers steadily on him while he was speaking, but now every so often she glanced nervously at her lap. At last he could see his Elizabeth; the familiar mannerisms were still there. Not a girl anymore, but certainly not quite the mature woman he had seen at first, either.

"Enough about Italy," he said. "I don't want to tell all my tales at one sitting. Tell me what's happened in London while I've been gone." He looked to his aunt to provide the news.

"Your grandfather writes that Henry has gotten himself into trouble again."

"Good old Henry," Nicholas said, shaking his head. "What's he done this time?"

"Young Henry is likely to be a disgrace to the title when he inherits."

"He's still young, Aunt Winifred."

"He's old enough to know better. I've written to Eversleigh and told him to stop coddling the boy."

"Aunt Winifred maintains my cousin should learn the meaning of responsibility before he inherits the family honor," Nicholas said. "I happen to disagree. He shall have so much money when he does, he shall have no need to."

"Nicholas!"

He grinned at his aunt. Besides Elizabeth, his aunt was the only woman in world he loved to tease.

"I should think a young man in his position ought to be responsible!" Amelia exclaimed.

"You're quite right, of course," he said, leaning toward her once again but keeping one eye on Elizabeth, who was trying without success to suppress a smile. "However, I find the subject of my cousin tedious." He waved a hand to dismiss the topic. "Aunt Winifred, what have you done for the Willards since they've been here?" He was listening to Mrs. Villines tell him about a dinner party when Elizabeth shifted on her seat and nearly lost her untouched plate of cakes.

"Beth," Amelia said, "why don't you put down your tea?"

"Perhaps, Elizabeth, you would change seats with me?" Nicholas offered at almost the same time Amelia spoke.

Elizabeth was so intent on rebalancing the plate, she did not hear either of them. She gave a sigh of relief and looked up to find everyone staring at her. She blushed. "Oh, dear, have I missed something?"

"Beth, dear," said Mrs. Willard, "Mr. Villines has offered to change seats with you."

"How kind of you. But I'm not uncomfortable at all." She was looking directly at Nicholas, and, her attention diverted, the plate began to slide off her lap. She grasped for it but missed. The plate hit the floor hard enough to break into pieces and scatter cakes over the rug.

"Oh, Beth!" Mrs. Willard exclaimed.

"It is nothing," Mrs. Villines said, rising to ring for a servant.

"I am so sorry." Elizabeth repeated the apology to the maid who came to clean to mess.

Every bit the girl he remembered, Nicholas thought.

"My dear little Elizabeth," Mrs. Villines said, "there is positively nothing to be sorry for." She patted her arm, taking her cup of tea as she did so. "Let Nicholas give you his seat. He's been terribly selfish to make you sit here while all the time he's had a comfortable chair by the table."

"Perhaps I'd better." She glanced at him and

stood when she saw him stand up. "Thank you," she said when he reached her side. "Someone must protect your aunt's china."

Nicholas was disappointed when the Willards left soon afterward. He turned to his aunt when they were gone. "I'm glad they're in London. Have they said how long they'll be here?"

"Likely until Amelia and Elizabeth are married."

"Elizabeth married? Don't be absurd, she's still a girl."

"She is just back from school," Mrs. Villines said on Elizabeth's behalf. "Give her time to adjust to London."

"Schoolgirls," said Nicholas, his tone expressing a full range of contempt for the limited charms of schoolgirls. "They giggle in a most annoying fashion."

"It was not Elizabeth I heard giggling."

"She restrained herself quite admirably from that vice. Elizabeth, thank goodness, is too sensible to giggle."

"Mark my words, Nicholas, she will be noticed."

"I do not calculate her career will be a very brilliant one if she goes about dropping things on all the carpets in London."

"Do you not think she is lovely?"

For some reason, it was important that his aunt not guess how Elizabeth had first affected him. "She was pretty when she was a little girl, too, you know." He shrugged. "But it is Amelia who has grown into a beauty."

Mrs. Villines dismissed the comment by shaking her head. "Surely you will allow Elizabeth is more than just pretty?"

"All right, Aunt Winifred, I will allow Elizabeth is very pretty. One day—when she is grown up, that is—she might even be exceedingly pretty."

"Elizabeth has something that Amelia, for all her beauty, does not have," Mrs. Villines persisted.

"And what is that?"

"Character," Mrs. Villines said firmly. "And character combined with beauty is a formidable thing for a woman to have."

"Well, I suppose, Aunt Winifred, that Elizabeth might have some small amount of beauty."

Mrs. Villines smiled and shook her head at her nephew.

CHAPTER
10
❧❧❧✕❦❦❦

EVERYONE WHO KNEW MRS. SMITHWAYNE AGREED
that she was a commanding personage. She was
widely admired for her firmness of character,
and her devotion to the poor and downtrodden
was really an inspiration to others; she made no
bones about it. No one could possibly be more
sure of God's intentions for the world—nor
more devotedly go about seeing they were carried out—than Annabelle Smithwayne. One
could count on her to know without hesitation
what was right and proper and when it was that
someone had not done it. She was stultifyingly
correct; even the smallest failure of deportment
was grounds for her thorough and unmerciful
disapproval.

Jane Smithwayne, who went everywhere
with her mother, looked nothing like her. She
was slender, for one thing, and for another, her
coloring was precisely the opposite. With her
milk-white complexion, pale green eyes, and

ash blond hair, she was pretty in a wistful sort
of way that completely escaped the notice of
her mother, who thought her daughter's lack of
heartiness only one of many shortcomings.
Much to the dismay of Mrs. Smithwayne,
Jane's mind was quick and her penetration
often acute. Fortunately her lack of education
generally disguised the defect. Jane herself be-
moaned what she felt to be her alarming ignorance, though she had, in fact, made the most
of what little education her parents had felt was
necessary for a daughter. Jane had many good
qualities that even her mother could not dismiss. She was tenderhearted, gracious, and always conscious of the feelings of others, even
to the detriment of her own. She knew, because
her mother told her so, that when she married
and had children she would have fulfilled her
sole purpose in life. Perfect obedience was required of Jane because her husband would
expect it from her. Jane tried her best to be obe-
dient, but sometimes she felt as though she
might suffocate under the tremendous burden
of making herself spiritually perfect for the
man who would one day be her husband.

It was not until the second time Mrs. Smithwayne called on the Willards that Elizabeth and
Jane became friends. When they came in Elizabeth was sitting on the floor near the fire petting
the kitten Beaufort Latchley had given to Amelia. Mrs. Willard and Amelia straightened up
from their perusal of a fashion magazine. Mrs.

Smithwayne frowned when she saw it, as she considered such occupations to be frivolous.

"Elizabeth." Mrs. Willard waved her hand in the direction of the fireplace. "Do get up and say good afternoon to the Smithwaynes."

"Oh, please don't," Jane cried when she saw the kitten curled up in Elizabeth's lap. She quickly sat down next to her and stroked the kitten's back. "What's its name?"

"Charlotte."

"She's so tiny."

"Jane is never more happy than when she may make the acquaintance of some small animal," her mother said, looking dourly at where the two girls were sitting.

Jane said nothing but reached to scratch the kitten's chin. "Such a ball of white fluff you are, Charlotte," she murmured to it.

Elizabeth decided Jane had just proved she possessed a great deal of sensitivity by knowing where to scratch and exactly the pressure to apply to make the kitten purr even more loudly. She'd already suspected that she might like Jane Smithwayne more than a little, and now she was certain of it. The two talked quietly while Mrs. Smithwayne kept up a one-sided conversation with Mrs. Willard and Amelia. By the time Mrs. Smithwayne rose to leave, Elizabeth and Jane had discovered they had enough in common to sustain a friendship.

They were fast friends by the time Jane gave in to her mother's prodding and asked Elizabeth to come to the Smithwayne Foundation for Abandoned Children one afternoon to help sort donated clothing. Elizabeth agreed only because of Jane. She did not relish the thought of being scrutinized by Mrs. Smithwayne. She arrived at the foundation feeling certain Jane's mother would lecture her about her many deficiencies. To her relief, Mrs. Smithwayne only frowned at her before leaving her and Jane settled in a room to themselves where they were to sort clothing.

"If this is a foundation for children, why is there so much clothing for adults?" she asked Jane not long after Mrs. Smithwayne had left them.

"Children are helped when their parents are helped. If we give clothing to parents, it's one less expense for them. It's the mother and father who must be convinced to send their children to school and to church."

"Do you think you do any good?"

"Sometimes. And many times not. For example, right now we are helping a man whose wife's death left him with two children to provide for, one twelve and the other but seven. He lost his job when he attended his wife's funeral. Now he's turned to crime in order to feed the two."

"But that's awful!"

"I know. Poor Mr. Howard—that's the man's name, Mr. George Howard. I'm not sure if we can do him any good. He makes more money housebreaking than he did working as a clerk. Apparently he's gotten better at it; he hasn't been arrested for weeks. He'll be transported if he's caught again, so perhaps he's more careful now."

"It would be nice if something could be done to help him," Elizabeth said.

"Yes, it would. Some of these clothes will probably go to him."

They were quiet for a time, until Jane put down the breeches she was examining to see what repairs would be necessary. "Your cousin is very brilliant," she said. "She always has a crowd of gentlemen about her."

Elizabeth had nothing to say in response. It was perfectly true, after all.

"Do you suppose she is in love with any of her admirers?" Jane asked.

"One might as well ask whether any of her admirers are in love with my cousin." Elizabeth laughed. "Amelia is always in love with this gentleman or that one. It seems to change from one day to the next."

That seemed to give Jane pause. "Do you suppose any one of them is in love with her?"

Elizabeth shrugged. She did not much care to discuss the subject. Jane's question made her think, very unwillingly, about how much attention Nicholas paid to Amelia.

"She will likely marry soon, I expect," Jane continued. "But with so many admirers, how is she to choose?"

"Well . . ." Elizabeth pursed her lips, not noticing how closely Jane was watching her. "At the present, I should say there are two or three gentlemen to whom she pays particular attention."

"Yes?"

"Nicholas Villines and Mr. Rutherford are two." She provided the names, though she was somewhat puzzled by Jane's curiosity.

"And the third?"

"The third is Mr. Beaufort Latchley."

"Oh. Does she show a preference between them?"

"I cannot say, Jane. But Nicholas is the finest of them, and I suppose Amelia will marry him." What it cost her to say that was incalculable, and she steeled herself against the pain it caused. She must get used to the idea. It would be no great surprise if they did marry; they made a handsome couple.

"Do you not think Mr. Latchley is a fine man?" Jane arched her nearly white eyebrows.

"Mr. Latchley takes himself, and life, far too seriously to suit me."

"It seems to me that Mr. Villines is dreadfully serious."

"Oh, but Jane, if you knew him, you would not say so. He isn't serious all the time. Nicholas is the kindest, most thoughtful man I know."

"Perhaps if you knew Mr. Latchley better,

73

you would find he has admirable qualities that would improve your opinion of him."

"No doubt I would, but I have no desire to know him better."

"If he is to be your relative, perhaps you had better," said Jane.

"Amelia will surely marry Nicholas. I think both families want it."

"Perhaps she will."

Elizabeth returned her attention to the pile of clothing in front of her. Jane seemed unaccountably relieved, she thought, and after a moment she smiled. Perhaps she shouldn't have spoken so harshly of Mr. Latchley.

"If you were in love," Jane asked, breaking their silence at last, "what kind of man do you think he would be?"

Elizabeth considered the question. "Naturally, he must be handsome," she said. "And I like dark eyes extremely."

"I agree that brown eyes are very fine."

"And if he is not fantastically rich, then, there is no hope for it. I should have to break his heart and turn him down."

"Should he not be a poet as well?" Jane laughed.

"Of course. But if he is not, then he must be something equally dashing."

"A sailor, perhaps?"

The image that came to mind was of a tall, mysterious man who could disappear into shadows without a trace. "A pirate captain," she said at last. She could hardly tell Jane she thought the Mayfair Thief was her idea of a dashing gentleman.

"A pirate!"

"Yes. Then we could sail away and leave the world behind. I think," she continued, "that if I am ever to be in love, he must have a sense of humor. Otherwise we should be very unhappily married, for he would not be able to appreciate me, with all my faults. If I am to tolerate his faults, he must tolerate mine."

"Elizabeth!" Jane exclaimed. "I can only say what a good thing it is that you're so quiet when you are out. I'm sure the many gentlemen who do admire you would be shocked to hear you speaking so."

"Well, I don't know why," she protested.

"Don't you agree that most gentlemen want a wife who has no faults?"

"If that is the case, Jane, I don't see how anyone ever manages to marry, and those who do must soon find themselves very unhappy."

"Haven't you two finished yet?"

Elizabeth jumped at the unexpected appearance of Mrs. Smithwayne. "Oh, my, is it late?" she asked when she saw the scowl on her face. "Do you happen to know what the time is, Mrs. Smithwayne?"

Jane looked at the watch hanging around her neck. "Half-past three," she said, snapping the cover shut.

"Half-past? I'm afraid I must go. Aunt Mary

expects me home for tea." She stood up, hastily arranging her shawl around her shoulders. "Will you come?" she asked Jane, feeling guilty because she was not really expected home for another hour.

"Thank you, no," Jane said. "Mother and I will finish here."

When Elizabeth arrived at Tavistock Square she had the house to herself. Havoc was gone for the day, and Amelia and Mrs. Willard would not be home for nearly an hour. She went upstairs to change into an old blue dress before going outside to work in the garden.

Mrs. Willard smiled broadly when Nicholas came into the sitting room after Mr. Poyne. "Mr. Villines!" she cried when the butler was gone. "What a pleasure to see you here."

"Good afternoon, Mrs. Willard." He bowed and then greeted Amelia warmly. She was wearing a dress of pink satin, a color he found to be particularly flattering on her. "Where's Elizabeth?" he asked when he saw she was not in the room.

"We are waiting for her to come home," said Mrs. Willard. "She's been helping Miss Jane Smithwayne, though she ought to have been home long ago. I can't imagine where she's got to. She's usually unfailingly punctual."

Amelia dimpled and laughed at her mother. "I should suppose, Mother," she said, "that Mr. Villines knows my cousin is apt to lose track of the time. She's quite . . ." She paused as she searched for a word to describe her. "Intense," she finally provided. It was clear from her tone she did not think it a good thing for Elizabeth to be. "More than once she's been late for tea because she was reading a book so interesting she quite forgot to look at the time and did not even hear the bell. Can you imagine that!"

Nicholas could but said nothing. Amelia's self-assured ignorance was, in an odd way, fascinating. She almost made him think a beautiful woman ought to be ignorant, a blank slate for her husband to write on as he wished—so long as he did not also want a wife he would be able to talk to.

"Beth is quite fond of reading," Mrs. Willard broke in. "It is a worrisome habit in a girl, and indeed Amelia is forbidden too much reading." Being a product of her times, Mrs. Willard thought cleverness a particular drawback in a woman, and she had taken great care to see her own daughter did not cultivate such a handicap. As for Elizabeth, well, she might have to support herself one day, and cleverness might come in handy in such an eventuality. Elizabeth was, as she often said, a poor relation, and poor relations, everyone knew, did not make good marriages—if they managed to get themselves married at all.

"I enjoy novel reading myself, Mr. Villines," said Amelia, "so I hope my mother does not think it too horrible a habit."

"Surely you do not, Mrs. Willard?"

"Not entirely." Mrs. Willard was unable to completely disapprove of the habit, though she might have if Nicholas had seemed to. Still, she felt it best to add, "A young lady would better spend her time improving her soul than her mind."

"Surely book reading cannot imperil the soul, Mrs. Willard."

"The right kind of books do not. You may rest assured I permit Amelia to read only the right kind of books." Evidently she considered the topic closed, for with hardly a pause to draw breath, she went on, "Amelia, it is such a lovely afternoon, perhaps Mr. Villines would enjoy a walk in the garden while we wait for Elizabeth?"

"That would be most agreeable, Mrs. Willard." Nicholas stood and extended a hand to her.

"I believe I shall stay inside to wait for Beth, Mr. Villines. But I'm certain Amelia would be glad to give you a tour." Mrs. Willard beamed at him from her chair.

"I should be simply too happy to show you the garden, Mr. Villines."

The garden at the back of the house was good-sized, with a recently trimmed lawn curving around both sides of the house and stretching out some fifty or sixty yards to the rear. The paths leading around either side of the house were bordered with blossom-laden flowers, carefully laid out and pruned back with exactness. Each plant almost perfectly matched its neighbor, and there was not a dead leaf or a wilting flower to be seen. Nicholas resolved to find out who their gardener was and to do his best to hire the man away.

"Beth is out here constantly," Amelia was saying, "sitting in the sun and digging about in the dirt. It's simply a wonder she isn't brown as toast."

Nicholas was admiring the rosebushes when Amelia came to a halt just as they were rounding a corner. He glanced at her, wondering why she had stopped and why she suddenly looked amused. He followed her gaze and saw someone sitting on the ground in the middle of the path, pinching dead leaves from the pansies lining the walk next to the house. Most of her face was shadowed by a wide-brimmed hat, but he caught a glimpse of her features when she sat up for an instant to push back the hair that was falling out of what had once been a rather severe chignon. She brushed impatiently at the wisps of hair and then pushed more pins into place. The gesture made him think of a woman he had known in Paris. She had arched her neck in just that same way. They had got along famously. He thought it odd that the Willards had hired a woman to work in the garden. Not that it made any difference, if the result was this garden.

She was leaning forward to reach the backs

of the plants, and as she did, the skirt of her faded dress tightened over her legs, bent underneath her so that she was sitting mostly on one flank. When she sat back again the material settled into folds of blue wool.

"Oh, dear." Amelia sighed when the girl shaded her eyes against the waning afternoon sun and waved at them with a gloved hand. Nicholas was shocked to see it was Elizabeth. "I'm sure she thinks you're Father," Amelia said. She shrugged and walked toward her. "I was just telling Mr. Villines how wonderfully you keep the flowers, Beth," she said when the two reached her. "He is here for tea," she added, to give her cousin a chance to stand up. "We decided to walk in the garden while we waited for you."

"Good afternoon," Elizabeth said while she brushed away the dirt that clung to her skirt. She extended her hand and blushed crimson when she realized she had not taken off her work gloves. She snatched them off and thrust them into a pocket of her skirt.

"And good afternoon to you, Elizabeth." He smiled at her. This time it was easier to make her back into his little girl. The tightening quiver of arousal was gone almost immediately.

"Well," Amelia said, taking Nicholas's arm again. "Perhaps we should go in for tea, now that we've found Beth?"

* * *

When Elizabeth came into the drawing room where tea was being served, she had changed from her faded blue wool into a watered silk and had combed her hair into a simple twist. Her dress was dark green and high-collared, and she wore a cameo pinned at her neck. For an instant Nicholas thought about how she had reminded him of that woman in Paris. The first thing he'd done after finally convincing the woman to leave with him was take down her hair and kiss her throat. It was strange that Elizabeth, of all people, should remind him of her.

"Elizabeth," he said, sitting down again when she took a place next to her aunt, "are you really responsible for the remarkable condition of the flowers here?"

"I suppose so."

"If you will forgive me for saying so, it's rather a pity. I'd promised myself I was going to attempt to hire away your gardener." The dark green of her dress made the familiar gray of her eyes even more piercing. She smiled. It had a disconcerting effect on him.

"You still might, I suppose. Mr. Hawley's quite good."

"Would you pour, Beth?" Amelia signaled the servant to move the tea things in front of Elizabeth.

"Where did you find the pattern for the laying out of the flower beds?" Nicholas persisted.

"It's my own. I had Mr. Hawley replant them when we arrived here, and I—" She glanced at her aunt and stopped. "Anyway, the pattern is mine."

"You have my sincere admiration."

She did not answer; she only blushed and stared at the sugar bowl.

"It's nothing to be modest about," he said. He felt as though he were trying futilely to reconcile opposites. There was Elizabeth the girl, he had told things he'd never told anyone else, who was his friend. And then there was the young woman before him, who clearly did not have the slightest idea she was almost painfully beautiful. It wasn't possible for her to be both girl and woman, and it was infuriating not to know which she was or which he preferred her to be.

"Tell me, Mr. Villines," Amelia said, "is your aunt well?"

He looked away. "Oh, yes, she's quite well."

"I like her immensely. Only she made you stop talking about Italy, and I would simply adore hearing more about your travels. I just know I should love to go there myself."

It was a relief of sorts to let himself be distracted by Amelia. She laughed at the proper time, shrieked if he intimated something only the slightest bit gruesome, and simply gazed at him the rest of the time. Yet her attitudes sometimes struck him as contrived. Each phrase was uttered for its effect rather than its meaning, each look was calculated to bring a particular feature into prominence. Amelia's features were, of course, quite worthy of admiration, and he was flattered she thought him worth all the trouble.

"Do you still drink your tea without sugar?" Elizabeth was looking at him, tongs poised over a cup of tea.

"Yes, but more milk than that." He watched her add the required amount of milk. Their eyes met, and he was relieved to see only Elizabeth in their clear depths.

Havoc Willard came in just as Amelia was telling Nicholas she was sure to simply die if she never got to Europe to see the places he'd talked about. A great deal of fuss was made over Mr. Willard, but soon he was comfortably settled with his tea and a plate of cold ham. The conversation flowed pleasantly from one subject to another, back again, over old stories, and off to new ones.

Nicholas smiled to himself. He was comfortable with the Willards, and he liked the tranquil feeling. He decided that if being married meant having a wife he adored and children as pleasant as Amelia and Elizabeth, then perhaps it was not a bad thing. He wanted to slow the passing of these moments. He'd not felt so at peace since before his father died. It was this sentimental turn of his thoughts that made him quickly agree when Mrs. Willard invited him to stay to supper.

His feeling of nostalgia increased during the meal. He had always liked Havoc Willard, and he liked him still, probably because it was so obvious he loved Elizabeth. Around him she joked, smiled, laughed, and did not spill a single thing. His memories of the times he had spent with the Willards were precious to him, and this evening they seemed dearer to him than usual.

"Perhaps," Nicholas remarked after he had made significant inroads into his beef, "I ought to try to steal away your cook as well."

Havoc lifted his eyebrows. "Which of the servants do you particularly want to steal away with, young man?"

"Well, your cook, for one. But gardening has become a particular hobby of mine, and this afternoon when I was admiring your garden I was informed Elizabeth was responsible for its remarkable condition." He grinned at her, and she smiled back.

"That's the truth," Havoc said, looking at Elizabeth. "So, you found yourself wanting to make off with our gardener, did you?"

"I'm afraid I was prepared to offer him vast sums of money to desert you."

Havoc turned to his niece. "How much would it take to get you off my hands, Elizabeth?"

She pretended to think about it. "Five or six pounds a month, at least, I should think, Uncle." She glanced at Nicholas, greatly amused, eyes fairly sparkling. This was the Elizabeth he remembered. There was nothing he would like better than to have everything back the way it was before his father died, and seeing Elizabeth laughing made him long for the days of his lost innocence.

"Five pounds a month and she's all yours, Mr. Villines."

"Father!" Amelia exclaimed. "And you, too, Beth. You should be ashamed."

"I hope you will keep this man away from our servants, Mrs. Willard," said Havoc.

"Is it true flowers are a hobby with you, Mr. Villines?" Amelia asked, giving her father a warning glance.

"Yes, I cultivate orchids in particular. I find it relaxing, especially after I've had a harrowing day."

"Do you really have harrowing days?" she asked. "You're so terribly stern, you don't seem the type to have them."

"I'm sorry to say I do indeed have the occasional harrowing day. It's working with my orchids that keeps me from tearing out my hair after a particularly bad one."

"So, you took your grandfather's advice after all," Elizabeth said.

"I suppose I did at that." He should not have been surprised she remembered. "My grandfather always encouraged me to take up gardening as a hobby," he explained. "He said it was a gentlemanly thing to do."

"I should love to see your orchids," Elizabeth said longingly and completely without the archness her cousin would have affected for his admiration.

"I've even built a conservatory for them. You must call on me, so I may give you a personal tour." He looked around the table as he issued the invitation.

"We should be simply too thrilled to come," Amelia said.

"Then you must. I'd be happy to show you the house as well."

The rest of the evening passed in a similar fashion, and even after he and Havoc had been left alone to sample the port and smoke one or two of his excellent cigars, it was not long before they joined the women in the drawing room. For a time they talked about London, then listened to Amelia play the piano and sing. At Elizabeth's insistence, Nicholas did some of his magic tricks. Elizabeth accused him of being a liar after he professed to be out of practice but managed to successfully carry off each trick. After he finished a complicated attempt, Elizabeth suddenly said, "Tell me, Nicholas, what do *you* think of the Mayfair Thief?"

"I'm afraid I don't know him," he answered.

She frowned at him. "You know what I mean. Mr. Rutherford says he admires him."

"Honestly, Elizabeth, I don't believe there's any such person. And I don't think Ripton does, either."

"But what if there were?"

"Thievery is hardly exciting," said Havoc.

"I concur with your uncle, Elizabeth."

"Well." She was blushing a little. "I still think he exists."

"I can see exhaustion has affected your brain, Elizabeth," he said, laughing as he stood up. "If I may, regretfully, say good night and thank you for a charming evening, I believe I ought to go."

"You must come and see us often, Mr. Villines," said Mrs. Willard.

"I believe you'll find I'll take advantage of such a kind invitation."

"Oh, but you must. We will be simply devastated if you do not," Amelia added.

"Watch out you don't run into the Mayfair Thief, Nicholas," Elizabeth called out as he was leaving.

"He only steals jewels, and I haven't any with me tonight. I'm leaving them behind at Tavistock Square," he replied with a smile.

"Why, thank you, Mr. Villines." Amelia giggled. "But do be careful!"

"I'll be quite safe, I assure you," he said, hardly loud enough to be heard. The sound of Amelia's laughter followed him out into the hall.

CHAPTER
11
➤➤❊❈❂❈❊⧏⧏

NICHOLAS LIVED ON CAMBRIDGE TERRACE IN ONE OF the stucco buildings facing the west side of Regent's Park. The house was really too large for a man living alone, but when it had become available after his improvement in fortunes, he'd rather liked the idea of having so much unused space. He was determined to have the purchase reflect the grandeur of the scheme that had made it possible, and the Cambridge Terrace house was certainly grand. But it was the view from the front parlor that had decided him. The way the evening light spread slowly over the green of the Park was a soothing sight to him and one he never tired of. It was worth every hard-earned shilling the place had cost. His favorite room in the whole of the house was the front parlor. It was high-ceilinged and spacious, and he kept it free of clutter. The large windows were curtained with a muted gold fabric and held open with tasseled lengths of

similar fabric. The rugs, too, had golden high-
lights. He had decorated the room with furniture from the last century; there was none of
that heavy, dark modern stuff in his parlor. A
large table dominated the center of the room.
His favorite armchair was by the fireplace, two
side tables flanked the windows, a few chairs
were scattered about, and a gold high-backed
sofa nestled against the wall opposite the windows.

He was sitting in his parlor with a book open
on the table before him. He was not reading; instead he was gazing at the Park. When his butler came in to announce the arrival of visitors,
he scowled and looked away from the view.
Though he took the card from the salver, he did
not look at it, glancing instead out the window
as if he expected to see his company standing
outside. He did not normally receive much before two o'clock, and he disliked having his
quiet mornings interrupted.

"Shall I tell the ladies you are not in, Mr. Villines?" Mr. Baker asked. He was thoroughly
used to his employer's moods, and he thought
he recognized this one. He waited for a nod of
assent.

"The ladies?" Nicholas finally troubled to
look at the card. "By no means, Baker, you must
show them in at once."

"Yes, Mr. Villines." He masked his surprise
at such a breach of custom. "At once, sir."

Nicholas stood up when Mr. Baker came

back with his guests. "Mrs. Willard, Miss Willard . . . I'm honored you've come. Good morning, Elizabeth." He bowed briefly to all three and took Amelia's arm to lead her to the sofa, commenting as he did that she ought to have a view of the Park. "Baker," he said, "please have someone bring refreshments. Perhaps some lemonade."

"Yes, sir."

"We were so intrigued when you described your orchids, we wasted no time in presuming on your offer to show them to us," Mrs. Willard said after she had taken a seat next to Amelia. "Beth, dear, do sit down so poor Mr. Villines may be comfortable in his own house." She waved a gloved hand while she spoke, taking in every detail of the room, from its old-style furniture to the portrait of Nicholas's grandfather that hung over the fireplace.

Elizabeth looked for a place to sit where she would be out of the way, but Nicholas quickly pulled out a chair for her at the table and seated himself at the head of it in order to have an unimpeded view of the three women.

"I should be more than happy to show them to you." A maid came in with a tray as he was speaking. "I'm ecstatic you've come so soon."

He was amused to see Elizabeth glance at Amelia and then at him, evidently imagining the comment to be directed at Amelia in particular. He was not sure it wasn't true. He returned Amelia's smile and wondered if it would be very hard to make her fall in love with him. The idea was not without a certain attraction. Amelia was very beautiful, and there would be the added benefit of frustrating Beaufort Latchley, who, if gossip were to be believed, was much enamored of her.

He was still considering the notion when he saw Elizabeth was not paying attention to the conversation. She was sitting with one elbow propped on the table, the side of her face cradled in the palm of one hand, examining the surface of the table. One slim finger lazily traced a pattern in the grain of the wood. Every now and then she would make some exclamation of interest, presumably for the benefit of Mrs. Willard. Eventually she turned her attention to the book he had left lying open before him. It was just close enough to tempt her into leaning forward to read the title. It was, of course, upside down in relation to where she sat, and it was just far enough away that she could not quite make out the legend at the head of the pages. She shifted so she was sitting at the very edge of her chair. Nicholas stopped midsentence to watch her. Biting her lower lip and squinting, she craned her neck, leaned forward one last inch, and almost toppled over.

"Beth! What in heaven's name are you doing?" Amelia's voice was sharp. "Do go on, Mr. Villines," she said when Elizabeth folded her hands in her lap and said nothing. "What you were saying was fascinating."

"I believe I was saying that if you enjoy the opera, you would like Paris a great deal. The opera there is superlative."

He reached for the book and, after replacing his bookmark, closed it. Certainly there had been no need for Amelia to snap at Elizabeth.

"Which city do you prefer, Mr. Villines, Paris or London?" Mrs. Willard asked.

"Next to London at the moment, Paris is my favorite city." With his forefinger, he pushed the book along the tabletop until it was within Elizabeth's reach.

"I should like to travel to Paris one day," Amelia said.

"I rather think Paris should love it if you did," he said.

"How very gallant of you, Mr. Villines." Amelia's smile made him think he could forgive her for continually calling Elizabeth "Beth" when she had to know full well Elizabeth hated the diminutive.

He waited until he saw that Elizabeth had put down the book before he rose to his feet. "Shall we go to the conservatory?" A few minutes later he was leading the three women to the back of the house. He held the door to the conservatory open for them, but as soon as he closed it, Amelia took his arm again.

"Goodness!" she exclaimed when the moist air closed in on them.

They walked down one of the aisles just ahead of Mrs. Willard, with Elizabeth bringing up the rear. Nicholas had spared no expense in fitting out his conservatory. It sported the very latest innovations for the cultivation of exotic plants. The ceilings were high, and panes of glass served as roof and walls so there was a profusion of light from all directions. The conservatory was not large; there were two aisles just wide enough to admit two persons walking side by side. Ferns planted in abundance softened the light to a gentle green, and water falling from heated pipes projecting over rough stonework was directed into a system of rills that made the air heavy with moisture and the scent of flowers. Most of the orchids were blooming, and there was silence while they looked around.

"Why, this is simply too lovely!" Amelia said. She halted before a brilliant pink flower.

"Cattelya skinneri," Nicholas said. "This particular plant is doing so well, I have become quite fond of it."

"I have a dress exactly this color."

He smiled. "If you tell me when you will next wear the dress, Miss Willard, I'll send some for your hair. They would look splendid."

"I would not dream of wearing a flower such as this in my hair," she replied, flashing him a brilliant smile. "I should wear it next to my heart."

"Mrs. Willard?" Nicholas asked, turning around. "Is there a flower you admire?"

"I believe this one." Mrs. Willard indicated

a flower similar in color to the one Amelia had admired.

"Like mother, like daughter. Shall I cut some for you now?"

"Oh, yes!"

Nicholas returned after retrieving his clippers, and after cutting several blossoms for Mrs. Willard and Amelia and handing them over with a small bow, he looked around for Elizabeth. He was anxious to know what she thought of his gentleman's habit. She had wandered farther down the aisle while he was busy with Amelia and Mrs. Willard and was examining the plants.

"Shall I cut you something?" he asked quietly when he reached the spot where she stood.

"I don't believe I could choose, Nicholas." She looked around. "I would want to take them all!" She was wearing the green silk again, and he could not take his eyes off the point where she had fastened a cameo. He thought of Paris again and found himself wondering how her hair might feel in his fingers. "They're all so beautiful," she said.

"May I choose some for you?" he finally asked.

"Yes, please do."

In a moment he was back with a spray of small white flowers. He handed them to her. "These, I think, ought to suit. Simple, but elegant."

She took them from him and bent her head to breathe in the sent. "They smell heavenly!"

He thrust his hands into the pockets of his coat and walked alongside her when she started down the aisle.

"What is the matter with this one?" She stopped before two plants that did not have so much as a single blossom.

"Elizabeth," Nicholas said with a sigh, "you have spotted the rarest plants in this room. This is *Vanda cerulea*. The blue orchid."

"Blue," she repeated softly. "It must be very beautiful."

"No one has ever seen it flower. Not in this country, anyway."

"It's difficult to grow, then?"

"Not if one knows the tricks, I imagine. The trouble is, no one seems to know them."

"Perhaps it doesn't like the climate in here." She shrugged.

"Orchids require such a climate."

"It seems to me, Nicholas," she said, looking fixedly at the two plants, "that since you've got two, you might try to experiment with different conditions."

"It took a fortune to acquire even one of these, let alone two!"

"Still, they both look poorly, do they not?"

"Perhaps this is how they ought to look."

"And perhaps not." She smiled at him. It was the familiar turning up of one side of her mouth that he had not realized he had missed quite so much. It felt good to see it again after so long. His little Elizabeth.

"Do you think you might succeed where every man in England has failed, Elizabeth?"

"I don't see why not." Her eyebrows rose in indignation. That, too, was a familiar expression.

"Just as stubborn as ever, I see."

"Am I stubborn because common sense tells me I might be right?"

"We shall see about that, little Miss Elizabeth!" He excused himself and in a moment was back with a pot and small trowel. She stood close by him, watching with some puzzlement as he carefully uprooted one of the blue orchids. He placed it in the pot and, turning, presented it to her.

Her eyebrows lifted in surprise this time. "Surely you don't mean for me to have this!"

"I propose an experiment. I shall turn over custody of this plant to you, which you are to treat in whatever manner your common sense dictates. The remaining one is to stay here, in my care. But, I warn you, there shall be dire consequences if you kill it."

"And if I don't?" She looked directly into his eyes, and for a moment he was caught in their depths, unable to answer her.

At last he spoke. "If, during the time you remain in London, you succeed in coaxing it into flowering, you will have half of any money resulting therefrom."

"But none of the credit?" Again that lifting of the corner of her mouth.

"Half the credit as well," he agreed. "But I reserve the right to take the plant away from you if I think it necessary."

"All right, Nicholas." She reached for the pot. "We'll just see who's right."

"Allow me to carry it for you," he said, holding the pot out of her reach. He was amused to see the color rising to her cheeks. "If you do have questions or need any advice, you must not hesitate to ask. I shall be positively inconsolable if it dies."

"Beth! Dear, come here and show us your flower." Mrs. Willard motioned to her from the end of the aisle.

Nicholas followed her, and when Elizabeth reached her aunt, he heard her say in a low voice, "You mustn't monopolize the conversation like that, Beth." She got a firm grip on Elizabeth's arm and did not relinquish it until they were saying their good-byes. The blue orchid had been consigned to the Willards' coachman for safekeeping, and as Nicholas was seeing them out, he left Amelia to approach Elizabeth.

He startled her by asking abruptly, "Did Monsieur Rousseau interest you? I only ask," he continued, 'because earlier you seemed so curious about the book."

"I apologize for that, Nicholas."

"There's nothing to apologize for. I'll send it on to you when I've finished."

"Thank you."

"Just remember, Elizabeth," he said as he waved off the coachman to hand up Elizabeth himself, "I shall pine away if you kill my orchid!"

CHAPTER
12

Nicholas was driving down Great Portland Street on his way to Cambridge Terrace after spending an afternoon visiting at Fitzroy Square when he thought he saw a familiar head of chestnut hair in the crowd on the sidewalk. He directed his driver to move to the side of the street, and when he was certain of the woman's identity, he called out: "Elizabeth! Elizabeth Willard! It is you," he cried when she turned her head. He signaled for the carriage to stop, then jumped out.

"Nicholas!" She came to a halt. "Good afternoon." She handed the package she held to Miss Lincoln and extended her hand.

"This is an unexpected pleasure," he said when he stood next to her on the walk. "Where are you headed on such a lovely afternoon?" He took off his hat.

"Home. And yourself?"

"I admit, I was sitting in that contraption"—

he motioned to the carriage—"gathering wool. It, too, is a gentleman's occupation, or so I am told." He brushed a lock of hair from his forehead.

"Will you walk with me, Nicholas?" she said after a pause.

He grinned at her. "I'd be delighted to."

"I'm sure Aunt Mary and Amelia, especially, would love to have you stay to tea," she added.

"It's kind of you to ask me." Nicholas fell into step with her, walking nearest the street. He signaled for his driver to follow them.

"How are your aunt and uncle?" she asked him.

"Quite well. I've just come from Fitzroy Square, as a matter of fact."

"I'd almost forgotten how much I missed your aunt, 'til we came to London. She was always kind to me, even though I was bothersome whenever we visited."

"You weren't bothersome, only exuberant."

"Oh, but I was. You need only ask her about that. I was always trying to help, and she let me, though I daresay I must have been more a hindrance than anything else. I always told myself that when I grew up I wanted to be just like her."

"Did you, now?"

"Yes."

They walked in silence for a few moments. He could still see the little girl he used to hold on his lap. She was older, of course, but not so very much. She had stayed innocent, and he had not. For some reason the burden of his guilt did not seem so heavy when he could see Elizabeth virtually unchanged. He hoped she never did change, for if she could be corrupted, what hope was there for him? "If I had known I would meet you, I would have brought the Rousseau with me," he said.

"Perhaps you will bring it another time." She shrugged. "Only if you do, don't tell Aunt Mary."

"Why not?"

"She thinks reading is a ruinous habit for a young lady." She did a fair imitation of her aunt's tone.

"I thought she only objected to the reading of novels."

"That too. But she's convinced I read entirely too much."

"Don't ever change just because someone thinks you should."

"I cannot help liking to read."

He briefly put an arm around her shoulders. "Will you promise me you'll never change, Elizabeth?" He could faintly smell the scent of violets in her hair.

"I can't promise that." She frowned at him.

"Yes, you can," he insisted. "You shouldn't listen to your aunt, Elizabeth. Promise me you'll always be yourself."

Her eyes opened a little wider. "That I can

promise. But, Nicholas, it's your fault if Aunt Mary does not like me the way I am."

"My fault?"

"Of course. You've always encouraged me to think for myself." She looked down to gently shake a wrinkle from her skirt. "It's only your opinion that ever mattered to me," she said softly.

"I'm flattered."

"You should be, Nicholas!"

He did not return her smile. "Always be my sweet little Elizabeth," he said in a low voice.

They had reached Tavistock Square, and Elizabeth paused at the door. She put a hand on his arm. "I'll always be Elizabeth," she said. "But it is unfair of you to ask me not to change when you have changed so much."

"I wish I had not," he said.

She reached to touch his cheek. "Sometimes I think you aren't the same person at all, Nicholas. Sometimes I think you're a stranger."

"Don't give up on me."

"Give up on you? Never. You are my friend. Nothing can change that."

"Is it true?" he asked, grasping her hand.

"Of course."

He raised her hand and, though he knew it was improper, pressed his lips to the tips of her fingers. When he looked up she was staring at him, a blush rising to her cheeks. "It means everything to me, to hear you say that, Elizabeth." The sound of Miss Lincoln clearing her throat behind him brought him to his senses, and he quickly let go of her hand.

"Will you come to tea?"

"It would be a pleasure," he said.

CHAPTER
13
⤜⤛✦⤜⤛

WHEN THE MORNING POST ARRIVED AT TAVISTOCK Square, Amelia and Elizabeth had already gone out for the early ride that was now a habit with them. Mr. Willard was gone for the day, and Mrs. Willard was alone in the sitting room. There were only three letters. One was from Mrs. Willard's sister in Exeter and one for her husband from someone she'd never heard of. The last was a letter bearing the insignia of Sir Jaspar Charles, Bart. She knew instantly only the third letter was important. Correspondence of any sort from a man of Sir Jaspar's stature was a triumph, even though he was already married.

It was an invitation, accompanied by a charming note from Lady Charles herself, expressing her wish that the Willards come to her party—she did so want them, especially her lovely daughter and niece, to meet the countess and earl of Lewesfield. She hoped they were not already engaged for the afternoon in question.

Mrs. Willard somehow managed to sit quietly until the girls came back.

"Hurry and get changed, my dear," she cried, jumping up and rushing into the hall when she heard Amelia and Elizabeth come in.

"What is it, Mother?" Both girls stopped on the stairs and stood looking at her.

"We are going out, so hurry along."

"But, why? What's happened?" Amelia asked.

"Why?" Mrs. Willard repeated. "Because we've an invitation to see Sir Jaspar Charles's painting on Wednesday. Lady Charles herself has written to me that Lord and Lady Lewesfield will be there and that she is anxious for us to make their acquaintance. Now, hurry along." Mrs. Willard gestured for Amelia to do as she said. "Lord Lewesfield!" she exclaimed half to herself.

"Ah! Amelia, you must make haste. You must have clothes fit for an earl to see you in," Elizabeth murmured.

"You know, Beth," Amelia said as they walked down the hallway to their rooms, "you oughtn't to take this lightly. You act as though you don't care that we are to meet Lord Lewesfield."

"Of course I care, Amelia."

"Well, it doesn't seem as if you do. Why, Mr.

Nicholas Villines tells me Lord Lewesfield is simply immensely rich."

"When did he say that?"

"Well, really! Mr. Villines may be the shining light of your life, Beth, but he does not spend all his time thinking about you, I can assure you of that. He and I talk quite a lot, you know."

"Yes, Amelia, I imagine you do." She said nothing more until she reached her room. "I imagine you do," she repeated to herself as she closed the door.

When the Willards arrived at Sir Jaspar's house in Mayfair, they made their way through the crowd to where Lady Charles was standing with another woman of about fifty years of age.

"Mrs. Willard, good afternoon. Allow me to say, Miss Willard," Lady Charles said to Amelia, "that you look lovely. And Miss Elizabeth." She took Elizabeth's hand and pressed it warmly. "Good afternoon to you as well, my dear. Lady Lewesfield, this is the charming family I was telling you about."

Lady Lewesfield fixed her gaze on them and nodded. "It is a pleasure," she said. "Are you enjoying London?" She seemed most taken by Amelia, so it was Amelia who answered.

"Oh, Lady Lewesfield! It is simply too wonderful."

"Well, now, you are a pretty girl."

Amelia dimpled and was about to say something when both Beaufort Latchley and Ripton

Rutherford arrived to greet Lady Charles and the countess.

Lady Lewesfield briefly lost interest in Amelia. "Good afternoon, Mr. Latchley," she said, pressing Beaufort's hand warmly. "Have you met these two young ladies?" She placed her other hand on Amelia's shoulder.

"Indeed, Lady Lewesfield, I have had the pleasure.' Beaufort turned to Mrs. Willard and bowed. Amelia was amazed to see how friendly he was with the countess, and she gave him a brilliant smile.

"Mr. Latchley is fast becoming a favorite at Portsmouth Square," said Lady Lewesfield. "We only wish he came more often."

"I might have known Mr. Latchley would make straight away for the loveliest women in the room." Ripton managed a sideways glance at Amelia while he bent over the countess's hand.

"Good afternoon, Mr. Rutherford," said the countess. She looked past Ripton. "Ah, Mr. Villines, you've come after all. Tell me, how is Eversleigh?" Lady Lewesfield extended her hand to Nicholas. "Lewesfield was asking after your grandfather just this morning. We had hoped we might see you both here."

"He has just left for Witchford Runs, my lady. He claims that not even the presence of women as charming as you can induce him to stay in London past November."

"I cannot blame him." The countess shook

her head. "Dear Mr. Latchley," she said, briefly grasping Nicholas's hand to prevent him from leaving her side, "do you not think Miss Amelia Willard would like to see Lady Charles's garden?"

"I would be delighted to escort you." Beaufort turned to Amelia and bowed stiffly.

"It would be an honor, Mr. Latchley," Amelia said with a giggle.

Nicholas glanced at Amelia, and when she giggled again, the corner of his mouth curled into what might have been a smile. Elizabeth would have given anything to understand the meaning of the glint in his black eyes when he looked at Amelia.

Amelia, conscious that she was the center of attention, tossed her curls, curtsied to Her Ladyship, and was gone. Ripton stared after them forlornly, wincing when Amelia placed her hand on Mr. Latchley's arm just before they were out of sight.

"Surely, Mr. Villines, you might take Miss Elizabeth out to see the gardens," said Lady Charles.

Nicholas nodded his assent and was turning to Elizabeth when the countess put a hand on his arm. "I promised myself I would have Mr. Villines for a partner at cards," she said. "Perhaps Mr. Rutherford will take Miss Willard around the gardens?"

"It would be a pleasure." Ripton looked at Elizabeth. "Shall we?" he asked.

"Certainly."

"I'll find you later," Nicholas said as Ripton led Elizabeth away.

"Which one of us do you suppose he was talking to?" Ripton asked.

"You, of course."

"Such a diplomat."

They were silent while they made their way through the room; the crowd prevented any further attempt at conversation. When they stepped out into the garden, Ripton looked at Elizabeth, who blinked in the sunlight and adjusted her hat to shadow her face. "Dashed bad luck, don't you think?" he asked, lifting his eyebrows quizzically.

Naturally, thought Elizabeth, he had really wanted to walk with Amelia, and here he was, stuck escorting the plain cousin. "We don't have to walk for long, Mr. Rutherford," she consoled him.

He looked startled. "Miss Elizabeth, I was referring to my arriving at the same time as Mr. Latchley. I can't abide the man. I assure you," he protested, "I consider walking with you to be a stroke of good fortune."

"Never mind, Mr. Rutherford." She patted his arm, sorry to have embarrassed him. "I wouldn't worry too much about Mr. Latchley. Amelia is so excited at the prospect of meeting Lord and Lady Lewesfield, I can assure you she's not thinking much about Mr. Latchley," she said.

"If he is the one who introduces her to Lord Lewesfield, she will think him a hero." He feigned dejection. "And I might as well have stayed home. Heroic men are the bane of my existence."

"One is hardly heroic simply because one introduces another to an aristocrat. Until Mr. Latchley saves someone from a burning building, he can hardly be a hero."

"Miss Elizabeth," he said after looking at her for a moment, "you really mustn't put up with such bad behavior from me." He shook his head slowly. "A gentleman ought not to carry on about another woman when he is already with a lovely young lady. Will you accept my apology?"

"Oh, I don't think that's necessary."

"But it is." He stopped walking and grasped her hand. "I do apologize, Miss Elizabeth." He bent to kiss her hand.

"Mr. Rutherford," she said in a low voice, feeling her cheeks begin to warm. She put her hand over his arm and continued walking.

"Nicholas tells me you've been to see his conservatory," he said after a few moments' silence.

"Yes, it was quite beautiful. I'd never seen orchids before."

"They are magnificent, aren't they? But to tell you the truth," he said in a confidential tone, "I prefer an uncomplicated flower. I limit myself to pruning the occasional rosebush, and then only when the gardener isn't looking. I do believe I'd come to some harm if the man caught me mucking about in his flower beds."

"I never knew gardening could be a dangerous hobby."

"It is at my house, I assure you," he said, returning her smile. He raised an eyebrow when she laughed. They had passed the roses and were walking on the grass toward a large elm. "Would you care to sit down?" He indicated a bench in the shade of the tree.

"Yes, thank you, I would. It's rather warm out."

Ripton sat down next to her and crossed his long legs at the ankles. "Now, tell me, Miss Elizabeth, do you still like London?" he asked.

"Yes, I suppose so."

"You don't sound certain."

"I don't know." She sighed, and Ripton looked at her quizzically. "It seems that everyone attaches such a lot of importance to the silliest things. I never knew how complicated choosing a pair of gloves could be until I came to London." She shook her head. "Do you know how often I find myself agonizing over such a silly thing, when I really ought to be worrying about a poor man who must steal in order to feed his children?"

"It's much easier to decide whether one is wearing the right gloves than it is to determine how one is going to help others."

"Well, I'm not doing enough." She bent to

pick up a leaf. "And what is worse, Mr. Rutherford," she said sadly, "is that sometimes I don't care." She was aware of him watching her examine the leaf.

"You seem to care a good deal more than most."

"Then I think most people must not care at all."

"They don't." Even he sounded faintly bitter.

"I'm sorry, Mr. Rutherford." She put a hand on his arm. "Forgive me for being so gloomy, will you?"

"There's nothing to forgive, Miss Willard."

"Anyway, I like London most of the time." She smiled up at him. "It's certainly a good deal more interesting than Miss Langford's School." She let the leaf fall to her lap.

"I imagine it must be," he replied, leaning against the back of the bench and clasping his hands behind his head. The ensuing silence was a comfortable one, and Elizabeth closed her eyes to listen to the birds in the tree above them. She was half-asleep when Nicholas found them.

"There you are, Rip," she heard him say. She opened her eyes. He was still several feet from where they sat. "I've been looking for you. Lady Charles is just about to give us a tour of the house and show us her painting." He looked at Elizabeth. "Has Ripton behaved himself?" he asked.

"Behaved myself?" Ripton said in insulted

tones. 'I've been a perfect gentleman, haven't I, Miss Elizabeth?''

"Yes, you have, Mr. Rutherford." She handed him the leaf, and he took it as though it were a tribute, tucking it away into the pocket of his waistcoat.

"I confess, I'm eager to see this painting of Sir Jaspar's," Ripton said as he helped her to her feet.

"Come along, then."

She took Ripton's arm again, and they followed Nicholas across the lawn and into the house.

The painting was in a drawing room, where it hung on a wall reserved for it alone. Several people were already standing before it, and there was some shuffling to make room. She lost sight of Nicholas when Ripton grabbed her hand and bullied his way to the front. He stood before the painting, paced about, and examined it from all angles. "Well," he said, turning to her, "what do you think of it?"

"It's lovely."

"Agreed."

"What do you think, Mr. Rutherford?"

"I think Sir Jaspar has gotten himself a bargain. He's been deuced lucky to get such a nice painting to go with this extraordinary frame."

More people came into the room, Amelia among them, and Elizabeth no longer had the undivided attention of Ripton Rutherford. As she made her way to the back of the room in order to leave the way clear for Ripton, someone jostled her, and in trying to recover her balance, she backed into what she assumed was an umbrella stand. It overturned, and she bent down to set it to rights. A cylindrical paper-wrapped package fell out of the stand, and she had to reach for it quickly to prevent it from rolling away and being stepped on. It was surprisingly heavy when she picked it up.

"Allow me, Elizabeth."

She looked up to see Nicholas setting the stand out of harm's way. "Thank you," she said when he took the package from her and carefully placed it back inside. He held out his hand and helped her to rise.

"There certainly are a dashed lot of people here," he said. "Are you all right?" He gripped her elbow.

"Yes."

"Let's walk. It's far too crowded in here." Elizabeth was happy to follow him outside. "Did you and Ripton enjoy your walk?" he asked when they were clear of the crowd.

"Of course."

"You were very quiet when I found you. I was afraid you had quarreled."

"Oh, no. I imagine he was plotting how to get Amelia away from Mr. Latchley."

"Oh?"

"He was afraid Amelia would fall in love with Mr. Latchley should he be first to introduce her to Lord Lewesfield."

"Do you think she will?"

Belatedly she realized that Nicholas and Ripton were in all likelihood rivals for Amelia. "If she does," she said hastily, hoping he did not notice her pink cheeks, "it will only be for an hour or two at the most. She admires you a great deal, Nicholas."

"Does she?" He took something out of his pocket and handed it to her without waiting for an answer. It was the Rousseau. "I remembered it just as I was leaving home," he said. "I wanted to give it to you before I left."

"Are you leaving so soon?" She fingered the ridges of the spine as she watched him, puzzled at the hardness of his eyes.

"Yes. I've a few things to attend to this afternoon that cannot be put off any longer." He stopped walking and turned to face her. 'Read it, and when you've finished we'll talk about what you think." For a moment the hardness of his gaze was gone, and she saw the Nicholas she loved. She was surprised when he suddenly grasped her hands. "Don't forget me, Elizabeth," he said.

"Forget you! Why do you say such a thing?"

"It's just that you look very pretty today, I suppose."

"Oh!"

"Soon enough, you won't want to spend any time with your old friend Nicholas."

"If you believe that, you do not think much of me."

"On the contrary, Elizabeth. Only, one day you'll be as grown-up as Amelia, and then I'll seem like rather dull company to you. I wish you would stay a little girl forever."

"Oh."

"Are we still friends?"

"You know we are."

"Are you sure?"

"Nicholas, we will always be friends."

Even after Nicholas had left her, it was some time before she went inside.

CHAPTER
14
※)X(≪

NICHOLAS ARRIVED AT REGENT'S PARK SHORTLY AFTER
nine o'clock. Amelia and Elizabeth were with
Miss Lincoln, and he waved as he rode up. At
Sir Jaspar's, Amelia had urged him to join them
this morning. He had not promised he would
come, and it irked him that Amelia had obviously never doubted he would.

"Good morning," he said. "Miss Willard."
He nodded at Amelia, who acknowledged his
greeting by smiling and lifting her riding whip.
He was certain it had taken her no small effort
to achieve her look of casual elegance. She always looked polished, with never a hair out of
place, unless it was artfully so. "Elizabeth." He
nodded to her. Her riding habit was stylishly
cut, very much suiting her slender figure. She
looked fresh, with her clear skin glowing from
the ride from Tavistock Square. The morning
air, Nicholas concluded, agreed with her.

"What a pleasant surprise to see you, Nicholas," she said.

Evidently Amelia had not told Elizabeth she had invited him on this morning ride.

"It isn't actually a surprise, Beth," Amelia said. "I asked Mr. Villines to join us."

"Well, then, I'm glad you came."

"Where shall we ride?" Nicholas asked.

"We usually go this direction." Amelia inclined her head to the right. She held back her horse until Nicholas was even with her.

"Let us go, then," he said just before they trotted off. He could not see Elizabeth, though he was aware of her riding a little to one side of them, hanging back with Miss Lincoln while Amelia looked at him archly.

"I was disappointed to discover you left Sir Jaspar's party so early," she said, gazing at him through lowered eyelashes.

"I'm surprise you noticed, Miss Willard.' He suppressed a smile at what he was certain was not genuine bashfulness.

"Of course I noticed!" Her blue eyes fixed on him. "I looked for you," she said, "but you were simply nowhere to be found."

"I'm sorry now that I left," he answered, returning her gaze automatically. He wondered if there was anything behind those soft, perfectly shaped eyes that would not become boring after a time. She was interesting now, but would she still be after even a year?

"And I, too," she said softly.

"You seemed occupied without my attentions."

"How little you notice, then, Mr. Villines," she said accusingly.

"Defend me, Elizabeth," he cried, turning to her. "Was she not constantly occupied?"

"You must admit, Amelia, there is something to what Nicholas says. But I wouldn't be disheartened. He did trouble himself to notice you were occupied."

"There, you see, Miss Willard? I had very little encouragement upon which to presume."

"Amelia," Elizabeth added, "is almost always occupied, though it's no fault of hers. 'None but the brave deserves the fair,' you know."

"Was I not brave to come here this morning?" he protested.

"Perhaps so," Elizabeth said.

"Perhaps?" He did his best to sound offended.

"It seems to me you might make any woman fall in love with you." She blushed, genuinely, as soon as the words were out.

"This is fascinating, Elizabeth, do go on. I should like to hear more about the power of my charms."

"He shall be vain as a peacock if you do, Beth," Amelia said.

The sound of someone hailing them interrupted Nicholas's response. Elizabeth first saw who was joining them. "Good morning, Mr. Rutherford."

"Good morning, Miss Elizabeth, Miss Willard."

"Good morning, Rip."

"Nick." By his expression it was clear that Ripton had expected to find Amelia and Elizabeth alone.

"Two surprises in one morning," Nicholas heard Elizabeth say. "It's quite overwhelming."

"What brings you to the Park so early?" he asked.

"The old boy needed some exercise." Ripton patted his horse on the neck. "And as Miss Willard was kind enough to invite me, here I am."

"Good morning, Mr. Rutherford." Amelia smiled fetchingly. "I'm so glad you could come. Will you ride next to me?"

Nicholas scowled. No doubt Amelia had also given Ripton the impression he would be meeting them alone. She obviously intended to make the two of them compete for her, and he did not like it in the least. If this was supposed to be a demonstration of her power to attract, he did not approve of her method.

There was a moment of silence before Amelia smiled and said, "Perhaps you might settle a dispute, Mr. Rutherford. Mr. Villines says I am too occupied with other gentlemen, and he dares not approach me for that reason. Do you think I am too occupied?"

"Miss Willard, the number of men who vie for your attentions is truly daunting."

"But, Mr. Rutherford," she cried, "that's hardly my fault."

"Be that as it may, it is daunting when a woman has so many admirers."

"Well then, what is the maximum number of admirers a lady ought to have, Mr. Rutherford?" asked Amelia.

"No more than a dozen or so," he answered.

"Only a dozen?" she said, pouting.

"How many admirers do *you* think a lady ought to have?" Ripton turned in his saddle to look at Elizabeth.

"No so many as a dozen, Mr. Rutherford. It would be too tiring. I don't know how Amelia stands it."

"You would prefer just six, perhaps?"

"I believe I should prefer to have a secret admirer. Then one might have all the excitement without any of the bother."

"Provided it isn't a secret from you as well," Nicholas added. He attributed his sudden vague anxiety to the fact that Elizabeth was young to be thinking seriously about having admirers.

"Do you really think having admirers is a bother, Miss Elizabeth?"

"It seems so to me, Mr. Rutherford. You were just now terribly abusing my cousin. And Nicholas was doing the same before you came."

"Beth is right, you two have been frightfully cruel. I shall have to think of some way for you to make it up to me."

"Perhaps a bit of unofficial news would suffice?" Ripton asked as the four of them continued riding through the Park.

"What news?" asked Amelia.

"It's all over London. Or it soon will be. Sir Jaspar's painting, you know, the one he was crowing over the other day. He claims someone's replaced it with a fake."

"A fake!" Elizabeth echoed.

"A forgery, Miss Elizabeth."

"Are you sure?" Amelia asked.

"Oh, yes. I had the news from my mother this morning. She's never wrong about such things. If she says it's so, then you may rest assured it's so. The morning after the party, he went to have a look at it before breakfast, and he discovered, so he says, that it wasn't the same painting at all."

"How unfortunate if Sir Jaspar spent all that money on a forgery," said Nicholas.

"Sir Jaspar swears he purchased the original."

"Clearly he did not," Nicholas said with a shrug.

"He's convinced someone switched paintings. Says he supervised the crating of it when it was sent over from Switzerland, and he knows the real painting went into the crate. He's called in the Metropolitan Police to investigate how his painting was stolen from under his very nose. The poor man's near to having apoplexy."

"Stolen? Could someone have stolen his

painting while we were there?" Amelia's eyes widened.

"I don't consider it likely, Miss Willard," Nicholas said. "There's quite a market for old masters. Someone working for the company that shipped it could have changed the paintings quite easily."

"I think it was the Mayfair Thief," said Elizabeth.

"Do you suppose it was?" Amelia asked.

"I thought he only stole jewels," said Nicholas.

"It isn't any great leap from diamonds to works of art," Ripton said with a shrug.

"It's only a matter of size and portability." Nicholas snorted. "If you want my honest opinion, I don't believe Sir Jaspar ever had the original. I think the painting we saw was already a fake, albeit a skillful one."

"I don't know about that, Nick. It looked real enough to me."

"Well, according to you, it's not the original now. How do you explain that?" Nicholas challenged him.

"Obviously, someone stole it."

Nicholas frowned. "Sir Jaspar never had the original, if you ask me."

"I think he did." Elizabeth surprised them with her emphatic statement. "The painting must have been changed after Sir Jaspar's party." The three were staring at her, but she continued. "The thief probably brought the forgery with him, hid it somewhere, then came back later to switch them."

"Oh, Beth, that's ridiculous."

"You've quite an imagination, Elizabeth," Nicholas said.

"What ever gave you such a fantastic idea?" asked Ripton, looking astonished.

"Because I—" She was blushing again, and she stared at the mane of her horse. "Just because."

"Because what?" Nicholas prompted. "A painting's a rather awkward thing to carry about," he said when she did not answer. "There were dozens of people there. I should think someone would have noticed a fellow carrying the thing into Sir Jaspar's house."

"Not if it wasn't in a frame, Nicholas."

"She's right about that," said Ripton.

"But there'd be a time of it getting the forgery into Sir Jaspar's frame," Nicholas pointed out. "It just isn't possible."

"But, Nicholas, don't you see? That's why it had to be the Mayfair Thief."

"Why? Because only a man who does not exist could steal a painting that was never really there?"

"No, because only the Mayfair Thief can do the impossible."

Nicholas stared at her, then broke into laughter. "Be careful, Elizabeth, you might wake up one day and find yourself in love with a myth."

"Well, perhaps I will, Nicholas," she retorted.

"I think you would be very unhappy if you discovered you were in love with someone cold-blooded enough to sneak into Sir Jaspar's home in the dead of night."

"He stole Lady Stinforth's tiara right off her head," Ripton said with a smile. "Sounds like a cold-blooded chap to me. Nicholas is right, Miss Elizabeth, you had better not fall in love with the Mayfair Thief."

"Ripton!" Nicholas scowled, but it did no good.

"Maybe Miss Elizabeth is right."

"I don't see why not," Elizabeth said. "Do you remember when I knocked over that umbrella stand, Nicholas? There was a package in it, and it was rolling away. You took it from me, don't you remember how heavy it was?"

"Could it have been a canvas?" Ripton asked.

"It might have been."

"And then again, it might not have," Nicholas said, glaring at Ripton. 'The two of you may believe whatever nonsense you like about this thief person. I don't even believe there's been a crime committed."

"I agree with Mr. Villines," said Amelia. "And I think it's time we changed the subject."

CHAPTER
15
❯❯❯❯X❮❮❮❮

PERCY JOHNS WAS FORTY-SEVEN YEARS OLD, AND HE took pride in his appearance. His clothes were always clean and neatly mended by his wife, his shoes were always polished, and his collars always starched. His hair, a nondescript brown that was slowly receding, was always combed perfectly into place. He was of average height and of somewhat more than average weight. By no stretch of the imagination could he be called handsome, yet his awkward features stopped just short of being ugly. Ale was his drink, a pint with lunch, a pint with the boys when he was off work, and another when he got home to supper and his wife. Percy was a man of confirmed habits, or rather, entrenched ones. Most particularly when involved in a thought-provoking case, he was a compulsive list maker. It was almost an unconscious habit with him to take pen and paper in hand whenever he sat down. He did not feel at ease unless he could make a list of his thoughts. His entire life was organized by the making of lists, chiefly because once he wrote something down, he never forgot it. Had he been born a gentleman, he might have gone to school and become a mathematician or perhaps a barrister, since the law was his consuming interest.

A detective with the Bow Street Runners until their dissolution in 1829 Percy was now a member of the recently established Metropolitan Police. He was good at his job; indeed, Percy Johns was unofficially responsible for the training of the younger officers. It was his habit to take one or two of the more promising men under his wing and instruct them in his methods. His most promising protégé at the moment was Alfred Wells. Mr. Wells was twenty-four years old, highly intelligent, eager to learn, and ambitious. Percy was reminded of himself when he was younger.

Percy sat at his desk, staring at a variety of lists spread out before him. One of them consisted of some fifty names, thirty of which were neatly crossed out. Another contained a succession of dates, followed by a description of a theft that had occurred on that date. One or two of those entries was crossed out. The first date was as early as 1837, when a bracelet valued at nearly five hundred pounds had been stolen from a Mrs. Snowden. Percy entered the date of the supposed theft of Sir Jaspar Charles's Van Dyck at the bottom of the list. He consulted a third list and, using a straight edge to keep the lines neat and parallel, crossed another seven entries off his list of names.

The theft of Sir Jaspar's painting was puzzling, and while it was possible the baronet had never actually had the original, a careful consideration of both his lists and the facts as related to him by Sir Jaspar made Percy think the man's painting had in fact been stolen. The one thing every theft on his list had in common was the seeming impossibility of it having happened at all. There were only two things Percy Johns knew for certain about the Mayfair Thief: he was an extraordinary man, and one day he would make a mistake. Percy intended to take full advantage of the mistake when it finally happened.

CHAPTER
16
※※※

"Come in for a drink, Rip?" Nicholas asked when the two arrived at Cambridge Terrace after having supper at The Phoenix, a club just off St. James's Street. It was still early, just past eleven-thirty, so Ripton agreed.

Mr. Chester was waiting for Nicholas, and as soon as they walked into the entranceway, he helped the men off with their coats.

"Did you have a pleasant evening, gentlemen?"

"Yes, Chester, we did."

"The Phoenix has got a new cook," Ripton added. "A most pleasant evening. I wish I had more like it."

"You will be staying up, Mr. Villines?" Mr. Chester inquired.

"Yes."

"Port, sir?"

"Yes."

"In the parlor, then?"

Nicholas nodded.

"Very good, sir."

A few moments later, Mr. Chester brought two glasses and a bottle of port to the parlor. Nicholas accepted the glasses and waved a hand to indicate Mr. Chester would not be required to stay.

"I don't mind if I do," Ripton said when Nicholas passed him a glass and the bottle.

They were quiet while they held their glasses. Fine liquor such as the port Nicholas bought needed to be drunk in silence, and Nicholas knew him too well to break such a necessary period of reflection. Nicholas stared at his glass for some time before drinking from it, but when he did, the port slid down his throat like the fine wine it was. It has been a pleasant day from the very start, he thought, and the evening was turning out to equally pleasant. He stretched out his legs and sank back into his chair.

"Lately," he said, "I have been thinking a great deal about getting married."

Ripton considered the statement. "Are we at last at an age when we ought to consider getting wives?"

"I believe so, Rip." There was silence while he emptied his glass. He refilled it but left it untouched. "I have all the comforts a man could want. I live in a house arranged exactly to my taste, surrounded by beautiful things, and"—he picked up his drink and lifted it to the light—

"I can well afford to consume the expensive port we are presently enjoying."

If everything went as planned, Nicholas thought, he would soon be able to lapse into the respectable idleness that would have been his long ago, had his father not squandered a fortune. He would be able to think about the seat in the House of Commons his grandfather kept urging him to seek. He would marry, have children, and one day pass on a fortune to his sons. He would have a family like Havoc Willard's.

"You don't think a wife would get in the way of your enjoyment of all this?"

"Not if she were the right woman." He sat up briefly to refill Ripton's glass. "I think it would please my aunt and uncle if I were to marry Amelia Willard. Even my grandfather would approve of her." A wife like Amelia Willard would be perfect for a Member of Parliament. She was exquisitely lovely, and she came from good family. She was soft-hearted, pliable, and utterly empty-headed, the sort of woman a man dreamed of marrying. It would be a good marriage to make.

"I see."

"But I do not believe I am in love with her, or ever will be." If only Amelia possessed even a little of her cousin's quiet fire, he would have fallen in love with her long ago. Elizabeth lacked neither character nor substance. There was not a vain bone in her body, when—to be perfectly honest—there was every reason for

131

her to be as vain as Amelia. "I think you might be in love with Amelia," he said to Ripton.

"Not yet," Ripton answered. "But I could be one day, if I put my mind to it."

The conversation, short as it had been, cleared the air of a tension that had been building since Nicholas had arrived in London. They smiled; as always, they understood each other perfectly.

Three-quarters of an hour later, the two had done away with nearly the entire bottle of port. Neither was feeling any ill effects. In fact, they seemed inordinately pleased with themselves.

"Nicholas?" Ripton leaned forward to replenish the contents of his glass with what little remained in the bottle.

"Hmm?"

"What do you make of Elizabeth Willard?"

"Elizabeth? Why?"

"I haven't had the opportunity to become as well acquainted with her as you have."

"She's like a sister to me. I've known her since she was this high—" He indicated with one hand. "She's turned into a sweet little thing, you know."

"A sister." Ripton shook his head.

"Of course, a sister. How else would I feel about her?" Nicholas wondered why he sounded so defensive.

"She's everything you said she was. Well-spoken, kind, thoughtful." He pursed his lips. "She's also remarkably pretty."

"But? . . ."

"I have observed she seems somewhat lacking in confidence."

Nicholas sat forward. "Do you know, you are precisely right. With a little more confidence, Elizabeth would be more than a match for Amelia."

"She would make someone an excellent wife."

"Well, someday, perhaps."

"I understand Lord Lewesfield is looking about for a wife for his youngest son."

"He's too stupid for Elizabeth."

"Well, there's Lady Charles's brother, Gerald," Ripton suggested.

"He's in the navy. That's no life for someone as delicate as Elizabeth."

"How about Mr. Westgate? He's got a few thousand a year; they'd never have to leave London."

"He's too old."

"How about Kelsy Raeford?"

"He gambles."

"And badly at that. Frederick Smithwayne?" Nicholas made a face. "Too young."

"And too stupid. I suppose your cousin Henry is too young as well."

"Henry?" Nicholas almost choked on the name.

"I admit, Henry doesn't seem right for her." Ripton shrugged. "I'm stumped, Nicholas. I don't know anyone who isn't too young, too old, or too stupid."

Nicholas peered at him over the rim of his glass. "She might be just the woman for you, Ripton."

"Me? I thought I was going to marry Amelia."

"Forget Amelia Willard."

"I'm not sure that I want to, Nick." He put a hand to his heart and looked upward longingly.

"When Elizabeth's a little older, she'll be a beauty, mark my words."

Ripton stared at his friend. "When she's a little older?" he repeated, putting down his glass. "Nick, are you blind?"

"Of course not, which is my point exactly. All she wants is a little confidence in herself."

"If I did not think you wanted her for yourself, I'd be playing the guitar and singing love songs under her window this very moment."

"Don't be maudlin." He made a face. "You might give her the confidence she needs."

"So could you."

"For God's sake, Rip! Elizabeth is my friend. One doesn't go about paying court to one's friends."

"Well, I don't know why not. I would if she was my friend!" He stood up without his usual grace and picked up his glass and the bottle. "Come with me, Nick," he cried.

Nicholas shrugged and followed Ripton to

his study, where he watched him open his desk,
carefully placing the bottle away from the edge.
When he had arranged writing materials on its
surface, he seated himself. "We shall need our
greatest literary efforts, Nicholas, so draw up a
chair."

"For what, if I might presume to ask?"

"To write a love letter to Elizabeth, of
course."

"But *I* am not in love with the young lady,"
he protested.

"That is strictly your own fault."

"Forgive me for my confusion, Rip, but when
did you fall in love with her?"

"Nicholas, you are very slow when you
drink."

"I? You're the one who's making no sense."

"I will write the letter because if you did, she
would no doubt recognize your writing."

"You don't wish her to know who is writing?"

"Good heavens, no. The whole purpose is to
make her think she has a secret admirer."

"A secret admirer? Oh, yes," he said
thoughtfully. "She did say something about a
secret admirer once, did she not?"

Ripton picked up the pen and dipped it into
the inkwell. "Yes, she did. And I suggest we
provide one."

A glimmer of understanding finally came to
him. "To give her more confidence in herself?"
he said slowly.

"Exactly my thought. We shall see then if you're correct about Miss Elizabeth Willard."

"Of course I am."

The letter was finally written to their mutual satisfaction, and after blotting and folding the page carefully, Ripton wrapped it with a blank sheet. He wrote the words *Miss Willard of Tavistock Square* boldly across its face.

Nicholas finished his breakfast the next morning and was about to get up from the table to go to his orchids when Mr. Chester came in.

"Do you wish anything else, Mr. Villines?" he asked.

"No, Chester. I won't be going out until much later this afternoon, so you may have the morning off, if you like."

"Thank you, sir."

"Is there something else?" he asked when Mr. Chester did not leave.

"Yes, sir. I found a letter on your desk this morning."

"Letter?"

"This letter, sir." He produced the letter from his pocket.

"Ah, yes, that letter."

"Perhaps you would prefer that I put it away for safekeeping?"

"No, Chester. You may deliver it."

"To Miss Amelia Willard, then?"

"No, to Miss Elizabeth Willard."

"As you wish, sir."

"And mind you," Nicholas added, "no one tells her whom it's from."

"You wish an anonymous delivery?"

"Yes, Chester, an anonymous delivery."

Elizabeth and her uncle were sitting in the drawing room arguing over the morning paper when Mrs. Poyne came in and handed her a letter. "What's this, Mrs. Poyne?" Elizabeth asked after taking it from her.

"It just came for you, miss."

"From whom did it come?" she asked, gazing curiously at the cryptic address.

"I don't know. He wouldn't say."

"Who wouldn't say?"

"The boy who delivered it wouldn't say, miss."

"What's this?" Havoc asked, looking up from the paper.

"Mrs. Poyne says this letter just came for me, but can't say whom it's from."

Havoc took the letter and examined the outside. "Well, Elizabeth, this is Tavistock Square, and you are Miss Willard." He handed it back to her. "Perhaps if you read it, you will discover who sent it."

"Thank you, Uncle Havoc. I might never have thought of that by myself."

"You may go, Mrs. Poyne. And I," Havoc said when she had gone, "shall sit here and read the paper in peace."

Elizabeth opened the letter and let the outer

wrapping fall to the table. "Goodness!" she said when she'd finished reading it.

"Well, whom is it from?" Havoc asked.

"I've no idea." She rang for Mrs. Poyne. When she came in, Elizabeth refolded the letter. "This wasn't for me, Mrs. Poyne. It's for Amelia." She handed it back to the housekeeper.

"But, Miss Elizabeth, the boy said it was for you."

"What does a boy know, Mrs. Poyne! I've read the letter, and it's obviously meant for Miss Amelia. Would you please give it to her? Tell her it was mistakenly given to me and that I apologize for reading her mail."

"Yes, miss."

"I say, Elizabeth."

"Yes, Uncle Havoc?"

"Listen to this." He had reached the editorial section of the paper. " 'I wish to express my deepest thanks,' " he read, " 'to the unknown benefactor who saved my life this Tuesday past. My faith in God and the decency and humanity of man was restored when I received in that morning's post a letter containing a sum of money sufficient to make it possible for me to devote myself to my painting. I wish my benefactor to know I shall not squander the gift and to know that I bless him with all my heart.' " Havoc put down the paper. "What do you think of that?" he asked.

"I think it's remarkable."

"I think the man's a simpleton to go throwing his money away on some fool artist."

"And I think, Thank goodness someone cares to help others who are in need."

"Pooh!" said Havoc.

"Listen to this, Mr. Johns." Alfred Wells snapped his paper to straighten it out and then looked at Percy to see if he had his attention.

Percy raised his eyebrows and sipped from his pint. "All ears, Mr. Wells."

" 'I wish to express my deepest thanks to the unknown benefactor who saved my life this Tuesday past . . .,' " he began reading. When he was done, he sighed loudly. "That sort of thing never happens to me," he said.

"The date of the paper?"

"Today." Mr. Wells shrugged, disappointed by Percy's reaction.

"Tuesday last," Percy mused.

"Are you going to put it on another list?"

Percy did not bother to answer the question. "Mr. Wells," he said, "do you think you could talk this artist into giving up the letter?"

"Whatever for?"

"Curiosity, mostly."

"I suppose I could try."

"Then do, Mr. Wells. Try your best."

CHAPTER
17
❖❖❖

Nicholas sat in his bedroom determined to be in a bad humor. He felt he did not really want to be alone just now, but he could not think of a single person with whom he might want to pass the evening. He wanted someone to amuse him but knew that any attempt to do so would only be annoying. He stood up and went to the window to stare into the darkness of his gardens. He wanted a change, was all. It was time for a change. Ten minutes passed during which he did not move so much as a finger, and he might have stood for another twenty had the sound of someone ringing at the front door not brought him out of his thoughts. He turned when the butler came in to announce the visitor.

"Show Mr. Rutherford up," he said.

"Nicky! Glad to find you at home," Ripton said as he came into the room after Mr. Baker. He tucked his walking stick under one arm and tipped his hat off with the other when Mr. Baker was gone.

"Good evening, Rip." Nicholas took a few steps forward and held out his hand. Ripton was always so affable, so easy-mannered, that he found it impossible to be irritated with him even when, as on this occasion, he felt determined to be so. They shook hands, and Ripton dropped sideways into an armchair, letting his legs dangle over one side. His walking stick and hat he balanced carefully on his lap.

"I was hoping I'd find you at your leisure," he said. "Because I've come to take you away from it. Call Chester and get dressed."

"I do not want to go out this evening."

Ripton waved his hand. "Nonsense! And anyway, you've been home all night. I'm going to the club for cards and drink, and I want you to be the one to cheat me out of my money." He struggled to reach into his waistcoat pocket and take out his watch. He looked at it, then at Nicholas. "Call Chester. I won't be put off tonight." He replaced his watch. "We two gentlemen are going out, and that's all there is to it, and, if you please, note that I say this with an air of finality. . . . Good," he said when Nicholas, after a sigh of resignation, rang for his valet. When Mr. Chester arrived, Ripton swung his legs to the floor. "Make haste, Chester. Dress Mr. Villines in his finest clothes."

Mr. Chester looked at Ripton. "Sir?" he said to Nicholas.

"Do as the man says, Chester."

"Where are we going?" Nicholas asked when he realized Ripton's carriage was not headed for St. James's Street.

"Oh, did I neglect to mention we are paying a call before going to the Phoenix?"

"Yes, you did."

"Well." He shrugged and grinned. "What does it signify if we do make a call first?"

"I am in no mood for any tedious society gatherings, Rip. Pompous old men, stuffy old women. I tell you, I'm in no mood for it. I shall be rude to all of them, and I promise you, you'll regret having forced me to come."

"You're too well bred to be rude, Nick."

"I shouldn't count on it, you scoundrel."

"One may rely on the breeding of a man whose cravat is always perfectly done."

"Damn it to hell," Nicholas muttered. Neither of them attempted to break the morose silence that followed until Ripton sat forward.

"Now, we're here," he said when the carriage stopped. "One hour is all I ask. Then we may go off to wherever you like." He waited while Nicholas stepped down beside him and then smiled at his surprise. "The Willards were having people over after the opera. I could not refuse the invitation when it was given me."

The house was blazing with lights, and when

Mr. Poyne pulled open the door to let them in, the sound of voices could be heard. They handed over their hats and coats and followed Mr. Poyne upstairs.

Amelia Willard was sitting in a corner of the drawing room surrounded by a group made up mostly of men. She was wearing a dress of dark red silk that lent an exotic cast to her features. The effect was completed by the jet curls reaching below her bare shoulders. The sound of her laughter floated over the room and would have caught one's attention even if the woman did not, but it was impossible not to notice her. Her azure eyes were sparkling, and the color in her cheeks was more flattering still. She half rose from her chair when Nicholas and Ripton approached her after greeting Mrs. Willard.

"Mr. Rutherford! Mr. Villines! It's simply too wonderful to see you!"

"It is wonderful to see you, Miss Willard," said Ripton, who was slow to let go of her hand.

"Good evening, Miss Willard."

"Good evening? Is that all you have to say to me?" She pretended to be hurt by Nicholas's mundane greeting. "I hope this does not mean you have stopped admiring me, Mr. Villines, for I would not have an easy time learning not to admire you."

"The night is especially wonderful now that I've seen you, Miss Willard." He bent over her hand a second time.

"That's much better." She giggled in delight. "Now, will you sit down?"

"We should love to, Miss Willard," said Ripton. He had somehow managed to find a chair, and he lost no time in placing it as close to Amelia as was possible given the crowd.

"I believe I shall stand here"—Nicholas leaned one elbow against the mantel of the fireplace—"so that I may survey all whom you have conquered." He intended that Ripton should have no more than his allotted hour, and he looked around for a clock so he could mark the nearest minute of their arrival. His attention was soon drawn to a second group that had formed on the opposite side of the room. Havoc Willard, the most conspicuous member on account of his height, stood with his weight on one leg, a hand resting lightly on the shoulder of his niece, the other hooked into the pocket of his waistcoat. They were all listening to something Elizabeth was saying, looking serious while she spoke. Whatever she said had provoked discussion, and the level of noise rose perceptibly.

Nicholas had a view of her profile from where he stood. She was wearing a gown of white satin trimmed with a modest amount of lace. A lace-trimmed scarf graced her hair, and she wore a small medallion on a ribbon around her neck. Mr. Beaufort Latchley was the one unmarried gentleman in the group around Havoc and Elizabeth, and he was watching her with an expression of interest on his somber face.

Latchley, though above thirty years of age, showed no signs of letting his figure go. He stood as straight and looked as trim as he must have been when he was twenty-five. His sharp dark features might even have warranted the appellation of handsome if only his smile were less like a grimace. He was wealthy enough to support a family in style should he ever choose to marry for a second time. Nicholas knew Latchley had pretensions to Amelia Willard and that Amelia had given him reason to think he might have her favor. He wondered why he was not with her now, fighting for precedence over all her other admirers.

Nicholas's musings on the subject were interrupted when Mrs. Benford-Smith and her daughter, Lucy, joined Havoc Willard's group. There was a noticeable stiffening in the attitude of the gentlemen; it was evident the conversation had been changed. Lucy Benford-Smith looked like her mother, light-haired, not tall, with large brown eyes whose expression seemed perpetually bubbling. She was ignoring Elizabeth, solely, Nicholas suspected, because her mother was doing the same. At last, though, Mrs. Benford-Smith turned to say something to Elizabeth. Whatever it was, it made Elizabeth color.

"Will you excuse me, Miss Willard?" Nicholas suddenly said to Amelia. "I should like to pay my respects to your father."

"Of course, Mr. Villines, but I shall miss you terribly if you are gone for very long."

"Good evening, Mr. Villines," said Havoc, shaking his hand with a firm grip. "A pleasure to see you here."

"Ah. Mr. Villines," Mrs. Benford-Smith cried before he could say a word to Elizabeth. "You were sorely missed at the opera. Was he not, Lucy?"

"Yes, Mother, he was." She smiled and held out her hand for him to take.

"And how is Lord Eversleigh?"

"Quite well."

"We are sorry he chooses not to stay in London." Mrs. Benford-Smith shook her head. "Well, and how is your dear aunt?" she continued.

"Fine, Mrs. Benford-Smith. I had supper at Fitzroy Square just the other night. In fact—" He turned to Elizabeth at last. "They especially asked me to give you their regards."

"And they have mine," she answered.

"I have been wondering, Elizabeth, if the orchid I gave you is doing well."

"If you mean have I killed it, no, Nicholas, I have not."

"He looks doubtful," said Havoc. "Perhaps you had better show it to him."

"Yes, please do," he said quickly. "Ladies."

He nodded at Mrs. Benford-Smith and her daughter. "Excuse us."

"I must tell you," he heard Mrs. Benford-Smith say to Havoc as he and Elizabeth walked away, "that Mr. Nicholas Villines is a confirmed bachelor."

"If all women were like her, I do believe I would be a confirmed bachelor," he muttered, taking Elizabeth's hand and tucking it under his arm.

"Aren't you?" she asked with a grin.

"It remains to be seen."

"This way." She indicated the direction. They left the drawing room and walked down the hall, away from the stairs. "I thought it ought to be in an environment opposite to your conservatory, so I've put it in the morning room. After my own, this room gets the most light." She stopped about halfway down the wall and opened a door. "Here it is." The servants had left lamps burning, and she crossed the room to where the orchid sat on the ledge of a window seat. "I ask you now," she demanded, "have I killed it?"

Nicholas bent over the pot and poked his fingers into the soil. "Perhaps you're on to something after all," he said. "It looks tolerable." He straightened when he heard the rustle of Elizabeth's skirts.

"Charlotte!" she said.

He looked around. She was by a low sofa near the window seat, bending over and holding out a hand to a small white kitten. "Well, who is that?" he asked.

She crouched down, tapping a finger on the floor in an attempt to entice the kitten to come to her. "This is Charlotte. She was a present from Mr. Latchley. Weren't you?" she said to it cajolingly.

"Mr. Latchley?"

"Yes." She settled herself on the floor when the kitten put its paws on her leg and sniffed her skirt.

Her legs were folded under her, just as she had sat that afternoon when he saw her in the garden. She was turned away from him, and though she could not see him, he saw with a piercing clearness the graceful semiprofile of her face and neck. "When did he give it to you?"

"Oh, not to me," she said with a quick glance back at him. "To Amelia." The kitten was in her lap, turning itself in a circle in preparation for settling down.

"You seem to have adopted it as your own."

He had not entirely shaken off his earlier mood of disquiet. He still felt curiously isolated from his surroundings, from people, even from Elizabeth. When he saw her mouth curving into a smile, he found himself reflecting lazily that it might be pleasant to kiss that mouth. He thought he ought to be shocked at his thoughts and that it was odd he was not. Quite the opposite; he was aroused by her, could feel it increasing, making his belly taut and his skin begin to tingle. But he was so comfortable with Elizabeth, he knew her so well, that his desire for her felt dreamlike and distant; real yet unreal. The tension was pleasant, exhilarating even, and he felt no compulsion to bring himself out of the mood.

"Amelia does not like cats." Elizabeth turned slightly to look at him. "It is the only thing about her that is not perfect."

He sat down on the sofa and smiled at her just before she returned her attention to the kitten. There was something so pure about her in that white dress. Her innocent glances at him, her perfect unawareness of his thoughts, were enticing. It was unthinkable, and still he let his mind linger on the image he had conjured up, of Elizabeth in his arms, of kissing her, of his tongue running over her teeth, into her mouth, enjoying the stealthy titillation of the fantasy.

The scarf in her hair was askew, and he reached to straighten it, leaning forward on the sofa so that his knees were on either side of her shoulders. "There. Now your hair is perfectly arranged." He touched one of the curls. "You've managed a complicated style," he said as an excuse to continue sitting as he was. He wondered what she would do if her told her that just now he wanted nothing more than to ravish her. To kiss her until they were both breathless and then to slowly undress her and teach her how to make him gasp with pleasure.

"It took simply hours."

He watched the rise of her breasts against the modest neckline of her gown.

"Well," she amended, "not hours, but quite long enough." She reached up and patted the scarf. "Enchanting, is it not?" Her backward glance at him was amused.

"If I were not so comfortable just now, I would throw myself at your feet." He tickled her neck through her hair. Oh, he thought, it would be enchanting indeed to whisper in her ear the thoughts on his mind.

"Now, wouldn't that be a sight?" She gave a small cry of disappointment as Charlotte suddenly got up and walked away. "Isn't that just like a cat?" she asked, turning to look at him.

He realized almost immediately that he had let too much show in his gaze. She knew him so well, not even her innocence could keep her from seeing something of the nature of his thoughts.

"This is an agreeable room," he commented into a deep silence.

"I love to read in here," she said at last. She held out her hand. "Help me up, Nicholas."

"I should think the room is at its most charming then," he said when they were both standing.

"Do men do nothing but think of flattering things to say to women?"

"Has someone been flattering you, Elizabeth?" She blushed, and he covered her hand with both of his. "Come now, who was it?"

"Nicholas . . ."

He did not let go of her hand when she tried to pull away. "Not until you tell me who's been trying to turn your head with compliments. Was it Mr. Latchley?" The look on her face told him he was right, and he snorted. "Oh, Elizabeth. You're a child compared to Beaufort Latchley. Besides, he only wants to make Amelia jealous."

"I did not say it was Mr. Latchley."

He knew she was thinking of that earlier moment, that she must have guessed something of what he had been thinking. It would be so easy to pull her into his arms, he thought. It was tempting, almost too tempting, the way she was looking at him, gray eyes questioning, cheeks beginning to turn pink again. He did not look away.

"Here you are!"

Nicholas turned around. It was hard not to believe the interruption was his punishment for wanting to ruin Elizabeth. It was perverse, he thought, to so badly want a girl as young and inexperienced as Elizabeth.

"Good evening, Mr. Rutherford." Elizabeth walked away from him.

"Miss Elizabeth." Ripton dipped his shoulders in a bow and stood in the doorway, looking from one to the other with an interested expression. "Miss Willard sent me to find you, Nick."

"She must miss your flattery." There was the merest hint of sarcasm in Elizabeth's voice.

Nicholas turned to Ripton. "You may tell Miss Willard you have found me."

"I had the distinct impression I was to bring you back with me." Ripton wandered into the room, watching Nicholas before letting his eyes settle on Elizabeth. "He's positively bent on being difficult, it seems, Miss Elizabeth. I had the devil's own time convincing him to come out tonight, and now he's going to make me break a promise to your cousin. I tell you, it's almost more than a man can take." He sighed loudly.

"I think, Nicholas, if only for the sake of poor Mr. Rutherford, you had better go."

"Truer words were never spoken," said Ripton. "With your permission, Miss Elizabeth." He bowed to her again.

"Good evening, gentlemen."

"I hope I did not interrupt anything important," Ripton said as he and Nicholas walked back to the drawing room.

"She thinks Beaufort Latchley has been making up to her."

Ripton looked at him, both eyebrows lifted in surprise at Nicholas's exasperated tone. He shook his head thoughtfully. "I see no reason why he would not, and perhaps several why he might."

"If he is, it's only because he wants to make Amelia jealous. She's just too innocent to see it. She's too young to have learned what men are like."

"A great many girls are married at her age, Nicholas. Some of them to men Beaufort Latchley's age."

"Elizabeth isn't just any young girl."

"So Mr. Latchley seems to have noticed."

CHAPTER
18
❯❯❯✖❮❮❮

ONE AFTERNOON WHEN THE WILLARDS WERE AT home, Elizabeth sat in the drawing room working on adding a lace border to a handkerchief. Mrs. Smithwayne and Jane had just left, and Mrs. Willard and Amelia were talking about the shocking decline in Jane's appearance.

"She always was rather too thin in my opinion," said Mrs. Willard. "But now I don't see how anyone can disagree with me." She shook her head sadly.

"She seems much paler than she should be," Amelia agreed.

"Her mother ought to take her out of this horrid London air before the poor girl wastes away to nothing."

"What do you suppose is the cause?" Amelia asked her mother.

"Surely, Amelia, you know the answer to that question," Elizabeth broke in softly.

"I'm sure I don't know, Beth."

"She is in love and believes he loves another."

"But who?"

"It is not my place to break Jane's confidence, Amelia."

"All the more reason, then, for Mrs. Smithwayne to take Jane from London," Mrs. Willard added. "If her heart is broken, it will surely do her no good to daily run the risk of seeing the man who has broken it. Beth, perhaps you ought to counsel Jane to have her mother take her away."

"Perhaps I should," said Elizabeth. "Though I would much rather counsel the gentleman." The sound of someone at the door made her pause. That their visitor was a man she could tell by the footsteps in the hall, and she found herself straining to hear his voice. Her heart leaped when for a moment she thought she heard Nicholas.

Mr. Poyne came in with Beaufort Latchley behind him. Elizabeth sat back, not so much surprised at having been glad to think Nicholas had come as she was dismayed by her disappointment that he had not.

He inclined his head. "Good afternoon, Mrs. Willard, Miss Willard."

"It's a pity you did not come a little sooner, Mr. Latchley. Miss Jane Smithwayne and her mother have only just left," Amelia said after Beaufort had nodded to Elizabeth.

"I'm sorry I missed them. Are you well, Miss Elizabeth?" he asked.

"Quite well," she answered, surprised to see him standing in front of her when she looked up. "And yourself, Mr. Latchley?"

He took a seat rather closer to her than she liked. "Fine, thank you." He seemed to be waiting for her to say something, so she used her sewing as an excuse to look away from him.

Mrs. Willard smiled cheerfully at Beaufort. "Miss Smithwayne did not look at all well."

"Miss Smithwayne's health may be more delicate than her mother believes," he said.

"Nonsense," said Mrs. Willard. "She has been foolish enough to fall in love with someone unsuited to her station in life, and now she suffers the consequences."

Elizabeth looked up from her sewing. "How do you know they do not suit, Aunt Mary?"

"Because, if they suited, they would be engaged."

"Perhaps they suit," said Beaufort, looking at Elizabeth as he spoke, "but he cannot return her feeling, however noble it may be."

He knows, thought Elizabeth. He knows Jane loves him, and he does not care. "Jane is the kindest person I know," she said. "I cannot imagine what man would not love her back."

To his credit, Beaufort reddened. "Miss Smithwayne is indeed the kindest of persons," he said. "But that does not seem to have prevented her from loving unwisely."

"I suppose not," she answered, wishing she dared let her scorn show in her voice.

"Whom do you suppose she loves?" Amelia asked.

"I do not presume to guess," Beaufort said, glancing again at Elizabeth, who picked up her handkerchief and pretended to be absorbed in her work. "We are not all lucky enough to fall in love with one who will love us back."

Beaufort became a frequent caller at Tavistock Square, and much to Elizabeth's surprise, he did not spend all his time with Amelia. His strategy for capturing Amelia's heart was obviously one of artful neglect, and as far as Elizabeth could see, it was succeeding wildly. One day, for example, when Beaufort was one of four gentlemen at the house, Amelia sighed loudly and, looking directly at Beaufort, said, "I do wish someone would take me for a walk in the garden. It is simply too wonderful a day to stay inside."

"Perhaps Mr. Stacey would be kind enough to oblige you," Beaufort replied. "Your cousin was just explaining Mr. Rousseau to me, and I should like to hear the rest of what she has to say."

Naturally Mr. Stacey was only too happy to oblige, and Amelia had to take her walk without Mr. Latchley. His indifference was almost more than Amelia could bear. She began to reserve her most fetching smiles for Beaufort. Her blue eyes were never more lively than when they were settled on him. She was careful not to let him become too certain of her, but her interest in him never flagged. Already captivating, she became more captivating still whenever Mr. Latchley seemed in danger of lapsing into his infuriating aloofness.

Three days elapsed without a visit from Beaufort Latchley. Then the Willards received an invitation to spend a week at Greenweald, the country estate of Mr. David Lillick. Amelia did not want her mother to accept the invitation until she discovered that Mr. Latchley had already sent his acceptance.

Greenweald had belonged to the Lillicks for over six generations, always providing its master with a generous income worthy of one of the oldest families in southern England. David Lillick, esquire, the current master of Greenweald, was a gentleman of about forty years of age whose wife, some ten years his junior, was devoted to him. Mrs. Lillick had married for love. She knew the match was considered beneath her husband, and she never forgot the favor he had done her by marrying her.

The primary purpose of the Lillicks' party was to allow Mrs. Lillick to show off her husband's generosity. She had at last given birth to a son, and Mr. Lillick had demonstrated his gratitude by presenting her with a diamond choker said by some to have cost upward of ten thousand pounds.

The Willards arrived at Greenweald to find

that most of the guests were already present. The Benford-Smiths, the Honorable James Aston and his wife, and one Mr. Stephen Martindale had arrived earlier that morning. To Amelia's joy, Beaufort Latchley arrived not long after they did. Of the guests, Elizabeth liked Mr. Martindale the most. He was a widower of about forty-five years who had taken it upon himself to see that everyone remained amused. Mr. Martindale was not handsome—his features were too uneven and his figure too round—but it was impossible not to like him and think him a very amiable gentleman.

The ladies had all been to admire young master Lillick, and afterward both ladies and gentlemen were taken on a tour of the house and gardens. Mr. Martindale had been a guest at Greenweald several times before, and he provided a commentary that kept Elizabeth smiling. He had it on good authority that the Greenweald flagstones dated back to the twelfth century and that one in particular had been stepped upon by a pope, though he could not be sure which it was, which went for both the pope and the flagstone.

When the tour was over and the guests were back inside, they were agreeably surprised to discover there was more than enough time for a game or two of cards before they needed to dress for supper. Elizabeth was glad they had decided to come to Greenweald. Once away from her mother, Lucy Benford-Smith was tol-

erable company, and Mr. Martindale alone was
worth the visit. Elizabeth was pleased when she
and Mr. Martindale were partners in a game of
whist against Miss Benford-Smith and Beaufort Latchley. She and Mr. Martindale won
both games handily because Lucy seemed to
take pride in playing poorly. Beaufort took the
losses with good grace, considering that he had
wanted to win.

Even after the cards were put away, Beaufort
lingered near Elizabeth. He grimaced at her and,
to Elizabeth's surprise, followed her to a seat by
the fire. "One day you and I will have to be
partners at cards, Miss Willard," he said with
another grimace she supposed was meant to be
a smile. "You played admirably."

"Thank you, Mr. Latchley. But Mr. Martindale also played well."

"Indeed he did. I very much dislike losing,
Miss Willard. I think with you as my partner
I must certainly win."

"You have more confidence in my skill than
I do, Mr. Latchley."

"I consider myself to be an excellent judge of
the ability and character of those whom I
meet."

"And you judge me to be a superior card
player, Mr. Latchley?"

Beaufort smiled. "Among other things, Miss
Willard, yes."

Elizabeth laughed. "I'm grateful you think so,
Mr. Latchley," she said, rising as she spoke. "If

you will excuse me, I believe it is time to dress for supper."

Once in her room, she sat at her dresser, gazing idly at her reflection. Curls, she decided, would be too much trouble. She was pinning her hair back when Miss Lincoln came in with her dress. The gown was her cousin's but Amelia claimed the color did not become her and had given it to Elizabeth without ever wearing it. Elizabeth did not think the color would have looked badly on Amelia at all. It was a muted rose-colored silk and exactly the kind of dress she had dreamed of wearing someday. The skirt had ruffles at the hem, and the sleeves and collar were trimmed with at least four inches of lace. There were even lace-trimmed bows arranged on the sleeves.

Though Elizabeth's waist was small, it had to be made smaller still to fit into the dress. Miss Lincoln cinched in her corset to make her waist the required seventeen inches and whisked the dress over her head without disturbing a hair. After the relative comfort of her day dress, the rose gown, however beautiful, was a torture to wear.

"How lovely you look, Miss Elizabeth!" exclaimed Miss Lincoln.

"I can hardly breathe," she gasped.

"It can't be helped, Miss Elizabeth. Your cousin could never get into this gown, no matter how much she moaned over it. You should be grateful for your tiny waist."

Elizabeth examined herself in the glass. The pale rose color brought out a similar tint in her own skin. A good thing, she thought, since the dropped shoulders exposed more of her than she was used to. Wishing that Amelia would discard more of her clothes, she pulled on a pair of gloves and went downstairs.

When Elizabeth entered the drawing room, she took a seat by Amelia and began talking with Mr. Martindale. Just as he asked Elizabeth how she felt about visiting a house reputed to be haunted, the steward came in to announce the arrival of Nicholas Villines.

"How wonderful that Mr. Villines was able to come after all!" Amelia exclaimed.

"I did not know Nicholas was invited," Elizabeth said.

"Why, yes, he was. But he said he would not be able to accept the invitation. I told him how disappointed I would be if he did not come." Amelia looked at Mr. Latchley for signs of jealousy.

He obliged her by saying, "I hope you will be too busy to pay much attention to him, Miss Willard."

Amelia's assurance that Nicholas had come on her account seemed to be well placed, for after he greeted the Lillicks he went directly to where Amelia sat. He was wearing evening clothes: close-fitting black trousers, a gray-striped satin waistcoat, and black cutaway coat trimmed with satin. His silk cravat had been tied in an elegant knot and arranged just so against the snowy whiteness of his shirt—in short he was perfectly, if soberly, dressed, every inch the proper gentleman. He looked severe until the moment he smiled.

"You are as beautiful as ever, Miss Willard," he said to Amelia.

She extended her hand to him. "And you are as handsome, Mr. Villines."

"Elizabeth." Nicholas let go of Amelia's hand and turned to her. "Have you been enjoying Greenweald?"

"Oh, yes," she answered. "It's beautiful. And Mr. Martindale has been keeping us all entertained with stories about ghosts, which, by the way, Mr. Latchley, I do not believe in." Nicholas's black eyes flicked to Beaufort, then back to her. "Except," she amended, "very late at night." She thought Nicholas was going to say something, but the announcement of supper prevented him from speaking.

"I seem to have arrived just in time," he said.

Beaufort rose and, after bowing and extending his hand to Elizabeth, said, "I believe I have the honor of taking you in to supper, Miss Elizabeth."

She stood, and as she did she thought she heard Nicholas say very softly, "It seems I was too late after all."

"It is so kind of you, Mr. Latchley, to take Elizabeth in to supper," Amelia said.

"I consider myself fortunate to have such an

exquisite partner." For some reason, Beaufort directed his comment more to Nicholas than to Amelia. "Though Mr. Villines is hardly more fortunate than I," he said while Nicholas helped Amelia to stand.

"I am surprised, Mr. Latchley," Elizabeth said as he escorted her to the dining room, "that you have given up the field to Nicholas without even a struggle. I would not have minded if you had taken Amelia instead."

"I do not believe I have given up anything, Miss Willard." To her surprise, he smiled again.

"Now, I am truly amazed."

"And why is that?"

"I have never thought of you as a man given to compliments for the sake of flattery." It was certainly true, but she blushed for saying it so bluntly.

"You are quite correct, Miss Willard, I am not. The truth is never flattery, however complimentary it might be."

If she had not known he was in love with Amelia, Elizabeth would have thought the compliment was meant to be taken seriously.

During supper, she was seated between Mr. Martindale and Mr. Latchley. Nicholas was at the far end of the table with Amelia, but she could not see him unless she deliberately tried. Mr. Aston was across from her, so there was much to distract her from that end of the table. From where she sat she had a view of Mrs. Lillick, resplendent in a pale green-and-blue satin gown with an almost alarming décolletage. She wore the diamond choker around her throat, reaching up several times to run a finger over the stones. When she moved, it sparkled in the light. It was a spectacular piece of jewelry.

To her chagrin, Elizabeth found Beaufort's efforts to draw her out were succeeding. He listened to her attentively, solicited her opinions, and expressed his own so well that by the end of the meal she could begin to understand why Jane had fallen in love with him, though she still believed he did not deserve the honor.

When the men had rejoined the women after having taken a surprisingly short time to enjoy their port and cigars, Miss Benford-Smith was asked to play the piano, and Amelia was easily persuaded to sing. Elizabeth had expected to sit unnoticed, but both Mr. Martindale and Mr. Latchley took seats by her. She had reason to be glad of it, for it gave her an excuse not to watch Nicholas turning pages for Amelia and Miss Benford-Smith.

"Your cousin Amelia sings very prettily," said Mr. Martindale.

"Yes, she does," she agreed.

"Can you be persuaded to sing for us as well?" Beaufort asked.

"It is an unfortunate fact that others do not love to hear me sing quite as much as I love to do so, Mr. Latchley."

"Oh, pshaw," exclaimed Mr. Martindale. "If your singing voice is anything like your speaking voice, I'll wager it would be a delight to hear."

"I am afraid, gentlemen, that where my cousin's singing lessons were a success, mine were equally a failure."

Amelia's song came to an end just as Elizabeth finished speaking, and the sound of Beaufort and Mr. Martindale laughing could be clearly heard above the polite clapping. Nicholas raised his head to stare across the room.

CHAPTER
19
-»»×««-

THE NEXT MORNING OVER BREAKFAST, MISS BENFORD-Smith suggested a picnic. The idea was greeted enthusiastically, and after Mrs. Lillick told them the ideal spot was to be found not over an hour's drive away, instructions for the preparation of a picnic lunch were sent to the kitchen.

They traveled in two carriages, with Mr. Benford-Smith, Lucy, Elizabeth, Mr. Latchley, and Mr. Martindale in the first. Havoc and Mrs. Willard both had decided to stay behind with the Lillicks. There was a moment when Elizabeth thought Nicholas would go in her carriage, but at the last minute he turned to answer a question from Mrs. Benford-Smith, and Mr. Latchley climbed in to take the last seat. It was nicely timed, she thought; Nicholas appeared to have ended up in the carriage with Amelia by accident.

The day was perfect for a picnic. Only a few

white clouds dotted the sky, and though the sun was out, there was just enough breeze to keep it from becoming too warm. Because they were driving in an open carriage, Mrs. Lillick had insisted they take along lap blankets, but it was far too lovely to use them.

The five of them kept up a lively conversation as they rolled past the green fields. Mr. Martindale, sitting between Elizabeth and Miss Benford-Smith, kept them amused during the hour's drive, and both Lucy and Mr. Latchley joined in the laughter at Mr. Martindale's jokes. The girls at school had talked about such excursions, or rather dreamed of them, and it was every bit as wonderful as it was supposed to be. Elizabeth knew Mr. Martindale liked her, and it was obvious that Mr. Benford-Smith admired her. Even the habitually somber Beaufort Latchley seemed almost light-hearted. It was impossible not to be happy when Mrs. Willard wasn't around to scold her for laughing too loudly or sitting too quietly, or whatever it was she happened to be doing that did not suit her aunt. She smiled at no one and everyone and peered over the side of the carriage to watch the ground go by. "Just smell this wonderful air," she exclaimed.

"Miss Willard!" cried Miss Benford-Smith with alarm. "Have a care you don't fall out."

"Oh, I won't fall," she answered.

"I daresay one of us gentlemen should essay

to catch you if you did," said Mr. Benford-Smith.

"Would you run the risk of falling out yourself?" She laughed but sat back against the seat.

"There are worse things a man might do besides catch you, Miss Willard," said Mr. Latchley with a smile less like a grimace than was usual for him. "The risk seems slight in comparison to saving the life of a lovely woman."

"Mr. Latchley, are you saying you would let an ugly woman fall?" Elizabeth asked with a smile.

"I'm sure Mr. Latchley would catch whoever might fall," said Miss Benford-Smith.

"Of course, you're quite right," Elizabeth responded. "I'm sure Mr. Latchley is too much a gentleman to let a woman fall to her death solely on account of her looks." She decided to attribute his previous comment to the effect of fresh air on a man obviously in great need of it.

"Thank you for your confidence in me, Miss Willard." He smiled yet again and looked practically pleasant.

They had been driving steadily uphill for the last half hour, and finally the driver pulled the horses to a halt. "Here we are," he said, twisting around in his seat to look at them.

"Already?" It seemed to Elizabeth that they had reached the spot for the picnic in much less than an hour. "But I thought Mrs. Lillick said it was an hour's drive."

Mr. Benford-Smith took out his watch and glanced at it. "Fifty-four minutes, to be exact, Miss Willard," he said.

"We must have had the better horses," Mr. Martindale observed. "The others seem to be a few minutes behind us."

"Shall we explore, Miss Willard, while we wait for the others?" Lucy Benford-Smith asked.

"Go along, dear," said Mr. Benford-Smith when Lucy looked at her father for approval of the suggestion. "But do not go out of sight."

"Yes, Father."

"Perhaps you ladies would care for company?"

"Well, Mr. Latchley," said Lucy, "normally I would have berated you for not asking sooner, but I have something of particular importance to say to Miss Willard."

"They must be alone so they may talk about us gentlemen, Mr. Latchley," said Mr. Martindale. "No doubt we would rather not hear what they have to say about brutes such as we."

"Come, Miss Willard." Lucy drew her arm though Elizabeth's and the two set off over a path headed downhill from the road. "Miss Willard," Lucy bubbled, "you are exceedingly nice. I believe I shall like you a great deal."

"Thank you. I certainly hope that is the case."

Lucy inclined her head toward Elizabeth's

shoulder as if she meant to impart a confidence
and said in a significant tone, "Well!"

"Yes?" said Elizabeth.

"Mr. Latchley seems to have formed an attachment to you."

"Oh, but you are mistaken, Miss Benford-
Smith." She laughed.

"I think not. I am rarely mistaken about such
things."

"As with most men, Mr. Latchley's attachment is to my cousin."

"Still, he likes you a great deal. He has made
that abundantly clear." Lucy stopped walking.

"What does it signify," she asked, "if Mr.
Latchley is determined to make a friend of
someone who may one day be his relative?"

"Nothing, I suppose, but the relation may be
a different one than you imagine, Miss Willard." Lucy, who had stood so she was facing
Elizabeth, suddenly clutched her arm. "Goodness! Here comes Mr. Villines. He's so handsome," she whispered. In a slightly louder voice
she said, "I used to be afraid of him, but now
I'm no longer frightened by handsome men. I
quite adore him." She delivered this last in a
whisper again. "Good afternoon, Mr. Villines,"
she said when he reached the spot where they
stood.

"Miss Benford-Smith. Elizabeth."

"Did you have a pleasant drive here, Mr. Villines? I should be very sorry to hear you did
not."

"It was pleasant, Miss Benford-Smith."

"Of course, it must have been. Miss Amelia Willard was in your carriage, was she not? She is most amazingly beautiful. Do you know, Mr. Villines, I was just telling Miss Willard"—she put a hand on Elizabeth's arm—"that she has succeeded in stealing Mr. Beaufort Latchley away from her cousin. What do you make of that?"

"Have you, now, Elizabeth?"

"I'm afraid, Miss Benford-Smith, that Nicholas thinks I am incapable of such a thing."

"Oh, Mr. Villines!" Lucy cried. "How can you? Why, Miss Willard is just the sort of woman Mr. Latchley might want to be his wife."

"And what sort of woman is that, Miss Benford-Smith?"

"Well, she is clever. No matter what you gentlemen say, that is generally an advantage in a wife. And she is beautiful."

"But," said Nicholas with a broad smile, "do you not think she is too young for Mr. Latchley? For that is what I think of the matter."

"Oh, no. Heavens, Mr. Villines, you talk as though she is a child. Why, I've had a proposal from a man Mr. Latchley's age, and I am a year younger than Miss Willard."

"You merely prove my point, as you did not accept him."

"But it was not on account of his age, Mr. Villines. Though I shan't tell you why I refused him, I think I may safely say he was neither as rich nor as handsome as Mr. Latchley."

"Then perhaps you ought to marry Mr. Latchley yourself."

"I daresay I would," Lucy giggled, "only he is in love with Miss Elizabeth Willard."

"How can you be sure? It seems to me Mr. Latchley spends a great deal of time with Miss Amelia Willard."

"Here come the others," Elizabeth said, relieved to have the chance to change the subject.

Mr. Martindale was the first to reach them. "We thought we ought to take your lead and go exploring," he said to them. "Mr. Lillick was good enough to tell me there is a wondrous view of the valley just a mile or so from here, and the others have agreed we ought not to miss it. It would be an ideal place to have our picnic."

"I should love to see the view, Mr. Martindale," Elizabeth said.

"Ah, Miss Willard. I did expect you would be of a kind to appreciate nature, and here I am, proven right."

It took some twenty-five minutes for the group to reach the vantage point, but it was more than worth the time. They walked partway up an incline until they reached a spot where the ground leveled out. There was a view of the valley, and to the north Greenweald could just be made out. They admired the view while the two servants laid out the blankets and took the food out of the baskets. Miss Benford-

Smith sat with her father and Amelia, while Mr. Martindale sat near Mr. and Mrs. Aston. Elizabeth hung back until Mr. Latchley finally positioned himself between Amelia and Lucy. Nicholas was the last to join them, and to Elizabeth's surprise, he did not sit with Amelia. He sat beside her and accepted the plate of food she handed to him. The luncheon was admirable; there was chicken, cold ham and beef, fresh rolls, fruit, and lemonade. Both Amelia and Lucy were talking to Mr. Martindale, and their laughter was the predominant sound for some time.

"Was that a new dress you wore last night, Elizabeth?" Nicholas asked after he had started on another piece of chicken.

"It used to be Amelia's." She handed him a napkin.

"Thank you. Would you pour me a glass of lemonade?" He held out his glass. "It looked well on you," he said when she handed him back his full glass. When he finished it, he put down his plate and lay on his back, hands clasped under his head, watching while Elizabeth cut a peach. "You ought to feed it to me," he said suddenly.

"Feed it to you? You lazy thing. Feed it to yourself." She held out a slice for him to take.

"Mr. Latchley will be jealous if you feed it to me."

"Not according to you."

"Do you love Mr. Latchley?"

"No." She laughed, dropping the fruit onto his plate.

He grabbed her hand and turned onto his side. "He's looking at us this very moment, Elizabeth," he said dramatically.

"Nicholas, don't." She tried to pull her hand away.

He pressed his lips to her hand. "There, now he shall be properly jealous."

"Nicholas!"

"If you don't love Mr. Latchley, why are you so distressed?" he demanded.

"It is cruel to tease me so."

He lay on his back again, still holding her hand. "I love to tease you, Elizabeth." He smiled.

"I don't know why."

"I can't very well tease Amelia." His eyelids drooped closed. "No, it simply wouldn't do to tease Amelia the way I tease you." He pulled her hand to his chest and covered it with both of his.

"Mr. Villines!" Lucy Benford-Smith called out. "Do come along, we are off to explore."

"Are you going, Elizabeth?" Nicholas asked in a low voice. She shook her head. "No, thank you," he called back to Lucy. "I am far too comfortable just now."

"Miss Willard?" Lucy implored.

"I think I will stay here."

Nicholas watched Lucy, Amelia, Mr. Martindale, and Mr. Benford-Smith walk away until they were out of sight, then let his eyes slowly close.

Elizabeth looked at him. His slight smile softened his mouth, but otherwise there was a hardness to his features that puzzled her. The years after his father's death must have been difficult for him, she thought, to have given him such a hard look. She reached to touch the thin scar on his cheek. "How did you get this, Nicholas?" she asked.

He opened his eyes, and for a moment she could not tell what she saw in them. "If I could tell anyone how I got it, it would be you."

"Poor Nicholas," she said.

"Do you pity me?"

"No. But things have been difficult for you, haven't they?"

"Yes."

"It's changed you."

"Experience will do that, Elizabeth."

"Was it as awful as that?"

"Sometimes I thought it was. Until I learned to like being alone, I was damned unhappy. I discovered one must like oneself in order to keep from going mad." He turned his head to look at her. "If it hadn't been for you and Ripton," he said, "I don't know what would have happened. You two were the only ones to stand behind me."

"You would still have survived," she said.

"I know I would have." He laughed. "But I would have been bitter, I think. I might have come to hate everyone. You kept me from that, Elizabeth, and I'll never forget it. I might have ended up a sour man like Beaufort Latchley."

"You don't like Mr. Latchley much, do you?"

"Latchley's bank held some of the mortgages on my father's property, so perhaps I dislike him by association. He was never malicious about it, but he never gave me so much as an inch in which to breathe. Not a bloody inch! There's no compassion in the man, that's why he became rich in direct proportion to my becoming poor. The most satisfying moment of my life was seeing the expression on his face when I paid off the last of the debt." He sat up. "Come, Elizabeth, let's go explore a little ourselves." He held out his hand when he had risen to his feet. "You've been awfully patient about listening to me."

"I wouldn't be your friend otherwise."

"And you are my friend, aren't you?" He stood very still, looking at her with an intensity that puzzled her.

She smiled at him. "I always have been," she said.

When they got back to Greenweald at nearly four o'clock, it was to find that Ripton had arrived during their absence. He and Mrs. Lillick had been busy making arrangements for dancing after supper and had made enough progress that they were awaiting only agreement from the musicians. Before tea was over, their confirmation arrived. Everyone thought it would be a perfect way to end the day, and the ladies retired to change somewhat earlier than would otherwise have been necessary.

Elizabeth stood in her room looking wistfully at the rose dress, wishing she had another gown even half as nice. She did not, and there was no help for it. For what seemed like the hundredth time, she wore her green watered silk.

When she joined the others in the drawing room, Amelia was already the center of attention. The arrival of Ripton Rutherford was just what her cousin needed to revive her flagging spirits. The dress she wore made the most of her figure, and she was shamelessly aware of the fact. She was busy promising dances to the men when supper was announced. Not even Lucy Benford-Smith could rival Amelia for her contributions to the conversation. Amelia sparkled. Nothing brought her to life like the prospect of an evening with handsome men about.

Several local families had been invited to attend the dancing, so there was a respectable number of people crowding the drawing room by the time the gentlemen came out of the dining room. The musicians were soon ready to play the first set. They proved to be surprisingly good, and by the second set of dances everyone was smiling almost as brilliantly as Amelia. She did not sit out a single dance, though it was no great wonder since there were slightly more gentlemen in attendance than ladies.

Ripton had just finished dancing with Amelia when he asked Elizabeth for a dance. "Is it true, what everyone is whispering about Mr. Beaufort Latchley being in love with you?" he asked as he swept her onto the floor.

"Goodness, no, Mr. Rutherford. Mr. Latchley is in love with Amelia."

"Do you really think so? I believe he admires you a great deal." He saw her blush and smiled. "I'd forgotten you think having admirers is a nuisance. Only secret admirers for Miss Elizabeth Willard." She did not answer him, and when the music ended Ripton took her hand. "May I get you something to drink?"

They were standing by the punch bowl when he said, "You blushed charmingly when I mentioned secret admirers, Miss Elizabeth. Dare I guess you have one?"

"You had better not, as you would be wrong." She looked up from her cup. "Amelia has got one, though."

"Amelia? Do tell."

"I found out quite by accident." She shook her head when Ripton took her glass to refill it. "Mrs. Poyne, our housekeeper, mistakenly gave me a letter meant for Amelia, and I read it before I realized the error."

"But how could such a mistake have been made?"

"It wasn't really her fault. It was directed only to Miss Willard of Tavistock Square."

"If it was directed to Miss Willard, how do you know it wasn't meant for you?"

"It was clearly meant for Amelia, Mr. Rutherford."

"So you gave it to her?" One blond eyebrow arched quizzically.

"Of course. She was furious with me for reading her letter. It was quite . . ."

"Yes?" He looked past her at the dancers.

"Complimentary." She followed his gaze. Amelia was dancing with Mr. Latchley for a second time. "Will you come outside with me, Mr. Rutherford?" she asked.

"Of course." He followed her without saying a word. They walked outside and into the garden until they were standing at the far corner, away from the lights of the house.

"Are you all right now, Mr. Rutherford?"

"Why?" He looked surprised. "Did I seem upset?" he asked, looking fascinated by his shoes.

"You seemed to be in need of some fresh air." Elizabeth had to smile. He walked a few steps farther to stand at the side of an oak tree. He thrust his hands into the pockets of his trousers and stared resolutely at the ground. "You should not worry about Amelia dancing twice with him," she said into the dark.

"Dancing twice with whom?"

"Why, with Mr. Latchley, of course."

"Beaufort Latchley." He emphasized the name "Beaufort" and leaned against the trunk of the tree, taking one hand from his pocket just long enough to unbutton his coat. "Do you not see the obvious, Miss Elizabeth?"

"I suppose it was because he asked her twice," she said, thinking that he was scowling because he was jealous of Mr. Latchley.

"Would you dance twice with a man merely because it happened to be the number of times he asked you?"

"And how many times did you ask Amelia to dance, Mr. Rutherford?"

"That, Elizabeth, is not the point."

She said nothing when he used her given name; they were friends, after all.

"There are no secrets in London society, you know." He reached up to tug at one the branches of the tree. "Mr. Latchley seems to visit you often enough."

"Maybe you ought to call more often."

"Well, however one chooses to look at it, Mr. Latchley spends altogether too much time at Tavistock Square. And if you want my opinion, he spends too much time with at least one of the two Miss Willards."

"Mr. Rutherford," she said with an exasperated sigh, "you will never make Amelia love you by sulking."

"I am not sulking." He continued to stare up into the branches of the tree. "I am despairing." He looked down for a moment when Elizabeth put a hand on his arm.

He sounded so bitter she felt sorry for him,

and she moved so she was standing directly in front of him. "You must be patient." She pulled gently on his cravat in order to make him look at her. "Amelia is not ready to marry. She does not want to distinguish any one gentleman yet." Ripton was looking at her, and encouraged because he seemed calmer, she smiled.

"I am finished being patient." He returned her gaze.

"Will you force her to love you, then?"

"No, I am giving her up," he said with a laugh and a shrug of his shoulders.

"If you really love her, I think it is not so easy as that."

"Perhaps not." He shook his head and was quiet for a long moment. "You are very kind, Elizabeth," he said at last. He let a hand fall lightly on her waist. "Why do you suppose that is?"

She ignored his question and reached up to straighten the cravat she had just a moment before set aslant. "You are twice as handsome as Mr. Latchley," she said. "But even more important, you are amiable where he is not."

"Flatterer," he said in a low voice.

"No, it is the truth."

"If I had any sense, I would have given her up long ago."

"One day, Mr. Rutherford, she will want the attentions of one man in particular, and there you'll be—handsome, kind, and a true gentleman. If that does not make her love you, she does not deserve you."

"I am already convinced she does not deserve me." He shook his head. "You know, when Nicholas and I were in school, he was always talking about you. 'Elizabeth is such a clever girl. Elizabeth can do this and that. Elizabeth is so kind!'"

"I did not know he talked of me."

"Talked of you! My dear young lady, I used to think if I ever met you, I would instantly dislike a woman so perfect."

"And did you?"

"I tried my best, but I failed. Everything he ever said about you is true. It is impossible to dislike you."

"Well, I'm glad you don't dislike me."

"I only wonder that Nicholas never mentioned how beautiful you are."

The tone of his voice, she thought, was odd, and while she was wondering just what it meant—if, indeed, it meant anything at all— she heard him whisper something.

"I'm sorry, what did you say?" she asked. She looked down in surprise when he curled an arm around her waist.

"I said, I think I've been a fool." He put his hand under her chin and lifted her head so that she was gazing into his blue eyes. "Have I told you I admire you?" he asked.

"Only that you admire my cousin, Mr. Rutherford." She laughed in order to cover her nervousness when he did not let her go.

"I do admire you, Elizabeth."

At first she was too shocked to do much of anything when he bent his head to hers. No one had ever wanted to kiss her before. At least never badly enough to actually do it, and she was surprised that Ripton Rutherford did. It was pleasant, and after a moment longer, she decided she like being kissed.

When he stopped, she looked into his eyes. "Oh, my," she said, lifting her fingers to her lips. She was glad her inane comment did not make him laugh. Quite the contrary, in fact. He grasped her hand and kissed her fingers, then moved to pull her close to kiss her again, more insistently than the first time. She had not gotten used to the fact that he had kissed her once, let alone that he immediately wanted to do it again. For an instant she relaxed against him, let him pull her tight into the curve of his arms, and for an instant only, she trembled as she wished it were Nicholas who was kissing her.

Her hands were against his chest. "No!" She pushed away from him, ashamed and embarrassed at her thoughts.

He let go of her, looking at her with a startled expression. "I'm sorry. Will you forgive me? I did not mean to take advantage—"

"It's I who ought to be forgiven."

"That isn't so." He reached for her hand and, when he had it, held it to his lips.

"It is. Please." She gently pulled her hand away. "Let's not talk about it."

"Why not?"

"Because I do not want to."

"All right," he said softly, a little sadly. "Shall we go inside?"

"Yes."

Once inside, she could think of nothing but what a fool she had made of herself with Ripton. He must think her a child, to have reacted to his embrace as if he had frightened her to death. She could hardly have explained that it was wishing he were Nicholas that had made her push him away.

Nicholas, whom she loved with all her heart, and who thought she was a child, was dancing with Amelia. She was gazing at him, every perfect feature of her face focused on him. And he seemed equally fascinated with her. How could he not be in love with Amelia? Amelia was beautiful and accomplished—and rich, everything Elizabeth was not. She saw him smile at Amelia. There was a dizzy sensation in her stomach at just the sight of his lazy grin. He would never look at her the way he did Amelia, no matter how much she wished he would.

When the dance ended she saw Nicholas look around, searching for someone. She could not bear to see him, and she walked quickly out of the room. There was a small parlor a short way down the hall, and she went inside to sit until she felt she could face him. Dwelling on her situation wasn't likely to accomplish anything, but it was impossible not to feel sorry for herself. It was all too appropriate that she should be reminded of Jane Smithwayne and how she sat by and waited for Beaufort Latchley to fall in love with her. She and Jane had much in common. What had she ever done to make Nicholas think of her as anything but his "sweet little Elizabeth"? Well, there was the rub. If she did anything, she might succeed only in making a fool of herself, and she did not know if that was a risk she wanted to take. It might ruin their friendship forever.

She knew by the sudden quiet and lowering of voices that the musicians had put away their instruments. She wished she knew what to do, she wished she knew whether Nicholas was in love with Amelia and whether there was even the slightest possibility that Nicholas might ever think of her as anything but his friend.

There were no voices to be heard at all now, and when she looked at the clock on the mantel she saw with surprise that it was well past two o'clock. She sighed and stood up. No one was in the room that had been used for dancing, and she climbed the stairs to her room. She was hardly ten steps down the hall when she heard a scream. She stopped, eyes open wide in fear. The thought of Mr. Martindale's ghost leapt to her mind, and there was a moment when she found herself listening for ghostly laughter. Another scream was followed by the sound of a woman sobbing. Then the door to Mrs. Lillick's room opened and Mrs. Lillick staggered out, clutching the neck of her dressing gown.

"Mrs. Lillick!" Elizabeth ran to her. "Are you all right?"

Another door opened. "What's happened?" Mr. Martindale was hastily fastening his robe as he came out of his room.

Mrs. Lillick fell sobbing into Elizabeth's arms. "It's gone," she moaned. "Stolen from underneath my very nose. He was right in the room with me. It was the Mayfair Thief."

"Good heavens!" Mr. Martindale put a hand on Elizabeth's shoulder. "Take her to the sitting room."

Mr. Benford-Smith came out of his room, and Mrs. Lillick repeated the story even less coherently than before. When Mr. Martindale put a hand on the door to Mrs. Lillick's room, Mr. Benford-Smith restrained him. "I've a pistol in my room," he said. "Wait here."

With one arm around Mrs. Lillick, Elizabeth led her to the sitting room and opened the door. "Oh, excuse me," she said.

"What's wrong?" Havoc stood up when he saw Mrs. Lillick's tear-streaked face.

"We thought we had imagined the screams," said Beaufort Latchley. He quickly crossed the room to help settle Mrs. Lillick on a chair.

"No, Mr. Latchley, you did not," Elizabeth said. "Someone was in Mrs. Lillick's room."

"Is there anything we can do here, Elizabeth?" Havoc asked.

"No, Uncle Havoc. Could you find Mr. Lillick and tell him where we are?"

Mrs. Lillick gratefully accepted the handkerchief Elizabeth handed to her when Havoc and Mr. Latchley were gone. "I was frightened half out of my mind to see someone in the room with me," she said, dabbing at her eyes. She looked up. "I must look a fright." Elizabeth patted her arm and murmured some words of comfort. "He stole the necklace! I took it off and left it on the dressing table. I wasn't away two minutes, but when I came back he was half out the window and the necklace was gone. He must have been in the room with me the whole time." She shuddered at the memory.

"Martha!" Mr. Lillick came in and sank to his knees, relieved to see his wife was safe.

She threw her arms around him. "Oh, David!"

"What's happened?" Nicholas whirled around when he heard Elizabeth close the sitting room door. "Is Mrs. Lillick all right?"

"Yes, I believe so. She's with Mr. Lillick now."

"Could you make any sense of what she was saying?" asked Mr. Martindale, who had been waiting in the hall with Nicholas and Mr. Latchley.

"Her necklace has been stolen. She left her dressing room for a moment, and when she came back it was gone."

"Has anyone sent for the constable?" asked Mr. Latchley.

"I sent one of the servants for him," Mr. Martindale answered.

The constable was a short balding man who listened to Elizabeth's relation of what happened with a skeptical expression on his face. By the time she had finished answering his questions and was told she was free to go, she was exhausted. She left the drawing room where they were interviewing the guests, intending to go straight to her bed.

Nicholas was waiting in the hallway. "Are *you* all right, Elizabeth?" he asked, taking her arm.

"Of course."

"Are you sure?" He stroked her cheek. The moment he touched her, her stomach tightened and she was entirely unable to speak for fear of what she might say. "You look pale. Come along, I'll walk you to your room."

"I don't think the constable believed a word I said, Nicholas," she said when they reached her door. "He just kept looking at me and blinking."

"It's his job to listen."

"Well, I think he was annoyed at being dragged out of his bed."

"No doubt he was."

"Have you given your statement?" she asked.

"Oh, yes. I saw and heard absolutely nothing, so it did not take even five minutes."

"The man must have no nerves at all to have waited calmly in an occupied room. He might easily have been discovered."

Nicholas shrugged.

"Do you believe in the Mayfair Thief now, Nicholas?"

"How do you know it was the Mayfair Thief?" He brushed a lock of hair from his forehead.

"Mrs. Lillick seemed certain it was. Even the constable mentioned the possibility."

"Well, whether it was the Mayfair Thief or only the Greenweald ghost, whoever it was," Nicholas snorted, "certainly wasn't very clever."

"What do you mean?"

"Because he made off with about five pounds' worth of paste."

"But Mrs. Lillick's necklace must be worth a thousand times that."

"If it was genuine, it would be."

"Of course it was genuine."

"No, Elizabeth, it was paste, and I should think a thief worthy of the name would know paste from the real thing."

"Are you sure?"

"All I know is that the necklace Mrs. Lillick

wore was paste, and that she has a brother who's in a great deal of financial difficulty."

Elizabeth stared, then said, "Surely you don't think Mrs. Lillick made all that up?"

He lifted his shoulders.

"But why would she do a thing like that?"

"So she could sell the real one for her brother."

"Did you tell the constable that?"

"Maybe I'm wrong. I'm not an expert after all. Maybe it wasn't paste. Perhaps it really was the Mayfair Thief."

"Perhaps," she said.

He brushed his hand across her cheek. "You must be exhausted, Elizabeth. I shouldn't be keeping you up with tall tales." He opened the door for her. They stood looking at each other. "I tried to find you tonight, but you weren't anywhere. I suddenly realized we have never danced, and I wanted to waltz with you." He reached for her hand.

"You did?" She could not look away from the blackness of his eyes. She felt that if only she could look into them long enough, she would see in them the answer to all her questions.

"I did." His arm suddenly snaked around her waist, and for an instant she found herself pressed against him. Just as suddenly, he let her go. "I'm glad you're all right," he said in a husky voice.

"Of course I am," she said. She was trembling from the effect of his brief embrace. Without knowing how she found the courage to do it, she went up on tiptoe and pressed her lips against his. "Good night, Nicholas."

"Elizabeth . . ."

"Yes?" She leaned against the door frame because her knees were suddenly too weak to support her.

"Nothing." He took her hand and pressed it briefly. "Good night."

She fought back her tears even after she shut the door. He did not love her, for surely if he did, he would have done something besides stare at her like that after she had kissed him. There had been something in those black eyes of his, only she did not know what it was. Surprise, perhaps, but something else as well. When she finally fell asleep, she once again dreamed of a mysterious gentleman who made his way quite freely through a crowded room. Try as she might, she could not catch even a glimpse of his face.

Ripton and Nicholas left Greenweald together early the next morning. Ripton was sitting with his feet propped up on the edge of the seat across from him, looking intently at Nicholas. Then he stared up at the roof of the carriage and let out a breath. "Lucy Benford-Smith was certainly full of tales, wasn't she?" he said.

"What? Oh, you mean about Latchley?"

"Yes, I mean about Latchley."

"If you ask me, he's just trying to make Amelia Willard jealous."

"Well," Ripton said slowly, "it's possible. But, Nicholas, we can't be the only two men who've noticed Elizabeth."

"I thought you were busy falling in love with Amelia."

"I haven't made up my mind to fall in love with anyone just yet." There was silence for a while, then Ripton cleared his throat. "Do you remember the letter we sent her?" Nicholas cocked his head. "I was able to discover she did receive it."

"And?"

"And she gave it to her cousin."

"Gave it to Amelia?"

"Yes. She read it and decided it must have been meant for Amelia."

Nicholas closed his eyes and let his head fall back against the seat. He opened them after a moment. "I ought to have foreseen that."

"I think she hasn't any idea how beautiful she is."

"She hasn't. Mrs. Willard sees to that," Nicholas said bitterly.

CHAPTER
20
※※※

THE DAY AFTER RETURNING FROM GREENWEALD,
Nicholas presented his card to Mr. Poyne. The
man nodded at him. "Wait here, if you please,
sir," he said. A few moments later he heard
much lighter steps coming down the stairs.

"Poyne." He heard Elizabeth's exclamation
of dismay before he saw her. "You shouldn't
have made Mr. Villines wait. Nicholas." she
called out from the middle of the stairs, "come
up."

He handed his coat and hat to Mr. Poyne and
started up the stairs.

"I'm so glad you've come." Elizabeth skipped
down a few stairs to meet him.

"Good afternoon, Elizabeth."

"Aunt Mary and Amelia aren't back yet," she
said. "But they'll be home shortly. Will you
stay to tea? Have you come to see the orchid?
Will you come upstairs?" She grasped his hand.

"Of course I'll stay to tea, and of course I'll

come upstairs. What is it that's got you so excited?"

"Come along and I'll show you." She tightened her hand around his and pulled him up the stairs after her. "It's *Vanda cerulea*. Oh, Nicholas, I think it's going to flower!"

He followed her into the morning room and, with Elizabeth hovering over him, examined the plant. "I'll be damned," he said under his breath, sitting down on the window seat. It wasn't exactly that it was going to flower, but there were obvious signs of new growth. When he looked up it was to see her shining eyes on him. This time he could not convince himself they were the eyes of a girl. It was quite possible for a man to lose himself in her eyes. They were large, expressive, thickly lashed, and the plain blue dress she always wore to garden in deepened the color to a smoky gray.

"Do you suppose we'll be rich?" she asked.

"If, in fact, it does flower, I expect so." He shrugged. "We would certainly be famous around orchid fanciers. I might even get a knighthood out of it."

"Sir Nicholas," she said slowly, testing the sound of it. "Oh! You would be unbearable if you were made Sir Nicholas!" She jumped up from her seat across from him and took his hand when he stood up. "Whom do you suppose was right, Sir Nicholas? Hmm?"

"You're being insufferable," he said.

She pretended to pout at him, and all he

could think about was how much he would like
to kiss those full lips.

"Are we really going to be rich?"

He laughed. "No doubt rich enough to buy
a castle or two, perhaps even to pay the servants
to clean it."

"Don't tease me, Nicholas." She let go of his
hand and threw her arms around his neck. "I
don't know how I shall stand the suspense."

He put his hands around her, sliding them
downward and briefly tightening them about
her waist. "I don't know how you shall stand
it, either," he said into her hair. It smelled of
violets, and he thought wryly to himself that
the scent was going to haunt him for some time.

She leaned back to look at him. "You don't
know how I'll stand it?" She slapped his chest
lightly and pouted at him again. "How will you
stand it?" she demanded.

"I don't know how I shall stand it, either."
He reached to brush his fingers over her cheek.
Soft, her skin was. That night at Greenweald it
had taken all his will not to pull her into his
arms, and this time was no different. He kissed
her cheek, sliding the fingers of one hand
around her neck when he did. She was looking
at him, a teasing smile still on her face. Just as
clearly as if it were actually happening, he could
see himself bending her head back so that he
could take her lips, could hear her moan of
pleasure as he caressed her. His knees felt weak
at the very thought of holding her body so close

to him. He watched her smile slowly fade and the look in her eyes become questioning. His fingers tightened around the back of her neck, and he let himself enjoy the incredible tension of his desire. Then he heard someone clear his throat behind them and looked up to see Mr. Willard. He moved Elizabeth away a little too hastily. "Elizabeth was just showing me the orchid."

"Have you seen it, Uncle Havoc?" she asked, turning quickly to bend over the plant. "Come and have a look, and tell me if you don't agree it will soon flower."

"Is that so?" Mr. Willard said to Nicholas.

One glance at Havoc told Nicholas that Elizabeth's quick reaction had saved him from making what might have been a rather uncomfortable explanation of his behavior.

"You will stay to tea, won't you, Nicholas?" Elizabeth asked.

"Please do," said Havoc. He returned his attention to his niece. "I came upstairs to find you, Elizabeth, because Mr. Rutherford is here."

"Is he? Well, we shall make a party, then, won't we? Oh! But I've got to change." She looked down at her dress with dismay. "I'll be downstairs in a minute, Uncle Havoc."

Nicholas followed Havoc to the drawing room, where Ripton was sitting with Mrs. Willard and Amelia. He was silent, happy to let Ripton guide the conversation away from him.

Ripton could always be counted on to sense his moods.

He recalled telling Ripton that he loved Elizabeth like a sister. Certainly what he felt was considerably more complicated than the affection he had claimed, and it confused him. He did not know precisely what he felt, he was torn between a guilty desire for her and their long friendship. Why he felt guilty he did not know; it made no sense at all. Elizabeth was beautiful; any man in his right mind would be drawn to her. Only, sometimes he did not know where to place the line between friendship and his growing attraction to her. It would be entirely too dangerous to involve himself with Elizabeth. He did not think he could bear her disapproval of the choices he had made, nor did he think he could keep them from her for long. As young as she was, she saw too much and knew him too well. It would be impossible to keep his secret from Elizabeth if they were to become anything more than friends. It was hard enough now.

When Elizabeth came in she was wearing a dress he had not seen before. The gold silk was high-necked and exceedingly plain. She looked youthful in it, but instead of convincing him she was too young for the kinds of thoughts he'd been having about her, he felt his attraction to her all the more strongly. Ripton was right: they couldn't be the only two men in

London who had noticed her. Could he bear it if she fell in love with some other man?

"Good afternoon, Mr. Rutherford," she said. Ripton took her fingers, and Nicholas saw his lips come perilously close to brushing the back of her hand.

"You said I ought to visit Tavistock Square more often, so here I am."

"How wonderful it is that you've decided to call more often, Mr. Rutherford," Amelia said.

Mr. Poyne came in to announce another visitor just as Ripton was retaking his seat. Mrs. Willard frowned when she read the card Mr. Poyne presented. "Who is Mr. Percy Johns?" she said. "I've never heard of him. Do you know him, Amelia?"

"I do not remember meeting him, Mother."

"He says he is with the Metropolitan Police, Mrs. Willard," said Mr. Poyne.

"The police! What does he want with us?"

"Show him in," said Havoc.

"So sorry to disturb you," Percy said when he was standing in the middle of the drawing room, looking out of place.

"Do sit down, Mr. . . ." Mrs. Willard glanced at his card again. "Mr. Johns."

"Thank you, madam. I have the honor of addressing Mrs. Havoc Willard, do I not?"

"Yes."

"And the rest of your company, if I might be so bold as to inquire?"

"My husband, Mr. Havoc Willard, our

daughter, Miss Amelia Willard, our niece, Elizabeth. And our guests are the Honorable Ripton Rutherford—"

"A pleasure."

"And this is Mr. Nicholas Villines. Lord Eversleigh's grandson."

"I am well of aware of Mr. Villines's background." He sat down at last. "It seems I've had a stroke of good fortune in finding Mr. Rutherford and Mr. Villines here as well," he commented.

"And why is that?" Havoc asked.

"Because I have all your names on my list."

"Goodness! Why?" Mrs. Willard was horrified at the thought of being on a policeman's list.

"You were all guests at the home of Mr. David Lillick on the evening of the alleged theft of Mrs. Lillick's necklace, were you not?"

"We've all given statements to the constable, Mr. Johns," said Mr. Willard.

"Yes, indeed you have. And he was kind enough to let me read them. However, it has always been my practice to speak to witnesses personally."

"Why are the Metropolitan Police even involved in the affair?" Havoc asked.

"Because of Mrs. Lillick's conviction that the Mayfair Thief is responsible for the theft of her necklace. It has fallen upon my shoulders to investigate the possibility that one man, the Mayfair Thief, as the public seems to call him, is responsible for several recent thefts. The idea that he absconded with Mrs. Lillick's necklace is not entirely without merit and so"—he shrugged—"here I am."

"What reason have you to believe it was the Mayfair Thief who stole the necklace?" asked Ripton.

"There are similarities in the modus operandi, if you will, most notably the boldness of the theft, that would indicate the Mayfair Thief."

"You sound as though you have doubts," Nicholas said.

"To be truthful, Mr. Villines, I do." He did not look away from Nicholas until Elizabeth spoke.

"You mean because of Mrs. Lillick's situation, Mr. Johns?"

Percy turned to her. "Astute, very astute, Miss Willard. The notion of Mrs. Lillick's brother somehow being involved in the puzzle is not without merit of its own."

"The only one of us who may have seen something is Elizabeth," said Mrs. Willard.

"Nonsense. None of us saw anything!" Havoc exclaimed.

"But, Mr. Willard, how do you know you saw nothing?"

"I saw nothing because I was in the sitting room with Mr. Beaufort Latchley for the entire hour before the theft."

"And what were you doing, if I might ask?"

"Discussing a private matter, Mr. Johns."

"Business, then?"

"No. It was a private matter."

"I see." Percy glanced at Elizabeth and Amelia. "You did not leave the room, Mr. Willard?"

"Neither of us did, until Elizabeth came in with Mrs. Lillick."

"Yes." Percy nodded. "That is what Mr. Latchley said as well. And you, Mr. Rutherford?" He turned to Ripton. "What were you doing on that evening?"

"I was in the process of losing twenty pounds to Nicholas in a game of cards."

"Mr. Aston and Mr. Lillick were playing with us," Nicholas said.

"And how long had the game been going on?"

He shrugged and looked at Ripton. "Half an hour, three-quarters of an hour, perhaps?"

"About that," Ripton agreed.

"You were all together when you heard Mrs. Lillick cry out?"

"To tell you the truth, we didn't hear a thing. We found out about it when Mr. Latchley came to fetch Mr. Lillick," Ripton said.

"We had no idea what was going on," Nicholas added. "When we got to the hall, Mr. Benford-Smith was just coming out of Mrs. Lillick's room. He said he'd seen nothing suspicious."

"Did he say whether he found the window open or closed, if you recall?"

Nicholas and Ripton looked at each other. "I don't know," Ripton said.

"If he mentioned it," said Nicholas, "I don't recall what he said."

"If I remember correctly, Mr. Villines, you did not arrive at Greenweald until very late the evening before the theft."

"That's so."

"And why were you so tardy in arriving?"

"Business in London delayed me."

"You, Mr. Rutherford, did not arrive until the very day of the theft. Was there any particular reason for your late arrival?"

"Yes. I did not know the Willards had accepted the invitation until then."

"I see. Well . . ." He glanced once more at Amelia and Elizabeth. "That is perfectly understandable, Mr. Rutherford." He shifted on his seat until he was looking at Mrs. Willard. "Did you see anything unusual, madam?"

"I retired for the evening at one o'clock, just as I told the constable."

"You heard nothing?"

"Nothing."

He nodded at Amelia. "Miss Willard?"

"I too had retired for the evening."

Mr. Johns sighed and turned to Elizabeth. "Why had you not retired as well, Miss Willard?"

"I was on my way to my room when I heard Mrs. Lillick scream."

"Once or twice?"

"Twice."

"You were coming from . . .?"

"A sitting room downstairs."

Percy raised his eyebrows. "And were you with someone?"

"No. I'd been there over an hour when I finally decided I ought to go to my room. I was halfway down the hall when I heard Mrs. Lillick. She was distraught, completely distraught, when she came out of her room."

"But you heard nothing before her cries?"

Elizabeth shook her head.

"And saw nothing?"

"Nothing." She leaned forward. "Do you really think it was the Mayfair Thief?" she asked.

"Truthfully, I am inclined to think not."

"But, Mrs. Lillick seemed so certain."

"Forgive me, Miss Willard, but how could she know who or even what she saw? No one has ever seen the Mayfair Thief, as you may know. In my opinion, he would not have been so clumsy as to have been seen. The mark of this man's thefts is timing, the most precise timing imaginable. The Mayfair Thief, you may rely on it, would have discovered a much more dramatic way to steal Mrs. Lillick's necklace."

"You don't consider the theft to have been dramatic?" Havoc demanded. "For, let me assure you, it seemed dramatic to us."

"Mr. Willard, I confess, at first I thought it was. But it was not so mysterious as it may have seemed to you. For example, there were a great many footprints on the ground underneath Mrs. Lillick's window, even a bent rosebush or two."

"Well, then. What more do you need?"

"I have followed the career of the Mayfair Thief for some time, Mr. Willard, and never once has the man left any tangible signs of his presence. The Mayfair Thief would never have been so inelegant as to leave footprints behind." Percy glanced at Nicholas.

"Perhaps he was careless this time, Mr. Johns," Nicholas said.

"While I do not discount the notion, Mr. Villines, I do not accept it, either. That is not the sort of mistake he is likely to make. No, when the Mayfair Thief finally makes a mistake, it will not be through clumsiness or stupidity. It will be serendipity."

"You sound confident, Mr. Johns."

"I am. Time, sir, is on my side. I have only to be patient."

"Perhaps he, too, is patient."

"I'm certain he is. But I, Mr. Villines, intend to be most patient of all."

CHAPTER
21
❖❖❖❖❖

"HAVE YOU BOUGHT A GOWN FOR LORD LEWESFIELD'S ball?" Havoc suddenly asked Elizabeth during tea the day after Mr. Johns's visit.

"I was going to wear the one Amelia gave me."

"What? Wear a gown you have already worn?" He pretended horror at the thought. "It won't do, Elizabeth. It just won't do. Tomorrow morning," he announced, "I shall take you all shopping for ball gowns."

He was true to his word. When they arrived at the Regent Street shop, he made a show of supervising the choices, but it was only Elizabeth's he watched over. She chose a pattern he approved of, but while she was looking at fabric, he told the shopkeeper exactly what he expected the dress to look like. When she had chosen a bolt of silk, he silently pointed out to the clerk the fabric he had seen Elizabeth lingering over before she chose a less costly one.

Both Amelia's and Mrs. Willard's gowns were delivered the day before Lord Lewesfield's Christmas ball. Elizabeth did not say anything, but she could not help thinking her dress ought to have arrived even before theirs.

By three o'clock the day of the ball, Elizabeth's gown still had not been delivered. It finally came while she was in her bath deciding what to wear instead. She hurried to finish, and when she had toweled herself off, she hastily donned her dressing gown. She unwrapped the box eagerly, anxious because she was afraid there was something wrong with it. She was just lifting off the top when one of the servants came in to tell her Mrs. Willard was asking for her.

When Elizabeth arrived to help her finish dressing, Mrs. Willard was already wearing her blue satin gown. "There you are," she said. "I thought you'd never get here."

"I came as soon as I could, Aunt Mary."

"Help me decide what to do with my hair, Beth."

"Yes, Aunt Mary." She took the brush Mrs. Willard handed her.

"Tonight, Beth," said Mrs. Willard, "Mr. Latchley will propose to Amelia."

"Do you think so?"

"What else could my husband and Mr. Latchley have been talking about at Greenweald?" She waved her hands to punctuate her words.

Elizabeth nodded. "What does Uncle Havoc say?"

"He refuses to tell me. It only convinces me I am right." Mrs. Willard sighed. "If only Mr. Villines were not being so slow to declare himself. Tell me, Beth, do you think he is holding back because Mr. Rutherford is also in love with Amelia?"

"I don't know, Aunt Mary."

"It's the only explanation. Mr. Villines had better get over such niceties, or he will lose her. Perhaps you might say a word or two to him?"

"I couldn't!"

"Of course you could, my dear."

Nearly an hour later Mrs. Willard's hair was done to her satisfaction. Elizabeth glanced nervously at the clock on the mantel. Tonight her aunt was bent on discussing every choice. Should it be this scarf or that one? this pin or that brooch? the tan gloves or the white ones? Should she wear more than one ring? Which necklace should it be, her pearls or her diamonds? The litany seemed endless. When at last Elizabeth was free to return to her room, there was little enough time to take her hair out of its paper curls. She was relieved when Miss Lincoln came in to help her just as she was beginning to pin up her hair.

"There is my dress, Miss Lincoln." Elizabeth pointed to the box still on her bed. "There's hardly time to get it pressed." She prayed there was nothing wrong with the gown; Lord Lewesfield's Christmas ball was the event of the season, and she wanted to look her best.

"Don't you worry." Miss Lincoln tucked the box under her arm and was gone almost before she had finished speaking.

Elizabeth was just putting the finishing touches on her hair when Miss Lincoln came back. She shook her head. "Your hair will never do. Not for this dress."

"Uncle Havoc," Elizabeth said. No wonder the gown had been late in coming. The fabric was much finer than the one she'd actually chosen. It was the shimmering blue-black shot silk she had wanted and tried to match with a less expensive bolt. The dress had the kind of detailing she could not afford, the kind she had dreamed of. The pattern was not at all like the one she had chosen. The flat, pleated collar—if such it could be called, for it was immediately obvious it would come nowhere near her neck—was wide with a small edging of black lace at the bottom edge. The bodice, which came to a sharp V at the waist, was embellished with black beadwork, and the sleeves, with three small puffs of fabric above the elbows, were also trimmed with black lace. The hem of the skirt was decorated with the same black beading that decorated the bodice.

She looked at Miss Lincoln. "We shall have to tighten my corset." A few moments later she stood in the center of the room taking rapid breaths as she struggled to breathe. In another moment the dress was over her head, anchored firmly to her petticoats and being fastened up the back.

"If you don't find yourself a husband tonight, Miss Elizabeth, then there's something wrong with men," Miss Lincoln said when she stood back to examine her.

"What does it matter, if I suffocate before I can be married?" she asked.

Miss Lincoln ignored her sufferings. "Now, we must do something with your hair. Sit down."

"Gladly!"

"A dress such as this does not require anything elaborate." Miss Lincoln began taking down the curls that Elizabeth had spent over half an hour putting up.

"But, Miss Lincoln."

"Understatement will turn the heads of the gentlemen tonight, Miss Elizabeth. You will look beautiful without seeming as though you are trying, and that will make you the most fascinating woman at the ball. Where are your scarves?" She rummaged through the drawer until she found one that suited her needs. "Believe me, Miss Elizabeth, you will not have to try hard at all."

There was a knock on the door, and Mrs. Poyne came in to tell them the carriage was ready and that the rest of the family was waiting for her.

"We are not ready yet," cried Miss Lincoln.

"You'd best hurry. Miss Willard is impatient."

"Mrs. Poyne," said Elizabeth from her seat, "would you be so kind as to get my black shawl from the dresser?"

"A moment yet, Miss Elizabeth." Miss Lincoln secured the scarf by winding it through a plait of hair and tucking the second of the two twisted coils up with a comb and letting the ends of the diaphanous black scarf hang down her back.

"Will you fasten my necklace, please?" Elizabeth held up the two ends of the gold chain with her mother's ring suspended from it.

Miss Lincoln stood back when she was done. "Is she not a vision?" she asked Mrs. Poyne, who was holding the shawl ready.

"She is," she answered as she helped Elizabeth wrap the shawl around shoulders that were as bare as most of her back.

The two women followed Elizabeth as she flew down the stairs, and they stood together after the Willards were gone. "Miss Willard won't like it," said Mrs. Poyne, shaking her head slowly.

"No, she won't. And I should think you'd be glad of it, too."

CHAPTER
22
❱❱❱❈❰❰❰

When the Willards arrived at Lord Lewesfield's house on Portsmouth Square, there was a line of carriages stretching out past the gates and into the street. It was nearly a quarter of an hour before they were standing next to a footman who bellowed their arrival in order to be heard above the noise. He grinned at them and pocketed the pound note Mr. Willard had slipped him to ensure a proper announcement. Almost as soon as they stepped into the room from the front hall, they were greeted by a group of young men who, though more interested in Amelia by habit, quickly regarded Elizabeth with interest.

"Do you mind, Mr. Willard, if we take your lovely girls away?" one of the young men asked.

"Indeed, no, Mr. Stacey. I shall be glad to have them off my hands," Mr. Willard replied.

"Shall we, then?" Mr. Stacey was the first to

offer his arm to Amelia, and there was some bustle while the other three offered their arms to Elizabeth.

"I must say," said the gentleman who ended up taking Elizabeth's arm, "it seems this year Lord Lewesfield has invited quite a different sort to his Christmas ball."

"Do you think so, Mr. . . .?" She could not remember who this thin, overgroomed man was.

"Mr. John Gayle, *à votre service.*" He bent at the waist as he pronounced the words.

"Mr. Gayle."

He nudged her with an elbow. "There is Lord Stepping. He is wearing a coat by that man Poole." He nodded wisely. "We shall have to wait for the next set," he said when they reached the ballroom. He stood stiffly erect, hands clasped behind his back, turning his head to survey the crowd. "There goes Sir Wesely," he said. "I should not have worn that shirt with that waistcoat. Do you not agree?"

"I can't imagine you would, Mr. Gayle."

"And there is Mr. Godling. I should have thought he might dress better."

These words were uttered in such an indignant tone that Elizabeth could only shake her head and hope he understood it to be dismay at Mr. Godling's shocking attire. It took Mr. Gayle only a few moments longer to realize it was the woman standing next to him who was attracting the stares of so many gentlemen, rather than his own exquisitely tailored jacket. He regarded her with a stare something like mingled reproach and surprise. "Who is your father, Miss Willard?"

"Why, Mr. Willard, of course," she answered. "I imagine he would be quite shocked to discover he was someone else." To her relief, he did not seem to take offense at her flippancy.

"I meant, what is his background?"

"I do not know. I have never met him."

"Then you are entirely in the care of your uncle?"

"Yes. He has raised me as if I were his own."

"I suppose, then, your uncle will be as generous to you as he is to your cousin?"

Elizabeth stiffened. "I haven't any money of my own, Mr. Gayle."

"I assure you, Miss Willard, I was not thinking of—"

"No," she interrupted, "I don't suppose you were." He ought to have had the decency to pretend he was interested in her for reasons other than money. "Let me put your questions to rest. I am not at all rich, nor will I be. Now, Mr. Gayle, forgive me, but it is beyond my power to dance with you." With those words, she walked haughtily away.

The ballroom was crowded, and she had to push her way past several people before she came to a spot where she could stand without being jostled. Understatement indeed, she thought. She might as well have been wearing sackcloth for all the notice Mr. Gayle had taken of her. She sighed, feeling more than a little sorry for herself. She felt awkward standing alone and glanced around for someone who looked familiar. Considering the number of people here, it was no surprise that she did not recognize a soul. She completely disagreed with Mr. Gayle. She thought everyone was brilliantly dressed; all the men were handsome, and all the women were beautiful. Never in her life had she seen so much bejeweled skin. If the Mayfair Thief had any sense at all, she thought, he was here somewhere. She began to study the men in particular. Any one of them might be the thief.

Suddenly she saw someone she recognized. The policeman, Mr. Percy Johns. He was in formal clothes and, like her, was standing alone, surveying the crowd. Mr. Johns suddenly turned, almost as if he had sensed her interest. He was near enough that she could not be so rude as not to acknowledge him. He returned her tentative smile.

"Miss Elizabeth Willard, is it not?" he asked, eyebrows lifting.

She nodded. "Good evening, Mr. Johns."

His gaze darted to where she was nervously fingering her necklace, then lifted to her face. "Have a pleasant evening, Miss Willard." He moved off into the crowd, leaving Elizabeth alone once more. He must have the same idea she did, Elizabeth thought. Somewhere among this press of exquisitely dressed men and women was the Mayfair Thief.

After several more minutes of scrutinizing the gentlemen, she was struck by how many appeared to be interested in something near where she was standing. She glanced over her shoulder in order to catch a glimpse of what they were looking at. A tapestry hung on the wall behind her, but it hardly seemed worth staring at; certainly one could not get the full effect of it without being a good deal farther off than these gentlemen were. She turned back, and as she did it occurred to her that they were looking at her. All thought of the Mayfair Thief left her. As a sort of test, she smiled at the next man to look her way, just a small lift of the corner of her mouth in case she was wrong. His eyes widened, and he nodded, giving her a look that was almost positively a leer.

"Elizabeth." She recognized Nicholas's voice before she saw him. He was one of the few men wearing black, his white shirt and cravat in stark contrast with the rest of his clothes. Even his waistcoat was black and like the lapels of his coat was trimmed in black satin. His hair was tousled and curling over the top of his stiff collar. He looked devilish and so handsome that Elizabeth almost lost the power to speak. "How long have you been here?" he asked when he had kissed the back of her gloved hand. He seemed to take his time lifting his eyes to hers.

"Long enough to have been rude to one poor

gentleman already." She clasped her hands tightly, suddenly nervous because she had often seen Nicholas look at Amelia the way he'd just looked at her.

"I can't imagine you being rude to anyone."

"I'm afraid I was, Nicholas." She resisted the urge to reach up and brush the hair from his forehead.

"Then he must have deserved it." He spoke quickly, with hardly a pause before he continued. "Are you engaged for the next waltz, or am I too late?"

"There you are, Mr. Villines."

He frowned and turned. A smile was quickly in its place when he saw Amelia.

"I have been looking for you simply everywhere," she said when she reached them. She paid no attention to her cousin. "Is this not the most elegant house you have ever seen?"

"Good evening, Miss Willard."

"I positively adore this music. Lord Lewesfield has hired a most remarkable orchestra, do you not agree? You simply must dance this set with me." She put a hand on his arm and looked at him so imploringly that Elizabeth did not see how he, or any man, could have refused her. And, of course, he did not.

"Excuse me, Elizabeth." Nicholas looked apologetic. "Will you promise me the next waltz?" He grasped her hands. "Well? I shan't let you go until I have your promise."

"The very next one," she said. The look he

gave her before he turned back to Amelia made her stomach suddenly tighten. She took a deep breath against the sensation as she watched the two walk to the dance floor.

She was not alone for long. Beaufort Latchley approached her, taking her hand and holding it firmly. "Good evening, Miss Willard." She colored when she felt his lips against the back of her hand. "One imagines a woman as lovely as you is engaged for every dance," he said.

"Does one?" She was still trying to catch a glimpse of Nicholas.

"Indeed." He inclined his head. "Therefore, I shall not presume to engage you to dance until after supper." He looked at her thoughtfully. "Perhaps," he said, "you will save me the one just after?"

Elizabeth glanced at him inquiringly, too engrossed in remembering the way Nicholas had pressed her hand for so long to pay much attention to Beaufort Latchley.

"If that one is promised, perhaps the one after that?"

What had Nicholas meant by holding her hand so long, and by looking at her with such a penetrating gaze?"

"I would consider it a great honor if you deigned to dance with me," he added with another smile that barely curved his lips.

A waltz, he had asked her for a waltz.

Beaufort took her silence for agreement.

"Thank you, Miss Willard. I look forward to it."

She and Beaufort stood talking—aimlessly, it seemed to Elizabeth—until Mr. Stacey came to ask for a dance. She had several partners after that, none of whom she paid any more than polite attention. She looked constantly for Nicholas. Was she daring too much to think he felt something more than friendship for her? She ought to suppress such a hope at all costs; disappointment would be too unbearably cruel. She refused the dance just before the waltz. She did not want to miss Nicholas.

Nicholas had no trouble finding Elizabeth for their waltz. She was surrounded by gentlemen. Even Mr. Stacey, whom everyone knew was smitten with Amelia, was a member of the crowd around her. "There you are, Elizabeth," he called out when he was still several feet from where she was standing, listening to something Mr. Stacey was saying. She turned when she heard him.

"Nicholas!"

"You promised me a waltz, you know," he said when he reached her.

"Did I?"

"You know you did." He held out his hand. "You would break my heart if you did not dance with me." He thought she almost might.

"I should hate to break your heart, Nicholas," she said softly.

"Would you, now?" He smiled what he was sure was his first genuine smile of the evening. His tension dissipated enough for him to be aware he was glad to be with Elizabeth. It seemed he must have been waiting for this moment since he arrived. He puzzled over what a relief it was to finally be with her until the music began and they were close. Then he ceased to think about it at all. She danced well. It was effortless to move around the floor with her in his arms; her cousin did not dance half so well. He glanced down. Her eyelids were lowered so that her eyes were nearly closed. There was a dreamy expression on her face, as though she were remembering some long-ago pleasure or, maybe, savoring a present one. Another time he might have teased her about it, but now he was content just to watch her. It was magical, this sense of well-being; he was not used to it, nor did he know what to make of it. He pulled her closer when a couple danced too near, and though it was improper, he did not immediately relax his embrace. She looked up when his arm remained tightened around her waist. He gazed into the cool gray of her eyes, wondering as he did whether it was possible for two people to be any closer than were he and Elizabeth.

"Is something the matter, Nicholas?"

"Nothing at all," he replied, smiling because her cheeks were turning pink.

When the music ended they were standing

by a doorway. He walked with her into the hall. "You're flushed," he said, raising one hand to touch her cheek with the backs of his fingers. Her skin was still impossibly soft.

"Am I?"

"Yes."

He signaled to a passing footman, frowning when he saw there was only champagne on the tray he carried. "Can you tell me," he said to the servant as he took a glass of champagne, "who the devil that is?" He pointed to a man standing resolutely at one end of the hall.

"Him?" The footman glanced down the hall. "Don't know, sir. Probably one of the policemen."

"Policemen?" echoed Elizabeth.

"Yes, miss."

"Will you bring a glass of punch?" Nicholas asked.

"Directly, sir."

"You know, Nicholas, Mr. Percy Johns is here this evening. I think he expects to catch the Mayfair Thief tonight."

"Perhaps he will." The footman returned with the punch, and Nicholas handed it to her.

"That wing of the house is closed off." The servant nodded to the end of the hall where the policeman stood guard. "So you might prefer to walk in the other direction."

"Thank you, we will."

"Why did you make him bring this?" Elizabeth complained when they started walking slowly toward the open end of the hall. She made a face at her punch. "I'd rather have champagne."

"Does your uncle permit it?" he asked.

"Why ever not? I was permitted to come to this ball and even to dance with you."

It seemed incredible to him that she could be so nonchalant when his own nerves felt stretched to their limit. He somehow managed to adopt her bantering tone. "I don't believe you."

She laughed and wrapped her free arm around his. "Naturally, you're right, Nicholas. Uncle Havoc said that on no account was I to dance with you."

Her teasing made him feel slightly ridiculous for keeping her from having a glass of champagne, as though she really were a child. He would not have questioned Amelia if she had asked for a glass. He looked for another footman, but they had walked some distance down the hall and none was in sight. "Here," he said. "You may have mine." Her nearness to him was making the skirt of her dress brush against his leg, and that, more than anything else, made him uncomfortably aware of her.

"Thank you, sir." She held out her punch until he took it from her. He placed it on a nearby table and watched her take a small sip of his champagne. She stared into the glass before taking a second sip. "It's quite good," she said with a surprised look at him.

"Lord Lewesfield would hardly serve inferior champagne."

"I'm afraid I wouldn't know the difference. I've never had it before."

He whirled to stand in front of her. "Give me that!"

"Uncle Havoc never said I could not, Nicholas." She held the glass away from him, but he reached around her and took it.

"I should hardly like to be accused of corrupting a young lady's morals." She was laughing, and he could not keep a stern face. "You ought to be ashamed, Elizabeth," he said, putting the champagne down on the table.

"Yes, I suppose so." She spoke matter-of-factly. "But I'm not."

"It's a wonder your aunt and uncle let you come."

"Not really. Have you noticed my dress?" She spread her fingers over the skirt of her gown. "It seems Uncle Havoc thinks there's hope for me, if I display a little more bosom than I like." She flushed pink.

"What do you mean, 'hope for you'?" He tucked her hand back under his arm. A faint wisp of the violet scent she used made him wish he dared move closer to her.

"I'm not beautiful or charming like Amelia," she was saying. "If I were rich, Aunt Mary says I might be married . . ." She finished the sentence with a shrug. "It isn't likely, but hope springs eternal in Uncle Havoc's breast."

They had reached a corner where there was a window, and Nicholas stopped to open it. "What makes you say that?" He turned to face her. She took a step forward to let the breeze from the open window cool her, closing her eyes for a moment. It was almost painful to look at her.

"There are some things, Nicholas, that one simply knows." She opened her eyes. "I'd thought about it even before Aunt Mary and I talked." She sighed.

"May I ask what she told you?"

"Mostly that a poor girl will not have many offers of marriage."

"Do you think a man will marry only for money? There are other reasons besides that." Well, so, she looked undeniably grown-up in that dress. If her uncle was responsible for the gown, he seemed to have known too well what he was doing.

"Perhaps so." She smiled. "But so far, no one has fallen in love with my lack of fortune."

He scowled, angry to hear evidence of how successful Mrs. Willard had been in keeping Elizabeth humble. "Don't joke about it, Elizabeth. There are a thousand reasons for a man to fall in love with you, even before he knew you." He leaned into the corner to look at her because she did not answer him. "You don't believe I mean it," he accused.

"If you do, I wish you would not say such things to me."

"Why not?" He reached to take her hand and pull her to him. Strains of music from the ballroom could be heard even from their corner. He pushed one end of her scarf back over her shoulder. "I do mean it." She shivered when his fingers brushed over her bare skin.

"You should not talk to me so."

"Surely I have the right to tell you the truth, Elizabeth? My God! Have you seen yourself tonight?" He grasped her shoulders. "You might have any man you wanted. Even bloody Mr. Beaufort Latchley." And to himself, he thought, She might have me.

She was looking at him, but when he mentioned Beaufort Latchley, she glanced away. "Please don't tease me, Nicholas."

"What makes you think I am?" She lifted her eyes to his, and it came into his head that if he was in love with her, he ought to tell her so. "Elizabeth . . ." His fingers slid across her cheek to curl around the nape of her neck.

He had few inhibitions about the satisfaction of his appetites, and he was not, he believed, any stranger to sexual passion, but his upbringing had been scrupulously correct about the differences between ladies and the women to whom a man might properly make love. Therefore, he knew it was wrong to want to make love to Elizabeth; but there it was, he did want to, and badly enough to risk everything to have her. He did not know if she took a step closer to him or if he pulled her to him, but they were suddenly so close it was a simple matter to tip her head so that their lips would meet. She did not pull away from him as he was afraid she might. Instead her arms went around his neck, and she melted against him.

It was not a chaste kiss. The propriety, or the stupidity, of passionately kissing a woman in a place lacking even a semblance of privacy did not occur to him. It was natural to be kissing her this way, and it was more than a little arousing that she obviously felt the same. She fit perfectly in his arms, exactly the right height for him. He deepened their kiss, opening her lips under his, oblivious of anything but the feeling of his tongue moving over her teeth, then past to explore her mouth, of being completely and exasperatingly excited. He could not get enough of her; just kissing her would never, could never, be enough.

He brought his hand up between them, letting his fingers settle gently around her throat before sliding them down over the curve of her chest. He stopped kissing her, pushing her to arm's length because it was impossible to speak if she was so close. "Elizabeth . . ." It was on the tip of his tongue to ask her to leave with him, which would have been madness, absolute madness, but at that moment he was fully prepared to do it, and damn the consequences.

The sound of someone walking down the hall startled them both, and he was not at all certain he was glad of the interruption. It was a sobering realization. He could not live with himself if he ever did anything to hurt Elizabeth. And that would be the only possible result if he were to let things between them go any further. He stepped away and closed the window before turning back to say the first thing to come into his head.

"I promised a second dance to Amelia. I'll not forgive myself if she's disappointed." Her gray eyes were fixed on him, not reproachful, not even hurt, only watchful. "I'm sure the others must have missed you by now," he added. "I should not have taken you away from the dancing."

"No, I suppose not," she said after what seemed an eternity.

Not another word passed between them until they reached the ballroom. He bowed over her hand and was turning to leave when she prevented him by grasping his arm.

"What were you really going to say to me, Nicholas?"

He had a panicky feeling that she knew.

"Tell me," she demanded softly.

It would be insane. Better that he should bewilder her now than hurt her later. "I don't remember."

"You're lying." She said the words evenly, without any hint of uncertainty.

"Elizabeth, I'm sorry, but I don't remember." He shrugged and laughed. "If it was important, no doubt I would recall."

"Go, then!" She pushed him away. "Go to Amelia!"

"I'm sorry—" He stopped, began again. "What happened—"

"What did happen, Nicholas?" She turned away when he did not answer. He took a step to follow her because he could not bear to have her think he wanted Amelia, stopping before she was lost in the crowd. He did not know if he was making a mistake by letting her go, he only knew he felt as if he were shutting a door that ought to have remained open.

It was ironic that Amelia found him not long after her cousin had left him. She dimpled with pleasure and readily convinced him to help her to the dining room, where he piled a plate with food she did not eat. They talked pleasantly enough since it took no effort of will to remain calm with Amelia. He was barely listening to her chatter when she suddenly leaned forward to put a hand on his arm.

"Tell me, Mr. Villines," she said earnestly, "what do you think of my cousin tonight?"

For an instant he thought she had seen him with Elizabeth, and he stared at her, dumbfounded. "Pardon me?"

"I mean, her dress, Mr. Villines."

Of course, she had not seen them. "It is a stunning thing," he answered.

She frowned. "Yes, the gown is stunning, but do you not think Elizabeth seems, well, out of place in it?"

"In what way do you mean, Miss Willard?" He was startled into sitting upright.

"You know she has nothing from her father, at all."

"I don't believe I follow you." He was afraid he followed her quite well enough. It was no wonder Elizabeth thought no one would be interested in marrying her.

"I mean," she said, leaning forward again to deliver her judgment in a confidential tone, "the dress only shows she has pretensions above her due, Mr. Villines."

"Elizabeth is the least pretentious person I know." He spoke stiffly, hoping it would make Amelia realize he disapproved of the conversation.

"I am afraid she will be hurt. If she does attract the notice of a gentleman, she will only be disappointed when he discovers her position."

"You talk as though you think she is a peasant." He let his dismay show in his voice and expression.

"Not a peasant, of course."

"Mr. Latchley is said to be quite enamored of her." He did not know that it was true, but as soon as the words were out he was certain it was.

"Mr. Latchley? Oh, my goodness, Mr. Villines." Her dimples appeared. "That is simply impossible. Beth?" She lifted her hands. "She isn't capable of attracting the notice of Mr. Latchley. I assure you, if he pays attention to

her, it is only because he wishes to attract—"
She glanced at her lap. "To attract the notice of
someone else."

"Indeed?"

"Yes. Beth has quite lost her mind if she
thinks a man like Beaufort Latchley has any interest in her."

Nicholas stared at her. "Let me remind you,
Miss Willard, your cousin has been a particular
friend of mine for nearly fifteen years."

"Exactly, Mr. Villines."

"I assure you, Elizabeth is more than capable
of attracting the serious attention of any man
in this room."

"Mr. Villines." She shook her head sorrow-
fully. "I only hope I can prevail upon you to tell
her of the danger she exposes herself to."

"Danger?" He drew his eyebrows together.

"Yes. The danger of making a fool not only
of herself, but of my father, who has been so
misguidedly kind to her."

"This seems to be such a serious matter, perhaps you ought to tell her yourself."

"I have considered it."

"And?"

"I believe she would not take it well from
me." She bit her lip. "I would hate to have her
misunderstand my motives. That is why I am
asking you to talk to her. You are, as you say,
her particular friend."

"Miss Willard, I will think very seriously
about your suggestion. But you judge Elizabeth

far too harshly. Ripton Rutherford, whom you know adores you, is by his own admission half in love with Elizabeth. Why, if you can believe it, I'm more than a little in love with her myself." He rose. "If you will excuse me, I have something to attend to."

"Mr. Villines." She pulled him back to his seat.

He sighed. "Amelia, you are one of the most beautiful women I have ever met. You have breeding and the grace and accomplishment other women only dream of. With all that you do have, I confess I fail to understand why you are not as charitable toward your cousin as she is to you. Now, forgive me, but I must go."

"Then, you'll speak to her?" she asked anxiously.

"Amelia . . ." He leaned forward and kissed her forehead. "You may rely on me to say exactly what needs to be said."

"Miss Elizabeth!" Ripton stood back to look at her. "My compliments," he said. His eyes expressed what little admiration had not been in his voice. "Will you dance with me?" The contrast of his dark clothes and his fair hair made his eyes seem almost unnaturally blue. It was lucky for him he was handsome enough that his eyes did not overshadow his looks. "I am in luck," he cried as he led her to the dance floor. "A wicked waltz is the very dance a gentleman ought to have with the most beautiful woman at a ball."

"Do you really think I'm beautiful?" she asked wistfully.

"Indeed I do," he answered. He broke the moment by smiling at her. "I'm sure," he said, "that we must be positively wicked-looking together."

He took her hand as the music started. His hand on her waist was firm, and although he held her just a little too close for good manners, Elizabeth did not mind. He did not seem to notice it himself. Ripton was not quite as tall as Nicholas, and she found herself looking directly into the blue of his eyes.

"You waltz beautifully," he told her. She smiled back at him. "Is there anything you do not do well?"

"I consider myself to be a model of perfection, Mr. Rutherford."

"Rightfully so, Miss Elizabeth." When the music ended, he bent over her hand. "It is with a great deal of reluctance that I hand you over to that fellow." He looked pointedly at the gentleman who had come to claim his dance.

"Good evening, Mr. Rutherford, and thank you for all your gallantry," Elizabeth said. "You've cheered me up more than you know."

"Then my evening has been an unqualified success."

Ripton was standing in the same spot, watching Elizabeth dance, when Amelia Willard put a hand on his arm.

"I saw you dancing with my cousin, Mr. Rutherford." She dimpled at him.

"Oh?"

"Yes, and I must say it was very kind of you."

"It is my habit to be kind to beautiful women," he replied.

"Now you are being too kind." She wrapped her arm around Ripton's.

He lifted his eyebrows. "Not at all, Miss Willard."

"I find it unsettling when a woman tries too hard. Do you not think so, as well? I mean," she said when Ripton gave her a blank look, "that Beth is stepping out of character tonight. She has always been content to stay in her place before. I would never have thought her head could be turned, but London seems to have done just that."

"Ah, now I understand you. You mean Elizabeth is at last not bothering to hide her beauty. Yes, you are quite right to notice it, quite right, Miss Willard. It shows what a discerning eye you have."

"Why, thank you, Mr. Rutherford. Do you not think it sad? I am greatly concerned for her." Amelia pursed her lips. "I should hate to see Beth's kind nature spoiled, would not you?"

"I share your concern. It's only a wonder she hasn't been spoiled yet, considering what she has been exposed to."

"Yet I fear it is inevitable, Mr. Rutherford."

"There I must disagree. Elizabeth Willard is the finest woman I know, and if anyone can endure such circumstances, it is she, to be sure."

"Would you be amenable, Miss Willard, to a stroll rather than a dance?" Beaufort tucked Elizabeth's hand under his arm.

Elizabeth did not much care what she did, so she nodded her agreement. A short hall led to a brightly lit room that opened into a courtyard, and Beaufort headed toward it. There were several others sitting, standing, or walking about, but the space was large and afforded no small amount of privacy. Beaufort came to a stop just before the open doors, where he let go of her arm and turned to face her.

"Miss Willard, I am a man of few words," he began. He paused until Elizabeth looked away from the courtyard and he had her attention. "I beg you, forgive me if I seem to speak abruptly." He winced as if he keenly felt his professed awkwardness. "I admit that when we were introduced you did not inspire in me any of the higher sentiments. Oh, I thought you a pretty enough girl, that certainly is true. But I am a man who admires spirit in a woman, and I mistook your quietness for something other than what it is. My error was not soon discovered, nor did I discover it suddenly. I have gradually come to hold you in increasingly greater esteem, to the point, Miss Willard, that I now think of you in terms quite different from what I felt even a month ago." He stopped.

He seemed to think his pause a significant one, and, uncertain what precisely he wanted her to say, Elizabeth spoke cautiously. "Mr. Latchley, such a high opinion of me is not justified."

"I have no doubt it is justified, Miss Willard," he said. "I could not hold you in higher esteem if I wanted to." He paused again, as if weighing the effect this was having on her. "Neither my family nor my fortune is old, though as to the latter, there is the advantage of its amount. If there is to be some connection between us, it would, I daresay, suffice."

"Mr. Latchley!"

Beaufort took her hand. "I will be a happy man, Miss Willard, if you do me the honor of consenting to be my wife."

She was at a loss for words. "I think, Mr. Latchley, I can make you no answer at all, absolutely none," she finally managed to get out, "without first speaking to my uncle."

"I have already acquainted your uncle with my intentions toward you."

She was nonplussed. "May I ask what he said?"

"He gave me to understand his approval was contingent only upon yours." He considered her obvious confusion. "I see, Miss Willard, that my declaration has taken you very much by surprise."

"Yes, it has."

"Is it impossible for you to tell me in what light you view the matter?" he asked.

"I had no idea you had formed any attachment to me," she said slowly. "I am honored, truly honored. But . . ."

"You have formed no similar attachment to me?" He smiled wryly. "That is something that may be changed over the course of time, do you not agree?"

"Perhaps so." She did not feel as flustered now. "But is it not odd for you to do me the singular honor of asking me to be your wife without once having said you love me?"

"You demonstrate your youth, Miss Willard. Love is an emotion best left out of marriage. It never lasts. When it does wear off one is left miserable, and the object of former passion serves only as a daily reminder of one's condition. If, at your tender age, you had ever been in love, you would know what a wretched thing it is." She did not answer, and Beaufort took her arm again. "If it is agreeable to you, we will talk of this again after you have come to know me better."

"I think that would be best, Mr. Latchley. But I must first speak with my uncle."

"That is only as it should be. Shall we go back?"

Elizabeth was grateful when Beaufort led her into the dining room, and when she saw Amelia, for once she was glad.

"Beth!" Amelia waved back at her. "Good evening, Mr. Latchley," she said when the two reached her. "Where have you been?"

"We have been walking, Miss Willard."

"How kind of you to take Beth along. I'm sure she was glad for the fresh air. Do sit down, Beth. You look simply exhausted. Poor Mr. Latchley. I hope you did not look so poorly while you were with him."

"In my opinion, you cousin has never looked lovelier."

"Oh, nonsense. Why, she looks positively wretched, I'm sure."

"I am a little tired," Elizabeth said.

"Please excuse me, ladies." Beaufort bowed to them. "I hope to see you tomorrow." He was looking at Elizabeth, but it was Amelia who answered.

"I should be simply delighted, Mr. Latchley." They both watched him leave. "Have you seen Mr. Villines?" Amelia asked. "I believe he is looking for you."

"Did he say why?" In spite of herself, her heart leaped.

"No. But perhaps I have an idea. Nicholas has the most ridiculous notion that Mr. Latchley admires you. Can you fancy that?"

Elizabeth was so shocked to hear Amelia using Nicholas's given name that she could say nothing.

"Do you not agree Nicholas is handsome?" Amelia leaned back in her seat and sighed.

"Of course." It was all Elizabeth could do to speak without letting her voice tremble.

"Do you know, Nicholas has kissed me?" Amelia closed her eyes and sighed again. "And told me I am the most beautiful woman he has ever had the pleasure of knowing?"

There was no response from Elizabeth but silence.

Amelia opened her eyes and sat up. "Well," she said, "and if you are supposing that I am also in love, you might be right. Are you not happy for me?"

"You are to be congratulated, Amelia." She stood up.

"Thank you, Beth. I think I must be the happiest woman in the world."

Elizabeth nodded and walked out of the dining room. The crowded ballroom made her almost frantic to be alone; not for a moment longer could she tolerate these laughing, smiling people. She made her way through the room as quickly as the crowd would permit and did not halt until she saw she was at the very corner of the hall where she and Nicholas had stood before. She whirled and went the opposite direction. The last thing she wanted was to be reminded of how she had let herself think he wanted to be anything more than friends. It was Amelia he loved, Amelia he wanted to marry. Tears burning behind her eyes made her hurry down the hall. She twisted the knob of the first door she came to, sobbing with relief when it opened.

When the door was closed behind her, she leaned back and squeezed her eyes shut against tears she could no longer keep away. Her misery was utter for wanting to believe that Nicholas had meant his attentions to her to be anything but what they were. He was going to marry Amelia. She did not know how she would stand it, but stand it she would. Stand it she must. There was nothing else she could do.

"I wish I were dead!" Pulling a handkerchief from the pocket of her skirt, she balled it up and pressed it to her eyes. At last she willed the tears gone and let her head fall back against the door. When she opened her eyes, it was a moment before they adjusted to the darkness. She was in some sort of anteroom; she could just make out an open door on the opposite side, leading to the main bedroom, no doubt. There was a lamp on the table near the door, and walking slowly because of the darkness, she made her way to the table. She found matches and in a moment was putting flame to the lamp. A noise made her fingers pause just above the wick.

"Is there someone here?" she called out. Nothing. She shook out the match and lit another. The lamp flickered, then caught, suffusing the room with a dim light. Another noise made her freeze. She was not alone. Before she could call out to let the person know she had intruded, she was grabbed from behind and fingers were pressing tightly over her mouth, holding her head back against a hard shoulder.

"Don't make a sound," a voice whispered in her ear. "If you value your life, not a sound." Paralyzed with fright, she nodded. He took his hand from her mouth, and for a moment his fingers pressed into her shoulder.

"Who are you?"

There was no answer; then a black-gloved hand was holding something in front of her. The light from the lamp flickered off it, making a mysterious green seem to leap from the stones. Emeralds, she thought. They must be emeralds!

"Do these answer your question? They are beautiful, aren't they?" he whispered when he heard her intake of breath. His low voice, seductive and soft, was that of an educated man, a gentleman. The necklace flashed in the dim light. "On you, they would be even more so." He put the emeralds up to her throat. "Against such skin as yours, they would be spectacular."

For one eerie moment, she was certain she knew the voice, but it was impossible to be sure when he spoke only in a whisper. She gasped when she felt his fingers brushing against the back of her neck, unfastening the clasp of her own necklace. She knew she ought to scream, but she could not. Then she felt cold metal against her skin, shivered when he fastened the clasp and let the heavy weight settle around her neck. His fingers were holding her shoulders, pulling her against him. The buttons of his coat dug into her back. His hands slid slowly down her shoulders, and with the fingers of one hand he traced on her chest the outline of the largest, bottom-most stone. She shivered again. His hand lingered, moving caressingly over the curve of her breasts. "I should like to have you wearing only this," he whispered, breath hot in her ear. Again she felt that she knew the voice. "Naked in my bed." Hot mouth on her shoulder, sliding up to the side of her neck. "I have never wanted a woman the way I want you. I thought I would go mad with desire for you when I saw you tonight."

Quickly he unfastened the necklace. One of his hands disappeared for a moment. His voice was hardly loud enough for Elizabeth to hear as he held up her plain gold chain. "This, I will keep." Then it too was gone from sight. With one arm wrapped around her waist, he leaned forward and put out the lamp. She could see nothing in the blackness. Still holding her, he moved around the table. Then she heard the sound of a window being opened, felt the chill of the night air on her, the warmth of his breath on her cheek. "Oh, Elizabeth, I do love you," he said.

She was alone. There was nothing to show that anyone had been in the room with her. It

might have been a dream, except for the lingering sound of his voice in her ear. In her heart,
she thought she recognized the voice. She raised
a hand to her bare throat.

CHAPTER
23
>>>※<<<

IN SPITE OF NOT HAVING ARRIVED HOME UNTIL PAST two in the morning, Nicholas awoke at five o'clock. He groaned and rolled onto his stomach, pulling the covers over his head. He was half-asleep again when he began to think about Elizabeth. The way she'd looked, she could have made any man hunger for her, let alone one who was more than a little in love with her. It was not the first time he'd seen her wearing a dress that bared her shoulders, but it was the first time they had been bared so dramatically. She had felt so substantial in his arms, and he had not been able to resist the intensity of his desire for her. He wondered if she would have left with him. Of course. She trusted him too much not to have agreed to go. And she had been every bit as aroused as he, there was no doubting that. He should have taken her to Cambridge Terrace, where they would be undisturbed. Where he could unfasten her hair and tangle his fingers in it when it was loose and flowing. . . .

The back of her dress was fastened with dozens of tiny buttons, yet they fell away as soon as his fingers touched them. She was looking at him with parted lips as he pulled off her gloves because he wanted to feel her bare hands on him when she touched him. He was aching for her. She was so sleek, so perfectly willing to let him explore the soft curves of her. He pulled her into the circle of his arms, holding her tight against him. When he picked her up, she wrapped her arms around his neck and kissed him just as passionately as she had at Lord Lewesfield's ball. He was weak with desire as he let her slide down slowly when he reached the bed. Then she helped him to undress, whispering to him that she desired him, too. Her hands on him were hot and making him tremble. They fell onto his bed, his fingers were in her hair, the scent of violets in the air, the sound of her sighs in his ears as he entered her. What he wanted was to hear her crying out his name, to hear her gasping when he touched her.

When Nicholas woke the second time, it was past nine o'clock. He lay still, remembering, even savoring, his dream and not sure if he was sorry it had only been a dream. When Mr. Chester came in to help him dress, he was fully awake. He had his breakfast brought to him in the parlor, where he sat cradling a cup of coffee in his hand. One of the servants brought him the morning paper. The only article he was interested in was on the front page.

A valuable emerald necklace had been stolen from Lady Lewesfield's private rooms, in spite of heavy police presence at the house. The theft was the work of the Mayfair Thief, there could be no doubt of that. The writer scoffed at Mr. Percy Johns's vow that he was close to learning the identity of the Mayfair Thief. Would society ever be free of this mysterious thief, queried the writer, when the police had just demonstrated, yet again, their inability to capture him even when he was under their very noses?

Nicholas put down the paper and stared out over Regent's Park. He dared not ask Elizabeth to marry him, the risk for them both was too great.

He did not stir until nearly eleven-thirty. He gave strict instructions that he was not to be disturbed for any reason and spent the afternoon with his orchids.

CHAPTER
24
❧❧❧❧

ELIZABETH GLANCED OUT THE WINDOW BEFORE SITTING
down and pouring herself a cup of steaming
coffee. She added a liberal helping of cream and
asked for the morning paper to be brought to
her. The paper was duly brought, and with the
unusual luxury of being the only one yet about,
she was soon absorbed in reading the account
of the theft of Lady Lewesfield's emeralds. The
story occupied the better part of one page, and
she was rereading it when Mr. Poyne came in.

"Miss?"

"Yes?"

"A gentleman is calling."

"At this hour?" She put down the paper.
"Who in heaven's name is it?" She looked at
the card Mr. Poyne had brought her.

"Shall I tell him you are not at home?"

"No, Poyne. Show Mr. Rutherford in. And
would you ask Mrs. Poyne to please bring some
toast, if it isn't too much trouble?"

"Yes, miss." Mr. Poyne nodded and left. When he returned, it was with Ripton Rutherford close behind him.

"Mr. Rutherford."

"Good morning, Miss Elizabeth," he said after Mr. Poyne left. He stood looking at her, hands clasped behind his back.

"Do sit down, Mr. Rutherford. Will you have some coffee?" She was already reaching for the pot when he nodded.

"Thank you, yes." He seated himself on the chair across from her, readjusted his position once or twice, and took the cup she held out. "I hope I find you well this morning."

"Very well, thank you."

"Not too tired from the ball?" He put several lumps of sugar in his cup and stirred the mixture.

"No." She shook her head. "And yourself? How are you?"

"As well as one might expect under the circumstances," he said.

"Oh?" There was a strained tone in his voice that surprised her. "What circumstances are those?"

"The usual ones, I suppose." He took a sip of his coffee and immediately put it down. "Did you sleep well?" He added another lump of sugar to his cup.

She was not certain if it would be best to pretend there was nothing unusual about his behavior, but she answered him as if there were not. "Yes, I did. And you?"

"Not well, I'm afraid." He looked up briefly from his study of his spoon. "Actually, I slept quite well, once I did fall asleep, but it was a deuced long time coming."

"How terrible for you." His awkwardness was beginning to make her feel ill at ease, too. "I'm afraid, Mr. Rutherford," she said, hoping it would prod him into telling her why he had come, "that Amelia is not up yet." She refolded the paper carefully and placed it by her cup, determined to show him by her manner that she was perplexed.

"Oh, I haven't come to see Amelia. In fact, I'm rather glad to have had the good luck of finding you alone." He was startled when a servant came in with the toast Elizabeth had asked for, but he recovered himself quickly.

They were silent until the woman was gone, and then, to put an end to what was becoming an uncomfortable moment, Elizabeth said, "Then you are here to see me?"

"Yes," Ripton said. "I am." He seemed gratefully absorbed in transferring a slice of toast to a plate.

"May I ask why?"

"Certainly. It has to do, in a way, with what went on at the Lillicks'. I've not been able to get it off my mind."

"The Lillicks'? Oh!" She reddened when she

realized he must be referring to having kissed her. "There isn't anything to apologize for."

"Oh, I haven't come to apologize. Unless, of course, you think I ought to," he added hastily. "I should be happy to, you know, if you think I ought."

"No, Mr. Rutherford, I do not." She was now thoroughly embarrassed.

"Good, because I should hate to think I must apologize for something I enjoyed so immensely." He smiled brightly, picked up his coffee, and made a face after taking a stiff swallow of it. He put the cup back on its saucer and pushed it away. "Perfectly horrible," he murmured. She was going to pour him another cup, but he waved it off. "No, I would only render that undrinkable as well. I confess, I'm rather nervous. I'm afraid I shan't be able to carry this off well at all. I've never done this before. you know."

"Never done what before?"

"Why, this, of course."

"I see." She did not see at all but decided he would attempt to make himself clear in good time.

"I want to say, Elizabeth, I think you are an extraordinary young woman, and I consider it a great honor to know you. I respect and admire you for your kindness to me, especially when I've been so deuced difficult. As you know, I have expressed some rather strong sentiments in connection with your cousin, and I wish to assure you—" He cleared his throat. "A new leaf and all that, you understand. You needn't worry about it in the least.

"Well. Indeed," he continued. "I assure you, I only bring up the subject so it is perfectly clear it does not matter to me in the slightest. My own financial situation being what it is allows me to indulge my affections, if you will. I have nearly twelve thousand pounds a year from my grandmother, and I will, of course, come into possession of a good deal more upon the passing of my father. There's the baronetcy, naturally, and I am given to understand that I shall have in addition to my present income something like another twenty or thirty thousand a year. My father is a frugal man," he said wryly. "We might live quite easily on that, don't you think?"

Elizabeth blinked.

"I am convinced," he went on, "that it is possible to live comfortably—indeed, even elegantly—on the combined amount since I presently live extremely well on a lesser sum. I am merely trying to make the point that as husband and wife, two might live quite comfortably on the combination of my present fortune and, eventually, my prospective one, no matter what my wife might bring to the union. I do want to make it clear to you as well."

"Oh, dear." The only thing she could think was that he was talking about his apparently imminent proposal to Amelia. "I suppose two could live on just the twelve thousand. But, really, do you think you ought to be discussing this with me?" She knew too well that Amelia would refuse him.

"I thought it best to speak with you first. Not to put too fine a point on it, Elizabeth, it'd be deuced embarrassing to speak with your uncle only to be told no by the party most interested."

"Yes, I suppose you're right about that. But have you spoken with Amelia at all?"

"No!"

"Don't you think you ought to? You must, even before you speak to Uncle Havoc."

Ripton sat back in his chair and ran his thumb along the side of his jaw. "I see what you mean."

"It might save you a great deal of trouble, Mr. Rutherford."

"Your kindness is only one of the things that make me admire you. This only deepens my esteem for you, Elizabeth. . . ." He sat up and reached across the table to take her hand. "I'm only sorry I didn't have the sense to do this sooner. I might have been made a happy man weeks ago." He raised her hand to his lips.

"Mr. Rutherford!"

He dropped her hand immediately. "You're upset. A natural enough emotion under the circumstances, I expect. But I'd be a fool if I waited any longer to ask you to marry me."

Elizabeth stared across the table at him. "If

this is your idea of a joke, Mr. Rutherford, I don't find it the least bit amusing."

He blanched and quickly rose from his seat. He walked to the window, where he stood staring out at the street. "I've done this all wrong, haven't I? It was stupid of me to think anything but the truth would work." He turned to face her when he heard her stand up. "I thought I could bring this off in a more conventional manner, and I apologize for all that rot I just made you listen to. It's true, though. The emotion is quite genuine." She went to him, and when she was close enough, he grasped both her hands. "Has Beaufort Latchley asked you to marry him?"

She nodded.

He took a deep breath. "Have you accepted him?"

"No."

"I'm not foolish enough to think you love me. I know you're in love with Nicholas. But, Elizabeth, I'm in love with you, and I'll be damned if I wait any longer for him to come to his senses. If I did, I might wait until it was too late for us both, and I don't want to lose you to some clod like Latchley just because Nicholas refuses to see what it is he might have."

"Mr. Rutherford—"

"Ripton, for God's sake!" He dropped her hands.

"All right," she said softly, stepping away from him. She could hear her aunt Mary telling her that if a suitable man should make her an offer, she would be foolish to turn him down. "Ripton, I don't know what to say." He was more than suitable. He was handsome, rich, and he loved her. She turned to him. "Except, I can't say yes," she said.

"I did not expect you to," he said. "Nicholas may be a fool, but I'm not. I know how I feel about you. But if you're going to marry someone besides Nicholas, at least let it be me."

She thought about Amelia and Nicholas. "I'll think about it, Ripton," she said gently.

"That's all I dared to hope. Well, then, I should like to speak with your uncle today, Elizabeth."

"All right."

"I'll come back later, at a more decent hour of the day."

When Amelia came in a few moments later, Elizabeth was back in her seat.

"Good morning, Beth." She leaned over her cousin's shoulder and kissed her cheek. "Mr. Poyne said Mr. Rutherford was here. Where is he?"

"He's left."

Amelia sat down on the chair Ripton had been sitting in and helped herself to some toast. "Why was he here?" She shrugged when Elizabeth did not answer. "I wonder why he didn't stay?" she said. "You know, he left Lord Lewesfield's so suddenly last night, it was really quite odd. And now he's called here and left suddenly again. Mr. Rutherford is so very handsome. Don't you agree, Beth? I admire him simply too much."

"You've never paid much attention to him, Amelia."

"But I've always thought he was handsome."

"Handsomer than Nicholas?" she snapped.

"Nicholas? No, I don't believe he's quite as handsome as that. And anyway, Nicholas's family is even wealthier than Mr. Rutherford's. Why, one day, he might even be a viscount."

"Mr. Rutherford will be a baron someday."

"True enough, but I like Nicholas better than Mr. Rutherford."

"I think you like yourself better than anyone."

Mr. Willard came in just as Amelia was retorting "Why Elizabeth Willard!"

"Amelia, will you excuse me?" Havoc said. "I must speak with Elizabeth."

"She's been very rude to me, Father."

"Not without cause, I'm sure."

"Well, I'm sure that it was with none. Beth is putting on airs. You ought to put a stop to it before she makes a fool of herself."

"Will you come with me, Elizabeth?" Havoc looked at her inquiringly. When she had followed him to his study, she stood while Havoc carefully shut the door. "Sit down," he said. He waited until she was seated. "Elizabeth," he began, "you are very dear to me."

"Please don't scold me, Uncle Havoc, I could not bear it. I promise I'll apologize to her."

"That isn't what I wanted to talk to you about." He looked at his fingertips. "You worry me, Elizabeth. No, not because of Amelia." He waved a hand to prevent her from interrupting. "Has Mr. Latchley spoken to you yet?"

"Yes. Last night."

"And what did you tell him?"

"I told him I could give him no answer until I had spoken to you." Havoc nodded his approval. "He said he had already spoken to you. In fact"—her voice rose—"he seemed to think you wanted me to accept him."

"I do, Elizabeth."

She gaped at him. "Why?"

"I think the marriage would be a good one for you."

"But I don't love Mr. Latchley."

"That isn't necessary for you to be happy."

"You sound just like Mr. Latchley," she accused.

"You could learn to love him, Elizabeth."

"How could I, when he does not love me?"

"He is reserved, I grant you that. But, my dear, though he might have had Amelia for the asking, he had the sense to ask for you. I could rest easy if you were married to him."

"Are you telling me to accept him?" She spoke softly, hardly able to believe it might be true.

"Mr. Latchley is not so old that the difference

in your ages concerns me overmuch; indeed, an older man might make you happier than a younger one. He admires you a great deal and is prepared to be more than generous to you."

She stood up. It seemed incredible that he wanted her to marry Beaufort Latchley. "Mr. Rutherford was here this morning," she said.

"So I was informed. But that has nothing to do with your marrying Mr. Latchley."

"It has everything to do with it. He told me he loves me. He asked me to marry him."

"Is this true?" His eyebrows drew together. "Did you accept him?"

"I told him the same thing I told Mr. Latchley."

"He ought to have stayed to speak with me."

"He is coming back later in the day."

"In my opinion, Mr. Rutherford is an irresponsible young man."

"Are you going to make me marry Mr. Latchley?"

"Elizabeth, it would be for the best."

"I would rather marry Mr. Rutherford than Mr. Latchley."

Havoc sighed. "Mr. Rutherford may, perhaps, have my approval when—if—he asks for it. Until then, Elizabeth, I want you to promise me you will not refuse Beaufort Latchley."

"Yes, Uncle, I promise."

CHAPTER
25
❧❀❧

NICHOLAS WAS DISAPPOINTED TO FIND THAT MRS. Willard was the only person home when he arrived at Tavistock Square. He considered just leaving his card, but it was not likely he would have another chance to call before he left London. A few moments later he was sitting in the drawing room with Mrs. Willard urging a plate of biscuits on him.

"I'm sorry to have missed Miss Willard and Elizabeth," he said, taking a biscuit he did not want in order to appease Mrs. Willard.

"I'm sure they'll be equally disappointed when they learn you've called and did not stay, Mr. Villines. Amelia will be devastated. She speaks of you in the most glowing terms, don't you know."

"It is especially disappointing not to see them, because it will be some time before I am back in London." Nicholas saw no reason to prolong his visit.

"Oh? Are you leaving us?"

"I'm afraid so. I leave tomorrow for Witchford Runs. My grandfather and I share the same birthday, and he would never forgive me if I missed our party."

"But you will be back after the holidays, of course."

"Afterward, I plan to visit Spain and perhaps Portugal. It may be several months before I am back in England."

"Amelia will be disappointed, most disappointed, when she learns of this."

"I have a great deal to do before I leave London, and I regret that I am unable to stay any longer." He rose and bent over her hand. "Please, give Amelia my regards, and tell Elizabeth— Tell Elizabeth I shall write to her."

Mrs. Poyne looked relieved when Elizabeth finally came home from her visit with Jane Smithwayne. "You're to go straight to your aunt, Miss Elizabeth," she said.

"Is something the matter?"

"Nothing serious, miss." Mrs. Poyne grimaced. "She's in her room."

"At last, Beth," Mrs. Willard cried when she came in.

"What is it, Aunt Mary?"

"Something awful has happened!"

"Is Uncle Havoc all right?"

"He's fine. Good heavens, nothing's happened to him. It's Amelia. My poor Amelia!"

"Amelia?"

"Yes. She's had her heart broken, Beth, and I haven't the strength to tell her."

"What do you mean, Aunt Mary?"

"Mr. Villines is gone! Leaving without even a word to Amelia. If he never comes back from Spain, it will be too soon for me, the way he's treated poor Amelia."

She did not know what to make of her aunt's declaration. "How do you know Nicholas is in Spain?" she asked.

"He was here this afternoon and told me so. Beth, dear, you must be the one to tell Amelia. They might have been so happy."

"If he was just here, how can he be in Spain?"

"It amounts to the same thing." She waved one hand limply in the air. "He's leaving for his grandfather's tomorrow morning, and then he's going to Spain. Beth, you must be careful when you tell Amelia. She's had her heart cruelly broken."

"Yes, Aunt Mary, I will be." Elizabeth felt as though a weight had been lifted from her shoulders when she realized Nicholas had not proposed to Amelia. There was not going to be any marriage. Far better that he should be gone forever than to have him married to Amelia.

"Promise me you will."

"Yes, Aunt Mary."

CHAPTER
26
※≫≫≪≪※

MR. CHESTER WAS JUST REMOVING THE LAST OF THE shaving cream from his employer's face when Mr. Baker came in and cleared his throat.

"What is it?" Mr. Chester demanded. He frowned at the interruption of his carefully constructed schedule.

"Excuse me, sir, but Mr. Rutherford is here."

"He is?" Nicholas glanced at Mr. Chester. "Send him up," he said. He stood up and offered his hand to Ripton when he came in. "Good morning, Rip. I hope you don't mind this." By "this" he meant Mr. Chester's helping him to finish dressing. "I'm taking the ten forty-seven to Witchford Runs, and Chester's got me on a strict schedule."

"By all means, Nick. I just thought I'd come to see you off." He took a seat on the edge of Nicholas's bed and watched the efficient Mr. Chester at work. "I say, Chester, when are you coming to work for me?" he asked.

"You don't travel nearly enough to suit Chester. Does he?" Nicholas looked to his valet for confirmation.

"Indeed you don't, Mr. Rutherford." Mr. Chester nodded and stepped closer to brush off Nicholas's coat. "I'm very happy with my present situation, sir."

"There, you see, Rip? You haven't a chance."

Mr. Chester pulled out his watch and, after glaring at it, snapped it shut. "The carriage is waiting, Mr. Villines," he announced.

"Will you come with me to the station, Rip?"

"I'd be delighted."

A few moments later they were heading for Paddington Station. "It's decent of you to see me off," Nicholas said when they were on the platform awaiting the arrival of the train.

"How long before you're back in London, Nick?"

"I don't know. I'm going to Europe after Christmas. I've thought of going to Spain. It might be several weeks."

"I hope it won't be as long as all that."

"Why?" The train was just coming into the station, and Nicholas had to raise his voice to be heard over the piercing whistle.

"I've got some news I hope will cause you to cut short your plans."

"What news?" The train was pulling to a stop, and there was a bustle of activity on the platform.

"Well, amazing as it seems, it appears I am getting married."

"Married?" Nicholas came to a halt and turned to face Ripton. "You?"

"Yes. And I must say, Nick, I am equally amazed."

"Congratulations, Rip!" Nicholas began vigorously shaking his hand. "But, tell me, who is this Venus who's captured your heart?" he asked, pulling Ripton along with him to the train.

"I'm surprised you can't guess. I took your advice, after all."

"My advice? What advice was that?" he said, stepping up into the train, where he stood, one foot still on the step, looking down at Ripton. He was smiling broadly.

"About Elizabeth."

"Elizabeth?" His smile slowly faded. "You're going to marry Elizabeth?"

"I asked her the day after Lord Lewesfield's ball. After I found out about Beaufort Latchley asking her first."

"What?"

"Frankly, Nicholas, I was surprised to hear about you and Amelia. I always thought you were in love with Elizabeth."

"That's ridiculous!"

"Which do you mean?"

Nicholas snorted. "When is the wedding to take place?"

"Well, to be perfectly honest, she hasn't actually said yes just yet. But she's given me a most hopeful response."

"Come along, now." One of the porters gave Nicholas a tap on the shoulder, and the last thing he heard before the train pulled out of the station was Ripton asking him to be best man at his wedding.

Nicholas had not been at Witchford Runs even twenty-four hours when he made his aunt exclaim, "Nicholas, will you stop pacing like that? What in the name of heaven ails you?"

"Nothing ails me, Aunt," he responded. He sat down. "I have just now recollected," he said after a moment's testy silence, "that I have some business to attend to in London."

Lord Eversleigh had been watching his grandson intently, and he now said, "Dear boy, sit here with me." When he had obeyed, the viscount leaned forward to pat Nicholas's knee. "Perhaps you would like to invite the girl and her family to our birthday celebration," he said.

CHAPTER
27
⟶≫≍≪⟵

PERCY JOHNS SAT ON HIS CHAIR WITH ONE ELBOW propped up on his desk. He picked up his pen and neatly added the date of the theft of Lady Lewesfield's emeralds to one of his lists. This time he did not cross off any more names. Every one of the remaining gentlemen had been at Lord Lewesfield's ball. Still, the Mayfair Thief had finally had some bad luck. Nothing that would allow him to knock on the man's door and make an arrest, but it had created for the first time an opening, a small crack in what before had been a solid wall. Patience. All he needed was patience.

"Mr. Johns, take a look at this."

Percy looked up and took the paper Alfred Wells was holding out to him. "What is it?"

"I was having a pint with Stubbs, from George Street Station, and I told him about how the artist fellow wouldn't give us his letter, and we got to talking, you know, and he remembered about a woman who came into the station with a letter. Well, I didn't say anything on account of how I thought it couldn't possibly be related, only I couldn't get your lists off my mind. So, Stubbs and I, we finally found her, Mrs. Dwight, the lady with the letter. Almost an accident, really. But she still had the letter, Mr. Johns. And she gave it to us, so here it is."

"Well." Percy smoothed the paper flat on the table. "Thank you, Mr. Wells." It was dated September 1840, and though there was no day written on it, the date was still the first entry on a new list. His second entry was the date of the artist's letter. Across from each entry on the second half of the page he wrote in the date of the nearest theft from another list. "How curious," he said to himself. A little louder, he said, "I have never in my life believed in coincidence, Mr. Wells."

CHAPTER
28
❊❊❊❊❊

HAVOC WILLARD WAS SORTING THROUGH THE AFTERnoon post when he came across the letter bearing the coat of arms of Viscount Eversleigh. It was addressed to the Willard family, so he took it out of the pile of correspondence and carried it to his wife. She was in the drawing room with Amelia and Elizabeth, and he handed it to her without a word, watching attentively as she opened and read it. She broke into a smile and let it drop to her lap.

"We are invited to Witchford Runs, Mr. Willard."

He frowned when he saw Elizabeth lift her head at her aunt's exclamation, then stare intently at the letter in her lap. "Witchford Runs? Where in the devil is that?"

"Don't pretend you don't know what this means," said Mrs. Willard.

"Of course I know what it means. We are in-

266

vited to visit an aristocrat with whom we have no acquaintance," he replied.

"Young Nicholas Villines is visiting his grandfather, the viscount. He could not bear to leave Amelia, it's clear."

"Then you will insist on accepting this invitation?" Havoc asked.

"For the sake of our daughter's happiness, we must, Mr. Willard. We shall leave tomorrow." She gazed happily at Amelia. "They shall be married, I feel it in my bones."

Havoc called Elizabeth into his study later that afternoon. "Mr. Latchley would like to have your answer soon, Elizabeth," he said when she had taken a seat. She looked at her lap, and Havoc sighed. "Mr. Rutherford and I have spoken at length about you, and I admit he impressed me a good deal more than I expected. Nevertheless, I have told the young man my preference is that you marry Mr. Latchley."

She looked up. "Uncle Havoc!"

He sighed. "Mr. Latchley is certain of his affection for you. He may be reluctant to tell you, but I believe he loves you. And he will make you happy."

Elizabeth sat forward. "Please, Uncle. I do not want to marry him. Don't make me."

Havoc rose abruptly and began pacing before her. "I am convinced it is the best thing for you," he said with as much emphasis as he could muster without raising his voice. "He is willing to give you a fortune of your own, Elizabeth. No matter what happens, he could never touch that. The money would be yours."

"No!"

Havoc sighed again and stopped his pacing to sit next to her. "I have told Mr. Latchley that he has a rival. . . ." He took her hand. "I have also told him that if you do not accept this other gentleman's offer, he shall have your positive acceptance when we return from Kent. I wish you to understand that if you accept Mr. Rutherford, it will be against my advice. Listen to me." He reached to stroke her hair, and when she looked at him, he took out his handkerchief to wipe her tears. "If Nicholas loved you, he would not have left you to Latchley or Rutherford," he said slowly, wanting to be certain she understood him. "My dearest Elizabeth," he said softly, "your heart is in your face every time you look at him. You must put your disappointment behind you. If you were to marry Rutherford, you would constantly see Nicholas, and I believe it would make you miserable." He stroked her hair again. "I could not stand to see you miserable."

"But he's asked us to his grandfather's!" She clutched his hand.

"Elizabeth," Havoc said sadly, "I don't think he can see past the little girl you used to be. Nicholas Villines is the kind of man who is determined to get precisely what he wants. If his feelings for you were something other than friendship, he would have made that clear by now. What is clear is that your aunt is certain he will propose to Amelia. Even Amelia has talked of nothing but Lord Lewesfield's ball and how he courted her. He'd not have done so idly, you may rely on that."

"I can't marry Mr. Latchley!"

"Elizabeth, you must."

CHAPTER
29
❧≫✕≪❧

LORD EVERSLEIGH'S ESTATE WAS IN SOUTHERN ENG-
land, in Kent, not far from St. Margaret's Bay.
The approach to the house was decidedly un-
spectacular until the drive crested and the
house and stables came suddenly in view.
Witchford Runs itself sat in the middle of a
slight depression. In spite of its closeness to the
sea, there was no view of the water from the
house. It was not an imposing building, it had
too much charm to be that. The walls were a
dull gray where they could be seen through the
moss and ivy. The corners of the house were
rounded, rising up to the red tiled roof three
stories above.

Witchford Runs just missed being the grand
manor house. The windows of the lower floors
were taller than they were wide, and they were
all of multipaned, diamond-shaped glass. Carriages passed under an ivy-covered archway
before rattling over the flagstones of the inner

courtyard and coming to a halt before two carved oak doors.

The main drawing room at Witchford Runs was octagonal with an alcove at one end overlooking willow trees and green lawns. The floor, of wood dark and satin smooth from years of use, was mostly uncovered. The furniture was French, delicate in design and painstakingly embellished; wherever it was not veneered it was gilded.

Lord Eversleigh was writing a letter at a Roentgen desk he had acquired during a trip to Paris some years ago. Russell Villines was slumped comfortably in an armchair reading a London paper while his wife sat on a gilt-legged sofa, intent on her sewing. Nicholas sat on the window seat in the alcove, one hand dangling over a raised-up knee, staring out the window at the lawn. He stood up so quickly it was as if he anticipated the opening of the drawing room doors. The steward stepped in, just keeping the doors held open behind him, and announced: "The Willards have arrived, my lord."

"Thank you, Carsons. You may show them in." Lord Eversleigh replaced his pen in its holder and blotted his letter. Mrs. Villines put down her sewing and smiled broadly. The viscount, Mr. Villines, and Nicholas rose when the Willards were ushered in.

Although Lord Eversleigh was approaching his mid-eighties, it did not appear that he had lost even a strand of his white hair. He stood erect, and his black eyes were clear and intelligent as he smiled pleasantly at Mrs. Willard, shook hands with Havoc, and complimented Amelia and Elizabeth on their looks. He smiled again when Nicholas took Amelia's hand and bowed over it.

"I'm so glad you've come," Nicholas said to her.

"And I to be here, to be sure." She tossed her curls and glanced at Lord Eversleigh, who returned the smile and looked as though he thought her dimples were quite the most charming thing he'd seen.

"Good afternoon, Elizabeth." Nicholas took Elizabeth's hand when she extended it, but he did not kiss it as he had done Amelia's.

"Nicholas." Their fingers intertwined for only a moment.

Lord Eversleigh's gaze rested on Elizabeth even after he had taken his seat at the desk. "I am pleased you were able to come to Witchford Runs," he said, turning on his chair to face the center of the room. "I hope your journey was not unpleasant." He directed the comment to Mrs. Willard.

"Not at all, my lord," she answered. "Kent is lovely. And we did enjoy the drive from the station."

Nicholas sat down near Amelia, but after several minutes of inconsequential conversation with her, he fell silent and watched Elizabeth. She had left her place by her uncle and was standing in the alcove, looking out at the same view that had so absorbed Nicholas before.

While listening to Mrs. Willard's expression of thanks for his invitation, the viscount followed his grandson's gaze. "We are glad to have you here, madam," he said to Mrs. Willard before saying sharply, "Miss Elizabeth Willard?"

She turned around with a start. "Yes, my lord?"

"You have been silent, Miss Willard. What do you think of Witchford Runs so far?"

"Sir, it is exactly as I imagined it would be." The viscount raised his eyebrows. "Perhaps even more beautiful."

"You may admire it to your heart's content at some other time. Will you please an old man and sit here?" He indicated a chair near him. It was not a request, it was an order.

"Yes, my lord."

Mrs. Willard frowned at Elizabeth when she sat down. The Willards remained only a few minutes longer before Carsons came in to tell them their rooms were ready, but it was long enough for Lord Eversleigh to see that Nicholas's attachment to the Willard girl was far more serious than he had believed, and that there was some rift between them.

Elizabeth's room was large and furnished in a more sober style than the drawing rom. The India rug was woven in shades of blue, and cream, and the walls were hung with a muted blue silk. The canopy of the bed was also a deep bluish gray. There was a French commode along one wall, into which she saw a servant had already placed her clothes. The rest of the furniture was Sheraton. Her things were laid out on the dressing table, plain silver brush, a silver comb that did not match the brush, two tortoiseshell hair combs, her most valuable possessions, and a scent bottle that had belonged to her mother.

Elizabeth was nervous, the unsettled state of her stomach told her that. No doubt the fact that Lord Eversleigh seemed to have taken a dislike to her had something to do with it. She walked to the windows and opened the curtains. The windows overlooked the western side of the house, and she stared at the green fields for some time. It was exactly as Nicholas had described to her in his letters. The drive, the house, Carsons, even Lord Eversleigh, were all as he had written.

She did not like uncertainty, and now that she was here, things seemed more uncertain than ever. She believed her uncle when he told her Nicholas did not love her, and she had spent the entire journey to Kent reconciling herself to the fact. All of her resolve to feel nothing but friendship for Nicholas had dissolved the moment she saw him. And to make matters worse, Nicholas had not acted as though there were any understanding between him and Amelia. It was impossible to stifle her hope.

Though she had thought of taking a walk before it was dark, the clouds that had been gathering while they drove to Witchford Runs were now dark and heavy with moisture. As she watched, the first drops of rain began to fall. Even the weather seemed to be conspiring against her peace of mind. She resigned herself to staying inside, but after a few minutes more of staring out the window, she decided she had better find something to take her mind off Nicholas and what this invitation to Witchford Runs might mean. She exchanged her cloak for a shawl and went to find a servant to tell her where the library was. Before long she was sitting in an armchair turning the pages of a travel book without having the faintest idea of what she seeing. The sound of the door opening made her look up.

"Good afternoon, Elizabeth," Nicholas said. "Forgive me if I startled you."

"No, you haven't." She placed the book on the table next to her and wished she could make her heart stop pounding.

"Do you mind if I join you?"

"No."

He approached the table and reached for the book. He smiled, but she could not do the same. There was so much she wanted to say to him, but the thought of his being in love with Amelia paralyzed her. She could not bear to hear him tell her so.

"Have you ever been to Italy?" he asked when he had seated himself with her book open in his lap.

"I have not." She was surprised at the question, since he knew full well she had never been out of England.

"Perhaps you will go there one day." He shut the book and tossed it on the table. "Elizabeth . . ." He leaped from his chair and began pacing. "Elizabeth, it seems to me something is troubling you." His hair fell over his forehead, and he pushed it away brusquely.

"Perhaps there is," she said softly.

"I wish you would talk to me about it." He stopped pacing. "We must talk." He took a breath and waited, but she said nothing. "You are special to me." He scowled. "You always have been. You're not like other women at all."

"Is that true?" Her heart was in her mouth.

"Of course it's true. I have always thought of you as a dear friend, surely you know that." He sat down again, leaning far back in the chair.

"I am glad for your friendship, Nicholas, but—"

"Your future happiness is of great concern to me," he went on. "I should hate to see you do anything to jeopardize that."

Her gaze on him was half-puzzled, half-hopeful. "Do you think that I will?"

"I have reason to believe so."

"Did Uncle Havoc ask you to speak to me about Mr. Latchley?" she asked suddenly.

He looked at her sharply. "Why would you think that?"

"I thought he might have asked you to talk to me about him. He wants me to marry him."

"And will you?" He sat forward.

"I have made up my mind."

"You, marry Beaufort Latchley?" He scowled even more furiously than before. "You would wither married to a man like him. It's unthinkable, Elizabeth!"

"It does not signify. I will not marry Mr. Latchley."

"He isn't good enough for you, Elizabeth."

"Have you come to tell me who is?" She smiled, but he did not seem to notice it.

"Certainly Latchley is not," he snorted. "But why are you even thinking of marrying, Elizabeth?" The tenseness in his manner was back. "You are too young to be married. You had better wait until you are older."

He was acting as if it were inconceivable that someone might want to marry her, and she was suddenly angry at him. "How much older should I be? I am twenty years old," she snapped.

He waved a hand at her. "I did not have good sense when I was twenty either."

"Twenty is more than old enough for a woman to marry."

"Be that as it may, it does not mean you're old enough to be wise in choosing a husband."

"Don't you dare patronize me, Nicholas Villines."

His eyebrows lifted in amazement. "No," he drawled, "you had much better wait to get married, I think."

She jumped up. "I am not a little girl, Nicholas. And you're the only one who seems not to have noticed."

"I happen to know very well you've grown up, Elizabeth."

"Then why do you think I'm not old enough to choose a husband? I'm older than Amelia, yet I've never heard you say she's too young to be married."

"We had best leave Amelia out of this conversation."

"Why?"

"Because Amelia is exactly the kind of woman who ought to be married, and the sooner the better for everyone concerned. She will be an ideal wife."

"And I would not be? How is it that I am so deficient? What's so horribly wrong with me? I daresay if I married, I would make my husband a very good wife!"

"Elizabeth—"

"Uncle Havoc thinks I am old enough to marry Mr. Latchley. And Aunt Mary often says it is better for a woman to be married unhappily than not to be married at all."

"And I think it is better not to marry at all than to be married unhappily."

"Aunt Mary says that I had better get married if I do not want to be poor my whole life."

Nicholas stood up. "She doesn't care whom you marry as long as you don't make a better match than Amelia."

"Aunt Mary says a rich woman can choose not to marry and be none the worse for the decision, but a poor one would not wisely make such a choice."

"Oh, blast your aunt Mary, Elizabeth!"

"But she's right. Even Uncle Havoc agrees. I don't want to be a burden to him, Nicholas. And what will I do when they are gone? I might try to support myself, but at what am I permitted to make a living? Your sex prevents mine from any work that might support me into my old age. I have been making inquiries, and I have not been encouraged. In service I might make twenty-five pounds a year and still have nothing when I am no longer able to work. I have no wish to be both poor and old." She shook her head sadly. "If a rich man wants to marry me, a man whom I happen to hold in the highest regard, should I refuse him?" She stood up and met his gaze.

"I thought you said you wouldn't marry Latchley."

"Mr. Latchley is not the only man who thinks I am old enough to be married."

"Elizabeth," Nicholas said when the silence

between them was almost unbearable, "you know that Ripton is my dearest friend."

"Yes. And you are his."

"Then you must believe me when I tell you he once declared to me your cousin was the woman he wanted for his wife."

"I am perfectly aware of what his feelings for Amelia were," she said stiffly. "I believe him when he tells me he does not love her anymore. And anyway, Amelia does not love *him.*"

"One does not fall in love in a moment, you know," Nicholas said, ignoring her last comment. "This proposal of his, it seems to me, is rather sudden. Can you love a man who is so inconstant?"

"I have not said I love Ripton."

He seemed to relax a little. "Then you will not accept him, either?"

"Ripton is kind, and I believe he loves me."

"Surely you wouldn't marry him for his money?"

"A woman who has not loved more wisely than I had better marry for money than not at all."

"Ripton deserves better than that, Elizabeth. He deserves a woman who loves him."

"Ripton is perfectly aware of the state of my heart."

"All right! Marry Ripton, then!"

"I wasn't aware I needed your permission to do anything," she said as scornfully as she could.

He rolled his eyes in disgust. "Far be it from me to talk you out of your infatuation with Ripton."

"I'm not a child, damn you, Nicholas. I am perfectly capable of making up my own mind."

"Then I suggest you do it before Ripton falls in love with someone entirely new."

"I do believe I have made up my mind." She walked past him, pausing when she reached the door. "It is only a pity that you and Amelia will not be as happy as Ripton and I will be. Good day, Nicholas."

It was not an auspicious start to their stay at Witchford Runs, but it was at supper that evening that Elizabeth began to get a sense of how difficult it was going to be. Before, she had not thought there was an understanding between Nicholas and Amelia, but it certainly seemed so now. He did everything but call Amelia his dearest. To Elizabeth, he hardly spoke five words. That, combined with the fact that Lord Eversleigh clearly regarded her with suspicion, if not downright disapproval, made Elizabeth long to leave Kent and return to London.

CHAPTER
30
❧❀❧

THE DAY AFTER THE WILLARDS ARRIVED AT WITCH-
ford Runs, Mrs. Villines and Elizabeth sat in
one of the drawing rooms enjoying the warmth
of a fire. They were talking amiably when they
were joined by Lord Eversleigh.

"Good afternoon, Winifred," he said cheerfully, taking the seat next to Mrs. Villines. Elizabeth was surprised to see him smile.

"Good afternoon, Eversleigh."

"Miss Willard." He nodded at Elizabeth and
smiled again, but the salutation seemed stern all
the same.

"Good afternoon, my lord."

"Shall I call a servant to build up the fire,
Eversleigh?"

"In a moment, perhaps. I want Miss Willard
to tell me how she likes Witchford Runs."

This time his smile seemed almost friendly.
"I think it is a romantic place."

"Romantic, eh? In what way do you mean that?"

"Well—"

"Here you all are." Everyone turned to the door. Nicholas took a step inside, then stopped. In spite of the dreary weather he was wearing his riding clothes. "Grandfather, Aunt Winifred." He glanced at Elizabeth but said nothing.

"Surely you're not going out, Nicholas?" asked Mrs. Villines.

"It's not raining." He shrugged. "And I am tired of being cooped up inside."

"You mean it's not raining *yet,*" she said.

"I only wanted to ask if anyone knew where Amelia has gone. We were going to ride together."

"She's gone into town with Aunt Mary and Uncle Havoc," Elizabeth answered.

Nicholas glanced at Elizabeth. "Do you know when they'll be back, Aunt Winifred?" he asked.

Elizabeth suppressed a gasp at the rebuke. Not even when she tried to catch his eye did he look her way again. Her heart sank, as it did whenever she began to think that the rift between them might be permanent.

"No," Mrs. Villines answered with a quick look at her, "but perhaps you might ride with Elizabeth instead. I'm sure she would love to see the estate."

Nicholas at last met her eyes, and when she

saw the hardness in his gaze, she thought her heart would break. "Oh, no," she said softly.

He looked away. "I would prefer to go alone, thank you. If you will excuse me." He nodded curtly.

She rose seconds after Nicholas was gone. "If you will also excuse me." She was blinking rapidly so they would not see her tears. "My lord." She curtseyed. "Mrs. Villines."

There was a moment of silence after Elizabeth was gone, then the viscount sighed. "I thought bringing them here would improve the boy's mood. It appears to have worsened it."

There was an answering sigh from Mrs. Villines.

"Is she not the same Elizabeth he always talked about?"

"Yes. He's known her since they were children."

"And the other Miss Willard as well, of course?"

"Yes, but it was Elizabeth and Nicholas who were always together."

"The attachment, whatever it was, appears to have worn off," said Lord Eversleigh.

"I don't know what's happened." She shook her head sadly. "Eversleigh, it breaks my heart to see him driving away the only woman who could possibly make him happy."

He looked thoughtfully at the door. "Does

she deserve as strong a recommendation as that?"

"Yes, she does."

"Miss Willard!" The viscount found Elizabeth in the library, and he stood in the doorway as he called out to her.

"Yes, my lord?" She put down her book and jumped up to curtsy. She stood stiffly, afraid she'd done something to anger him, for he was looking at her very sternly.

"I am given to understand you have an interest in gardening."

"Yes, sir." She breathed a sigh of relief at such an innocent statement.

"I thought perhaps you would like a tour of my conservatory. I am going there now."

"Thank you, my lord." If it were possible to refuse the request, she would have done so, but instead she meekly assented.

"Come along, then." He had a walking stick, and he placed both hands on top of it while he waited for Elizabeth to reach him. "I should appreciate the company of a lovely young lady." Elizabeth shook off the notion that his voice was less disapproving. "Shall we go?"

The first thing she noticed when Lord Eversleigh opened the door to the conservatory was the scent of roses. "Oh! It smells heavenly, my lord," she said in a half whisper. He held the door open for her, and when she stepped inside she exclaimed, "Why, it's just exactly as Nicholas described it."

"When did he do such a thing?" he demanded, letting the door shut behind him with a bang.

"You often took him here when he was a boy, my lord. He wrote to me about it." She felt as if she were speaking of something that had happened a hundred years ago. "You once told him gardening was a very gentlemanly habit to have, but that even if he never took it up, he must never forget to give a woman roses. And he said he did not know about gardening, but he was sure to follow the advice about giving roses to women." To her chagrin, she ended sounding quite mournful.

"And has he?"

"Yes, he has, as I'm sure you know. I have one of his orchids, as an experiment, to see if I can make it flower. He says we shall become famous if we succeed." She managed to put a more cheerful note in her voice, though there was no chance of any such thing now. She supposed she ought to send the plant back.

"I meant, Miss Willard, has he followed my advice about giving roses to women?"

She knew she was blushing, but there was nothing she could do about it. "I'm sure I don't know, my lord."

"He wrote to you often, did he?"

Elizabeth followed beside him as he began

walking along the rose beds. "We wrote nearly every month for ten years."

"And what happened?"

Again, she fancied he seemed more forgiving toward her. "Well," she explained, "his father died and, naturally, as he grew older he was less interested in writing to a little girl, so we did not write so often, only every six or eight weeks."

"Humph! I suppose you've saved all his letters."

There was no earthly reason why she ought to be apologetic about her correspondence with Nicholas. "I have." She stopped and bent her head over a blossom-laden rosebush.

"And tied them with a blue ribbon, no doubt."

"A red one, my lord."

"I understand you have lost both your parents."

The abrupt change in subject disconcerted her. "My mother is dead, but I believe my father is still alive."

"Are you not sure, Miss Willard?"

"I have never seen my father, nor heard from him, but Uncle Havoc would have told me if he had died."

The only sound after that was the soft thudding of Lord Eversleigh's walking stick on the ground, and out of desperation, Elizabeth began asking him about his roses. To her surprise, he did not object to the change in topic. They were soon talking naturally, almost enjoyably. Not until they were headed back to the house did he startle her with another abrupt question.

"Miss Willard," he said, "have you any idea why my grandson is so unpleasant to you?"

"Yes, my lord, I do." She knew he was expecting her to tell him, but she only shook her head sadly. "We disagree on a subject that could not possibly interest you."

"It's a nuisance." He sniffed.

"I apologize for that, Lord Eversleigh. I assure you, I would leave here if it were within my power to do so."

"I thought you were in love with him, Miss Willard."

"It makes no difference if I am, my lord."

"Are you?"

She stared at him, into eyes as black as Nicholas's, fighting down the lump in her throat. "Yes," she whispered at last.

At supper that night Elizabeth did her best not to appear as miserable as she felt. She did not seem to be able to keep her eyes off Nicholas. Tonight she saw the man who had once intimidated Lucy Benford-Smith. He was handsome in a dark blue coat, dark trousers, and a pale green waistcoat. The cravat, a small but complicated affair, completed the picture. But the lines of his face were hard, and despite his smiles, his eyes were emotionless, as black and as unfathomable as a moonless night.

It was not as difficult to keep up an appearance of normality as she had feared. Lord Eversleigh had lost the stiffness in his manner that had made her think he disapproved of her. He adroitly filled in the silences that occurred when Nicholas refused to speak to Elizabeth unless it could not be avoided. But, as the meal progressed, Elizabeth's silences became longer and more frequent until it was easier not to speak at all than to have Nicholas deliberately ignore her. She ate the food on her plate, but she had no recollection of tasting it. The long glances that passed between Nicholas and Amelia were worse than any of the rest. Nicholas and Amelia kept each other well enough amused without her participation in conversation. When at last the interminable meal was over and the ladies rose to leave the men to their cigars and port, she nearly cried with relief.

"Mrs. Villines," she said when they were in the drawing room, "will you please give my apologies to Lord Eversleigh? I do not feel well. I believe I had best go to sleep early tonight."

"By all means, Elizabeth." She patted her hand consolingly. "Shall I come up to see you later?"

Elizabeth shook her head. "No, thank you."

Mrs. Villines put her arms around her in a quick hug. "My poor, dear little Elizabeth," she murmured.

The pity in Mrs. Villines's voice decided Elizabeth. She wanted desperately to be far away from Witchford Runs. She would not, could not, stay past tomorrow. "I want to leave in the morning," she said to Mrs. Villines in a low voice. "Will you order a carriage for me tomorrow morning?"

"I wish you wouldn't go."

"I can't stay any longer. I can't bear it."

Mrs. Villines kissed Elizabeth's cheek. "I'll check on you in the morning. We'll talk then."

When the gentlemen were alone at the table, Lord Eversleigh signaled for the port to be brought immediately. Havoc raised his glass and stared at it without saying anything. At last he sipped from it.

"Your port is excellent, my lord," he said. Lord Eversleigh acknowledged the compliment with a nod of his head. "I shall miss this, truly, I will."

"Surely you aren't thinking of leaving?" Eversleigh asked. "We had hoped you would stay to the New Year, at least."

"I'm afraid a day or two longer is all we can manage."

"We shall be sorry to see you go," said Mr. Villines.

"Nevertheless, I've business to attend to in London."

"Could you not return here after you've concluded your business? Winifred will be very disappointed to have you leave so soon."

Havoc glanced at Nicholas. "Elizabeth and I

both have business to attend to, but I'm sure Mary and Amelia would be glad to stay."

Nicholas finally looked up from his glass, but he said nothing.

"Russell, Mr. Willard," said Eversleigh, "would you be so good as to rejoin the ladies? Nicholas and I will be out presently."

"Shall we?" Mr. Villines looked at Havoc.

Havoc rose with only a bare nod of his head to Nicholas and Lord Eversleigh before following Mr. Villines out of the room.

"You may go now, Carsons." When they were alone, the viscount cleared his throat. "What I have to say to you, Nicholas, I prefer to say in the strictest privacy." He took the bottle of port and refilled their glasses. "I'll not have it said that visitors to my home are being driven away with the kind of unpleasant behavior you've been displaying toward Miss Elizabeth Willard." He looked at Nicholas sternly.

Nicholas drew a breath and expelled it before answering. "I'm sorry," he said, lifting his shoulders briefly.

"Apology accepted. I'll not ask for an explanation, only for an end to it."

"Yes, sir."

"Now, then." He leaned to one side of his chair and peered intently at his grandson. "Dear boy, will you tell me why you have not made the young woman an offer?"

"I do not want to be married, yet."

"Good heavens, my boy, what do you think a long engagement is for?" he chided. "If she is your choice, Nicholas, you have my approval. You might have chosen someone with a greater fortune, but"—he shrugged—"I find I cannot object to her."

"Ripton has asked her to marry him."

"I see." He watched his grandson. "And has she accepted him?"

It was a moment before he answered, sullenly, "Not positively."

He considered what Nicholas had said. "She might do worse than Mr. Rutherford," he replied at last. "But, my dear boy, will that be of much comfort to you when you have finally driven her to marry him?"

Nicholas looked up, startled.

Lord Eversleigh put his hands on the table and stood up. "I think enough as been said on the subject for now. Shall we go?"

"I see our party lacks one of its most charming members," Lord Eversleigh said when he and Nicholas rejoined their guests in the drawing room.

"Miss Willard expressed her regrets, Eversleigh," Mrs. Villines said of Elizabeth, "but she is not feeling well and thought it would be for the best if she retired early."

"Ah, well." The viscount sat down. "Perhaps you, Miss Willard," he said to Amelia, "will favor us with a song?"

"Of course, my lord."

"Nicholas, sit a moment with me." Mrs. Villines patted the spot next to her on the sofa when Amelia had seated herself at the piano. When he had done so, she continued to speak to him in a low voice. "I have only one thing to say to you. You must cease this awful behavior toward Elizabeth. She adores you, she always has, and I cannot bear to see you treat her so poorly. She intends to leave in the morning, and unless you promise to apologize to her, I shall do nothing to stop her."

Nicholas sighed. "I've been positively horrid to her, I know."

"You certainly have."

"I promise you, Aunt Winifred, I will apologize to her."

Mrs. Villines smiled. "Well, then. I've said all I have to say." She looked at Amelia. "Go turn the pages for Miss Willard," she said.

"I am afraid I, too, am unusually exhausted tonight." He stood up. "Will you forgive me if I also retire early, Grandfather?"

"Good evening, Nicholas."

"Good evening, then." He bowed and was gone.

Nicholas knocked on the door to Elizabeth's room but did not open it until he heard her quiet, "Yes?" He stood looking into the room, tense, a little anxious. She was sitting on a sofa on the farthest side of the room, facing away from him with her feet tucked underneath her.

Her elbows were propped up on the back of the sofa, and she was staring out the open window. She had not put out any of the lamps yet, and he could see her loosely braided hair hanging down her back, dark against the white of her dressing gown.

"May I come in, Elizabeth?" He spoke softly.

She jumped at the sound of his whispered question, turning her head quickly, arm still resting along the top of the sofa. She was looking at him with wide-open eyes. "Nicholas?" She pressed the fingers of one hand briefly to her eyes. "Please," she said. "Just leave me alone."

He took a step into the room, holding the door open with one hand.

"What do you want?"

"I've come to apologize." He pushed the door closed behind him when a noise made him think someone was coming down the hall. "I've been behaving very badly to you," he continued, "and I want to apologize and offer an explanation." Elizabeth sighed miserably, and it occurred to him that he might be too late, that his foolish, petty behavior of these last days had cost him the thing he wanted most. He finally understood what it seemed everyone else already knew. There was no reason not to be in love with Elizabeth; if any couple were meant for each other, it was the two of them. Since she was thirteen years old, he had been trying to make her into the kind of woman he could love.

He was the worst sort of dunce if he thought otherwise.

"I don't think I want to talk, Nicholas." Her voice sounded flat, expressionless. She might have been miles away from him.

"Are you going to marry Ripton?" he asked abruptly.

"I don't know."

"I must know, Elizabeth."

She frowned at him. "Did you invite us here to keep me from saying yes to him?" she asked sarcastically.

"Maybe so."

"Ripton does not think I am too young to be married."

"Neither do I."

"What, then? Does it matter to you whom I marry?" She leaned forward. "I used to think I understood you, but I don't, not at all," she said fiercely. "I cannot stand this! I won't!" She jumped up and faced him. "What must I do to make you stop tormenting me?" The words were said evenly, but he could see the trembling of her lower lip. "Tell me and I will do it. Only do not say you don't want me to marry Ripton because it does not suit you."

"Elizabeth, will you at least hear me out?" He was afraid he might not be able to make her listen, or that she might not care to listen. It frightened him to think what his life would be like without her. Already it was stretching out in front of him, empty, lonely, and utterly without meaning.

She shrugged her shoulders. "If you've come to tell me about Amelia, you might have saved yourself the trouble," she said. "You've made no secret of your feelings for her." She sat down again.

"Amelia!" He lifted his eyes to the ceiling. "Why does everyone insist on bringing her up?" This time there was a flash of something in her eyes when they looked at each other from across that chasm.

"Did you really think she could keep quiet? She told me what happened between you at Lord Lewesfield's ball even before you'd left Portsmouth Square. Everyone knows you're in love with her."

"And what happened at Lord Lewesfield's ball?" He crossed his arms over his chest, feeling some of his confidence coming back.

"Nicholas . . ." She sat up a little straighter. "I don't want to talk about Amelia."

"But I do." He willed her to look at him again. "The night of Lord Lewesfield's ball, I told Amelia she was one of the most beautiful women I've ever met." When she met his look from across the room, he could see her eyes, dark, serious, and saddened. "It's true, Amelia is lovely. But she's not the loveliest woman I know. Not by any means. I told her she was accomplished and graceful, too. But I never told her I was in love with her."

"She said you kissed her."

"Kissed her?" It was the jealousy and despair of the words that gave him hope. "So I did. Shall I show you what happened?" He pressed his hands against the door to make sure it was shut before crossing the room to sit next to her. "This was all it was, Elizabeth." He leaned forward and kissed her forehead. Her eyes were wide when he sat back, the pupils large and luminous.

"Then why? Why have you been acting as though you do love her?" She looked down. "And hate me?"

"I'm not in love with Amelia," he said, taking her hand in his.

"Did you ever think you were in love with her?"

"Never."

She pulled her hand away and stood up. "If you aren't in love with Amelia, why did you invite us here?" He watched her walk to her dressing table and pick up one of her combs. Her fingers played with it nervously while she spoke. "Before we came here, Uncle Havoc told me he wants me to marry Beaufort Latchley. He doesn't like Ripton, he thinks he's too frivolous or some such thing." She shrugged. "He wants me to accept Mr. Latchley when we return to London. But—" She turned her head just enough to see him from the corner of her eye and said in a hushed voice, "If I must marry someone, I would rather it not be Mr. Latchley." She was watching him in the dresser mirror, and he saw her tense when he stood up. "Nicholas, if you don't love me, then tell me so and let me get on with my life," she whispered.

He went to her, took the comb from her, and placed it on the table. "My little Elizabeth," he said softly, taking her by the shoulders to turn her around and into his arms. He bent his head to breathe in the scent of violets and to hold her tight against him, wanting to hold her tighter still. It frightened him to think he might have done nothing and lost her to Ripton. It was a miracle that she had waited as long as she had. "Why do you think I'm here?" he whispered. Her arms went around his waist, and the moment she melted against him was almost more than he could bear. He let her go reluctantly when she pushed away from him.

"Tell me why you're here, Nicholas, so there can be no misunderstanding."

"I've never been in love before," he said softly, "and until now, I did not know what to do about it. I don't want you to marry Beaufort Latchley or Ripton, or anyone else, for that matter." Her hands were on his chest now, but they were clenched into fists. "I'm here because I think if I could spend the rest of my life with you, I'd have far more than I deserve."

She was looking at him, uncertain, lower lip caught between her teeth.

He reached for her again. "There's no turning back for me." He stroked her cheek with the side of his thumb. "And you? Could you stand me for a lifetime?"

"Do you mean it, Nicholas?"

He saw the lingering doubt in her eyes. "You're all I want." He took one of her hands, spreading out her fingers before intertwining them with his. "Just you," he said. She leaned her head against his chest, and they stood motionless until at last he sighed. Not letting go of her hand, he pulled her down next to him on the sofa. "Is it what you want, Elizabeth?" he asked.

"More than anything."

"I would not be an easy man to live with," he said.

She smiled a little wanly. "Could it be worse than these past days?"

"I'll speak to your uncle tonight, if it isn't too late," he said. "But I must tell you, both my grandfather and I are in favor of a long engagement." It would take time to extract himself from the tangle of things that complicated his life. He could not risk being married before then. "There are things about me—" How could he tell her? "I have secrets, Elizabeth." He would have to be sure his past stayed firmly in the past.

"Everyone has secrets. A secret is nothing."

"Are you sure? If you knew, you might not be able to forgive me."

"You are my friend, and nothing you have done in the past will alter that." There was an odd intensity about her words. "There is only one thing I could not forgive, if you told me a lie to spare yourself from telling me something *you* think is unpleasant, or might hurt me." Her fingers tightened around his. "It is for me to decide what I am to do about the truth." She sat forward. "Do you understand me? Such a thing would not be your decision to make. You must trust me, trust that I love you more than anyone in the world and would do anything for you. If you promise me this, you may have whatever secrets you like."

"You don't know what you ask."

"But, Nicholas, I do."

Looking at her, at her grave expression, he was certain she did. "All right, Elizabeth."

She sighed, shutting her eyes and tilting her head against the back of the sofa. "When I thought you were going to marry Amelia, I wanted to die. I thought I would die."

He rested his weight on one arm by propping his elbow against the sofa near her head. "I'm sorry I made you think I might." He trailed one finger down the line of her neck, stopping at the base of her throat to finger the collar of her dressing gown. She stayed still but opened her eyes to look at him, questioning. The faint color of her cheeks deepened when he did nothing but press his fingers lightly along her collarbone. Touching her like that was the sort of intimacy he knew he should not be so eager to explore. "How long have you loved me, Elizabeth?" he asked.

"Forever," she said.

He stroked the side of her face. "I feel as though I must have loved you forever, too." He leaned forward to kiss not her mouth, but the skin above the neck of her dressing gown. He had no intention of making love to her, but it was sweet all the same to sense her arousal when he kissed the back of her jaw, to hear her intake of breath when his tongue briefly touched her skin. The tips of his fingers were resting high on her chest, just below the collar of her dressing gown, and he could faintly feel the beating of her pulse. So he kissed her there, too. She sighed when his finger traced a line along the top of her shoulder. He became acutely aware of the sound of their breathing, of the soft warm flesh felt through her dressing gown. His arm circled her waist, pressing against the small of her back.

Before, when he had been trying so hard to resist her, to resist his desire, the sheer effort of it had been enough to remind him of his resolve. Now that there was no reason for it, it was difficult not to give in. He bent to kiss her, softly and without any urgency, not intending it to be anything more than gentle. He could not stop himself from letting it go just a little further. Her mouth opened under his, and he tasted her. She was eager in the way she responded to him, returning his own passion with

a pliancy, a soft relaxing against him that made
him think it would be near impossible to deny
himself such a certain pleasure. One hand
slipped down to brush over the swell of a
breast, just for the pleasure of hearing her gasp
and for the undeniable pleasure of touching
her. When he broke their embrace it was only
because he was in danger of forgetting himself
and allowing things to go so quickly it truly
would be impossible for him to stop.

Without quite knowing what he was doing,
he pulled on the ribbon she had used to secure
her braid. To his surprise it came off easily.
Surely there could be no harm in indulging at
least one of his desires? This one, at least, was
harmless. He began to unbraid her hair, and
when it was loose about her shoulders in thick,
glossy chestnut waves, he buried his fingers in
it. He was holding her head between his hands
when she leaned forward, tilting her face to his.
He kissed her again. Her lips parted beneath his,
and he heard himself groan when their tongues
met. She did not move away when he stopped,
and he found he did not want to let her go just
yet. He kissed the back of her jaw, letting his
mouth slide along the bare skin of her throat
to the thin material of her dressing gown, feeling the warmth of her.

"I should speak to your uncle before it gets
any later," he said, letting her go at last.

"All right."

She stood up when he did, and he could not

help himself, he pulled her into his arms to kiss her once more. The knowledge that she would not resist him if he were to unfasten her dressing gown was far too provocative a temptation. Even while his fingers were working at the buttons he was telling himself he would go no farther. When it was open, he slid his arms inside, bringing her a step closer to him as he did. Her waist curved to rounded hips, and he spread his fingers out over them, pulling her close enough to him so that a more experienced woman would have known just how exquisitely she was exciting him.

He had opened his eyes to look at her, to try to remember why it was he had been about to leave, when she reached to unbutton his coat, long fingers slowly pushing it down his shoulders. He shrugged it off and did nothing to stop her when she began to unbutton his waistcoat; he was too lost in the smoke gray passion of her eyes to think of anything but her touch. She unfastened his watch chain from his waistcoat and bent slightly to let the garment drop to the floor. His arm was curled around her waist while she worked at the knot of his cravat, finally pulling the strip of silk from his neck and letting it fall. Then her hands were on his chest, sliding down his stomach, and there was a quivering in his belly, an aching need for her. She was pulling his shirt from his trousers, and still he could not bring himself to stop her.

"Elizabeth, we mustn't," he managed to say.

He shivered when she kissed him through the fabric of his shirt. He grasped her forearms, intending to push her away, to put a stop to the torture it was to have her touch him. Her hands were still on him, still warm against him. Somehow his fingers had slid up her arms to her elbows, cupping them, keeping her hands on him. Through half-closed eyes he looked at her, and when he saw her parted lips all he could think of was how she had responded to him when he'd kissed her. He bent his head to hers, not really believing he would be able to stop but still comforting himself with the possibility.

Her dressing gown was slipping off her shoulder, and he gently pushed it off, feeling her move in his arms so that it fell to the floor. He moaned because she was sliding her hands under his shirt, touching his bare skin. It was indescribable, the thrill that went through him. Still holding one of her elbows, he walked the few steps to her bed and sat down. He had no illusions about the consequences of making love to her. It was wickedly wrong, and it meant an immediate marriage. But when society demanded that a woman feel no passion for a man, it was wildly exhilarating to be arousing it in the woman he loved to distraction.

Her chemise, a sleeveless white linen that fell to her ankles, clung to curves he longed to touch, and touch them he did. He wanted her to need him as desperately as he needed her. He pulled her between his knees and circled her waist with his hands. "Tell me you're mine, Elizabeth," he said. The thought of possessing her, of making her his, made his belly tighten. He leaned forward and growled into her ear, "Tell me!" He slid his hands up to her back, then around to where the swell of her breasts began.

"I cannot think when you touch me like that," she answered.

"And if I touch you like this?" He circled a finger over her breast. She gasped when he bent to flick his tongue over her suddenly taut nipple. His mouth found her, and when she moaned, he could think only of how it would be when he was inside her and she was crying out in passion. It was impossible not to want it, to long and ache for it. He grasped her waist again, gathering a handful of her linen chemise and pulling it over her head, almost forgetting to let it drop to the floor when it was off. He whispered her name—too softly, he thought for her to hear; but she whispered his name in return as he reached for her, drawing her onto the bed to lie next to him. He kissed her throat, lips moving down to her shoulder, then to her breast. She arched against him; it was almost unbearable, the feel of her skin, the taste of her, the curve of a breast under his hand, gentle swelling of her hips, the feel of her long legs. He bent to kiss her again. He knew when she slipped her hands under his shirt and in nearly one movement pulled it off, when he felt their skin touching, that it would be perfect between them. He sat up long enough to pull off his shoes and what remained of his clothes and to unfasten the canopy so they were enveloped in a soft darkness when it closed around them.

He hurt her more than he liked, but still it took all his control not to continue. Lying on his side, he held her back against him.

"I love you, Elizabeth," he whispered. He stroked her until he felt her relaxing. She turned to face him, and he slid his hands from the small of her back to her shoulders. "You must have been made for me," he said. He spread the fingers of one hand over her stomach. "How else could you make me feel this way?" She had a mole high on her belly, and she shivered when he bent to kiss it. There was nothing more he wanted than to be inside her, to be holding her in his arms, while he made her quiver with the same passion she made him feel.

When he entered her for the second time, he heard her gasp, its sound mingling with his own. She was tight around him, hot and slick. Her gazed into her smoky eyes, saw the faraway look of arousal in them, and felt an answering ache within himself. They quickly found a rhythm, and after that there was nothing but her arching against him, whispering his name, touching him, making him hold her tightly, him moving in her more urgently, of seeing her body beginning to glisten with sweat, feeling his heart pounding and his flesh beginning to pulse. He forgot that he meant to teach her what it meant to make love. There was only his joy at seeing and feeling her response to him and the certainty they were meant to be. There was not one moment of awkwardness, no fleeting thoughts that the act seemed absurd. They were perfect, and it seemed as if he had always known it would be this way with her. He was holding her, looking into her depthless eyes, when she came, bringing him along with her in an agonizingly sweet release.

Elizabeth woke because of the unfamiliar feeling of having someone else in bed with her. The lamps were sputtering out, and the only light penetrating the canopy was from the dying fire. Nicholas was asleep. She could see his dark hair on the white of the pillow. She slipped out of bed, letting the canopy close after her because she did not want to disturb him. The air was chilly, but not enough to make her uncomfortable. She quickly put out the lamps and was crossing the room to return to bed when she stepped on Nicholas's waistcoat and felt something cold under her bare foot. At first she thought it was his watch chain, but she saw her mistake when she picked it up. She honestly did not remember seeing anything around his neck, nor could she recall if he had at some point paused to take it off. She stared at the chain, wondering why it made no difference to her. It seemed as though it ought to. A shiver of cold brought her out of her thoughts. She started to tuck it back into the pocket from which it had partially slid, but then thought the better of it. Instead, she went to the dresser and placed it in her jewelry box.

She sat in the bed, arms curled around her tucked-up knees, waiting for the chill of the room to fade. She felt strange, and it was a moment before she identified her feeling as fear because she she had what she wanted most—Nicholas—and dread that when he woke up he would tell her it had all been a terrible mistake; it was Amelia he loved after all. She stared at him, hugging her legs even tighter, wondering if she dared to pray he would not wake up.

He moved, turned to face her. It hardly seemed possible that he had told her he loved her, that he had held her so tenderly, had wanted to kiss her, and more. In sleep, the hard look to his face that had so often puzzled her was gone. She stroked his cheek, wishing she could memorize every line of his face. She heard him sigh, then felt his hand curl around her ankle. He pulled her leg straight, and when she lay back against the pillow, he said gruffly, "Tell me you're mine."

"I'm yours, Nicholas."

Under the covers his hand moved slowly up her leg to her stomach, then over to her hip. "Your skin is so soft, Elizabeth," he whispered. "I cannot get enough of the feel of you." She said nothing, only tried to regulate her breathing as his hand continued to move over her. He curled an arm around her neck and pulled her head to his. "I ought to go," he said when he released her after a kiss that left her stomach feeling dizzy.

"I know." She sat up, and he pushed the covers off his legs, then stretched. He was lean, with long hard legs and slim hips. His abdomen was flat, and she could have traced the outline of muscles under the smooth skin of his chest.

He watched her watching him, his black eyes calm, interested. "What are you thinking?" he asked when she reached to trail a hand down the middle of his chest.

"Are you mine, Nicholas?" she whispered.

"You know I am," he said softly.

She leaned forward to kiss his chest. "I wanted to make you stay, before. No matter what."

His fingers touched her cheek. "I thought I was the only one consumed by desire." He smiled.

"Oh, no." She kissed his chest, letting the tip of her tongue slide along his skin. He sighed and leaned back, propping himself up with his arms. She drew her fingers over his skin, testing the shape of his muscles, letting her mouth follow her hand. He groaned and did not resist when she pushed him down until he was supine. His fingers came up to tangle in her hair when she began kissing him where the ridges of his belly started.

Was it dangerous, she wondered, to feel as though nothing else mattered but making him want her? His skin was cool, firm. His eyes began to close as she caressed the hard muscles of his thigh. She wanted just to look at him, but the dizziness starting again in her stomach made that impossible. It was warm where their skin touched, hot where she kissed him to taste the slight saltiness of him.

"Come here, you!" He pulled her on top of him, and then Elizabeth groaned herself as he brought her up high enough to enter her. He held her hips, guiding them both, whispering to her how and where he longed to touch her, how he longed to have her touch him. She saw the desire in the curve of his mouth, in his parted lips. His hands on her were warm and solid. His movements inside her made her stomach tighten, made her being flame into a desire so strong she wanted to weep with it, weep with happiness that it was Nicholas who held her, who was making her cry out. It was every bit as overwhelming as it had been before. She was lost in his caresses, abandoned to their passion.

"It has never been so exquisite before," she heard him say. She looked into the black of his eyes and saw that it was true. His mouth took hers, kissing her even more fiercely, his fingers pressing into her shoulders, holding her to him.

She wasn't able to think of anything but him and how incredible it was that it should be so. He was calling her name, and she held him when the sweeping rise of their passion took her away from everything but them.

They lay quietly, his fingers gently stroking her back. She was still holding him, lips so close to his shoulder she could have kissed him had she not been so deliciously tired.

CHAPTER
31
❯❯❯❯❯❯❯

MRS. VILLINES WAS ALWAYS AWAKE EARLY WHEN SHE visited the country, and her stay at Witchford Runs was no exception. She lay in bed for a while, thinking about Nicholas's incomprehensible behavior and worrying about Elizabeth. She had for so long assumed that Nicholas and Elizabeth would marry that she had done little to let him know her wishes in the matter. Now it seemed unlikely there would be any marriage. Nicholas had been doing his utmost to make it seem he was captivated by Amelia. She did not believe he was in love with Amelia, but even if it were true, it was no excuse for his treatment of Elizabeth.

Mrs. Villines sighed. Elizabeth was going to leave Witchford Runs—if she were in Elizabeth's place, she would do the same. One day Nicholas would learn what a tragic mistake he had made, and it would be too late. No one, absolutely no one, except Elizabeth Willard was right for Nicholas. She threw the covers aside and got out of bed.

It was a quarter past eight when Mrs. Villines knocked on the door to Elizabeth's room. When there was no answer to a second knock, she tried the door, wondering if Elizabeth might really be ill. It was unlocked, so she stepped inside. She saw Elizabeth's dressing gown lying on the floor, and she walked across the room to pick it up. She must have been terribly upset last night, Mrs. Villines thought when she saw another heap of clothing a few feet away. She shook her head and picked them up, too, then examined them with a puzzled expression on her face. A man's coat and waistcoat, watch chain dangling from it, a cravat on the floor a little farther off. She turned and saw yet more clothing on the floor by the bed.

A gentleman's clothing might be here because Elizabeth was mending them, though it was difficult to explain why they were so haphazardly thrown about. But even if she were to believe that Elizabeth had thrown the clothes about in a fit of anger, there was no comforting explanation for the presence of a gentleman's shoes.

Still holding the clothes, Mrs. Villines walked to the bed, quietly because the drawn canopy meant Elizabeth was still sleeping, and bent to pick up one of the garments by the bed. She stared at what she held in her hand: her nephew's trousers. She recognized his tailor's label.

She opened the canopy just a fraction of an inch.

"Dear God, Nicholas!" She almost dropped the clothes, she was so startled when she saw him. He was startled himself, but he got out of the bed quickly, pulling the canopy closed behind him. Mrs. Villines caught only a glimpse of Elizabeth, who was fast asleep, but it was enough to notice that she did not appear to be wearing any more clothing than Nicholas.

"May I have my trousers, Aunt Winifred?" Nicholas asked softly.

Mrs. Villines was completely unable to summon coherent thoughts, let alone words. She held out his trousers, averting her eyes from the sight of her nephew's nakedness. When he had taken them from her, she quickly turned her back. "Nicholas," she said in a whisper, "what in heaven's name are you doing in here?"

"You may turn around now," he said. "I should think that must be rather obvious." He was looking down to fasten the buttons of his trousers. "A better question," he went on, "might be, how could I have neglected to bolt the door?" He extended a bare arm to take his shirt from her.

"Nicholas!" Aghast, she followed him to the far side of the room.

"Well, it is a rather obvious precaution." He turned to face her, waiting for her to hand him the rest of his clothes.

"Surely you don't mean that you've . . . that

this isn't the first time you and Elizabeth . . . ?"
She could not finish the thought. "Oh, dear
God!"

He sighed and ran his fingers through his
hair. "Yes, it is the first time." He put on his
shirt and coat, not bothering with any of the
rest.

"Nicholas, what could you have been thinking of? This is disastrous!"

"Of course it's a disaster!" His voice rose.
"It's the worst thing that could possibly have
happened!"

"We will need to discuss plans for your wedding, Nicholas. After you've . . . arranged yourself more decently, wait for me in the main
drawing room." She stood still while he tucked
his watch safely into a pocket, then walked into
the hall with him, putting a restraining hand on
him when the door was shut behind them.
"Elizabeth will make you happy, if only you let
her, Nicholas," she said softly.

"Aunt Winifred, I know that," he answered.

She watched him walk down the hall to his
room before going back inside to talk to Elizabeth.

Elizabeth was standing in the middle of the
room just fastening her dressing gown when
Mrs. Villines closed the door behind her.

"Well, Elizabeth, we must talk."

"What about?" She lifted her chin. She was
pale, but her gaze was defiant.

"I presume you know I found Nicholas in here?"

"Of course."

"What happened?"

She looked stubbornly at the floor.

"Did he force you?"

"Certainly not!"

Mrs. Villines did not know what to make of Elizabeth's expression. "You will be married, of course."

"I think not."

"Good heavens, of course you will." She approached Elizabeth and placed her hands on her shoulders. "Nicholas will do the right thing by you, of that I can assure you. He must marry you."

"Well, I do not have to marry him."

"Elizabeth, my dear, what if there is a child?"

She blanched. "Then I'll go away," she said. "You heard him. He does not want to marry me. You may tell him I have averted his disaster," she snapped, "for I refuse to marry him."

"Elizabeth!"

"I am leaving for London today, Mrs. Villines."

"My dear, think about what you are saying!"

Elizabeth frowned and walked to the window. She pulled open the curtains and stood looking out. "There's nothing to think about, Mrs. Villines. My mind is made up."

"It does not appear I can persuade you to change it."

"No, you cannot."

She shook her head even though Elizabeth could not see her. "You haven't any choice, I'm afraid."

CHAPTER
32
❖✦❖

"Well, Nicholas, have you anything to say?" Mrs. Villines sat down and looked at her nephew sternly.

He returned her level gaze as if he thought there were nothing extraordinary about their conversation. "I did as you advised me, Aunt Winifred." His hair, still damp from his hurried bath, was beginning to curl around his forehead.

"I hardly advised you to conduct yourself so improperly."

"I know." He sighed and sat back in his chair. "I never intended for things to go as far as they did."

"You had no business being in Elizabeth's room at all."

"Maybe not, but I assure you, I had the best of intentions."

"I have already seen how good your intentions were, Nicholas."

"I went to her last night to apologize and ask her to marry me."

"And did you?"

"Yes. And she accepted me. Grandfather approves, you know. We spoke about it last night."

"There is some consolation in that, I suppose."

"Naturally, under the circumstances, a long engagement is out of the question." He leaned forward. "I do want to marry Elizabeth, Aunt Winifred, only I did not think it would be so soon." He sighed again, putting his elbow on his knee and propping up his head in one hand. "I should like us to be married on the thirty-first," he said, looking at her.

"If only Elizabeth would agree."

He sat up. "What do you mean? Does she want to be married even sooner than that?"

"She does not want to be married at all."

"What!" He looked at his aunt skeptically. "That's ridiculous."

"She insists she is going back to London today. And *I* cannot persuade her otherwise."

"You are mistaken."

She put a hand on his arm. "Elizabeth overheard us, Nicholas, and she is hurt by what you said. She does not believe you want to marry her."

"But I did not mean it. She ought to know that."

They both stood up when the door opened.

"Here you are, dear boy!" said Lord Eversleigh. "Are you aware that Miss Elizabeth Willard has asked to be driven to the station this morning? She's in her room packing this very moment." He took in Nicholas's expression, then looked quizzically at Mrs. Villines. "What in the devil is going on?" he demanded.

"Please, come in, Eversleigh."

"Has something happened?" he asked, shutting the door behind him.

"Elizabeth refuses to marry Nicholas."

"Indeed?" He looked at Nicholas after Mrs. Villines sat down. "This is disappointing news. Did she give any reason for her refusal?"

"Last night she accepted me."

There was a pause, then: "You must not have been persuasive, if she's changed her mind already."

"My lord," Mrs. Villines broke in, "let there be no misunderstanding. Last night, Nicholas was far too persuasive!"

"What do you mean? Explain yourself, Winifred." He looked to his daughter-in-law for the explanation.

"She means, sir, that when she went to Elizabeth's room this morning, I was still there."

Lord Eversleigh's eyebrows lifted. "Still there?" he echoed. "Indeed?"

"I asked her to marry me last night, and she accepted. We agreed to a long engagement, which, as you know, was entirely my inclination."

"It took you all night to do that, did it?"

"No, Grandfather, it did not."

"I see," he said slowly. "You understand, dear boy, that when a man and a woman have passed the night together there is only one conclusion to be drawn about the events of the evening, irrespective of what may actually have occurred?"

"Yes. But it doesn't matter, Grandfather. We are going to be married." He turned to Mrs. Villines. "And I don't believe she's changed her mind, either."

"What do you propose to do if she has?" the viscount asked.

"They must marry, Eversleigh."

"I agree, Winifred. But he can't very well marry her if she isn't here."

"We can put an end to this immediately." Nicholas rang for Carsons and, when he arrived, spoke to him in even tones. "Mr. Carsons, will you ask Mr. Willard to come here directly?"

"Very well, Mr. Villines." He bowed and was gone.

Nicholas turned to his aunt. "Go to her, please, Aunt Winifred?"

"That girl is as stubborn as they come."

"Just don't let her leave."

"I'll do my best, Nicholas."

"This makes things awkward, does it not?" Lord Eversleigh settled his dark eyes on Nicholas when they were alone.

"We came to a positive understanding last night. It's impossible that she's changed her mind."

"It appears she has. Miss Willard asked for a carriage to take her to the station this morning."

"She's not gone, is she?"

"On my instructions, the carriage won't be ready for another hour at least." He crossed his legs and rested his hands on his knee, gazing thoughtfully at his grandson. "If you were Henry," he finally said, "I'd insist you marry the girl, with no dithering about, either. But perhaps you'd best leave things as they are. Let her refuse, she may know what's best. If it's necessary, I could arrange to have her stay in Europe."

"No!"

"You could delay. A long engagement isn't necessarily out of the question."

"People always talk when there is an early birth. Should it come to that, I don't want anyone wondering whether we married for love or for necessity."

"Well, then, I hope you can convince her to change her mind."

Mr. Willard came in just as Lord Eversleigh finished speaking. He glanced at Nicholas, then quietly took a seat across from the viscount. "What can I do for you gentlemen?"

Nicholas came directly to the point. "Mr.

Willard, I wish to inform you that Elizabeth may be with child."

Havoc's only sign of emotion was a slight lift of his eyebrows. "And if she is, would it be pointless to ask who the father might be?"

"It is myself, sir."

The gray eyes, so like Elizabeth's widened. "I see." He looked at Lord Eversleigh. "It grieves me to hear you tell me this news, Mr. Villines." He rose, hands clenching and unclenching inside the pockets of his coat. "Am I correct in assuming His Lordship's presence here means the acquaintance between our two families has come to an end, in respect of the social amenities, that is?" He did not wait for an answer. "I cannot believe, Nicholas, that you would take advantage, not just of me and my misguided hospitality to you in the past, but of Elizabeth. That girl worships the very ground you walk on."

"Mr. Willard—"

"I love her as if she were my own." He appealed to Lord Eversleigh. "My lord, surely it would not be so objectionable a match? Elizabeth is not poor. I have for some time now been putting away money against the day of her eventual marriage. This sum now amounts to some twenty thousand pounds, an amount I am fully prepared to double."

"An admirable sum, Mr. Willard, but not persuasive. Last night Nicholas and I discussed your niece at some length. I told him then if he wished to marry her, I had no objections."

"I spoke to Elizabeth last night—" Nicholas began.

"You apparently did a bloody lot more than that! Mr. Villines, Elizabeth loves you, and I think last night you probably found it quite easy to take advantage of the fact. She loves you far too much to refuse you anything you might ask of her."

"The blame is wholly mine," Nicholas said. "In intended only to apologize for my recent bad behavior and to ask her to become my wife. I did both those things, and then . . . well, I've told you that." He took a deep breath. "We agreed to a long engagement, contingent, naturally, upon your permission. An engagement of any length is now out of the question. I should like to have your permission to marry Elizabeth on the thirty-first of this month, Mr. Willard."

"I fail to understand why my approval was not solicited last night."

"I assure you, Mr. Willard, I meant to do so."

"Do you love her?"

"Yes."

"Well, I'm not convinced of that. I've not been blind to your behavior toward Amelia. It seems to me these last weeks your intentions lay very much with her."

"I agree it might have seemed that way, a circumstance I find I regret extremely. But I have never been the least bit in love with your daughter."

Havoc's expression finally softened. "I only want Elizabeth to be happy."

"I assure you, I want the same thing for her."

"If she wants to marry you, I have no choice but to give my permission." He shook his head. "Under the circumstances, I must agree that the thirty-first is not too soon."

"May we have your blessing?"

"Does it matter?"

"Of course."

Eversleigh cleared his throat. "There appears to be only one further obstacle, Mr. Willard."

He turned. "And that is?"

"Miss Willard insists on returning to London this morning—without the benefit of marriage."

"Is that so?" Havoc glanced at Nicholas. "Elizabeth does not seem to share your feelings, after all."

"It is only a misunderstanding. It will be quickly rectified, I assure you."

"Did it suddenly occur to you that I might not let Elizabeth marry with nothing? Is it the prospect of forty thousand pounds that makes you so anxious to marry her?"

"If that were so, Mr. Willard, I would be rather better off if I married Amelia. I love Elizabeth, and I would marry her even if you refused your permission. And you and your money may be damned."

"Nicholas, sit down. Mr. Willard has given his consent to the marriage. You needn't convince *him* of anything."

"We had better call Elizabeth," said Havoc. "But if she does not want to marry you, I won't force her."

"No, you'd rather force her to marry a dried-up man like Beaufort Latchley."

"Please!" Lord Eversleigh lifted his hands. "Remember, if you will, that you both love the same woman. It does no good to argue over which one of you loves her the more."

All three men turned around when the door opened. Elizabeth hesitated when she saw them, then walked to the center of the room, where she stood looking from one to the other of them. She was wearing a dove gray traveling dress, her hair was hastily pinned up, as though she had not quite finished dressing when she was called.

"Elizabeth," Havoc said, "Nicholas has asked me for permission to marry you at the end of this month, and I have given it."

"And if I refuse?" In spite of her dry eyes, it was obvious she was near tears.

"Why would you refuse?" he asked gently. "Is this not what you wanted?"

She did not answer.

"Elizabeth!" Nicholas stepped forward. "What's happened?"

"Miss Willard, surely—"

Elizabeth turned to Nicholas. "I'm the worst

thing that ever happened to you, Nicholas. It would be disastrous if we married, or don't you remember saying that? Well, you needn't worry. I won't be the one to ruin your life."

"Dear boy . . ." The viscount sighed. "When you have spent the night in the arms of a beautiful woman, you ought never to tell her in the morning that it was a mistake."

"Elizabeth, I didn't mean it."

"You won't be forced to marry him," said Havoc, "but think carefully what your life would be like if you refuse and find yourself with child."

"Mr. Willard," Eversleigh said, "perhaps we ought to leave them alone." He took Elizabeth's hand and patted it consolingly. "Your uncle and I concur with Nicholas that your wedding should take place on the thirty-first of the month. I will make the formal announcement tonight—if you agree to be married to my grandson, that is. It is my hope that you will. Now, if you will excuse us. Mr. Willard?"

Nicholas turned to Elizabeth when they were alone. "You were awake when Aunt Winifred came in."

"Yes."

"I do want to marry you. How could you believe otherwise?"

Elizabeth said nothing.

"What did you expect me to think when she saw me in your bed without a stitch of clothing on me?" He crossed the room and put his hands on her shoulders. "It's true I did not want to be married so soon. It's even true that a short time ago, I did not want to marry at all. My grandfather offered to send you away. It would have been quite simple to arrange. He's done it twice for Henry." His fingers tightened on her. "But, Elizabeth, I would be miserable without you." He gathered her in his arms when he saw her tears. "Now, you must trust me," he whispered.

She sagged against him, arms tight around his waist. "I was afraid you had changed your mind," she said. "I thought you were sorry."

"Never, Elizabeth."

"We could wait, Nicholas." She looked at him, eyes glistening with tears. "We don't have to be married so soon."

"No. Even if we knew there was no child, I could not leave you alone. Not now." He held her face in his hands and, with his thumbs, stroked her cheeks. "Not ever."

"Will you tell me why you wanted to wait?" This time, he did not answer. When he started to speak, she put a finger to his lips. "I could stand many things from you, Nicholas, but never a lie. Say you cannot tell me, if you must, but do not tell me a lie."

"Then, I cannot tell you."

"Someday, Nicholas, you will." She put her arms around his neck and pulled his head down to hers. It was a long time before they stood apart. "Aunt Mary will be furious," she said when they did. "She believes you will marry Amelia."

He stood close to her and stroked her hair. "I expect she'll be over it before long." He chuckled. "She will still have me for a relative, you see."

Havoc closed the door to the drawing room and heaved a sigh. It was a peculiar and trying way to start the day. Nothing was going as he expected. Though he might never know what was behind those black eyes, Nicholas struck him as a man who was, above all else, consummately in control of himself. For him to have allowed things with Elizabeth to have come to such a pass bespoke a powerful emotion. Whether it was love, he did not know.

He found Russell Villines sitting with Mrs. Willard and Amelia when he went in to the breakfast room for coffee and some eggs. The significant look Mr. Villines gave Havoc told him he was well aware of the events of the morning. When Havoc shook his head he smiled ruefully before applying himself to the eggs piled on his plate.

"Good morning, Father."

"Good morning, Amelia."

"Goodness, it seems we are missing only Lord Eversleigh and Nicholas. Do you know where they are, Mr. Villines? We might have a rather grand party if they were here."

"The last I heard, Nicholas and my father were locked up in one of the drawing rooms."

"Were they?" said Mrs. Willard with a pleased expression. "Whatever for?" She glanced at Amelia.

"I believe it has something to do with Nicholas's future happiness." Mr. Villines ignored Havoc's warning frown. "There appears to be some difficulty."

Mrs. Willard looked alarmed. "Surely Lord Eversleigh would not stand in the way of his grandson's happiness?"

"I am afraid I cannot say, Mrs. Willard. Though I have the greatest hope the situation will have a happy resolution."

"Lord Eversleigh's celebration is tonight," Havoc interrupted. "Have you a decent gown to wear, Amelia?"

"We were hoping to send a servant into Dover this afternoon to pick up Amelia's dress," Mrs. Willard said to her husband.

"Perhaps you might make an outing of it and drive in yourself," Havoc suggested.

"An excellent idea," said Mrs. Willard. "Perhaps you will come with us?"

"Impossible." He shook his head. "I have some business to attend to that will occupy me for the better part of the day."

"What a pity," said Mrs. Willard with a broad smile.

"But, here." Havoc reached into a pocket for his notecase and drew out two ten-pound notes. "Do your best to spend it all." He could not bring himself to tell his wife how things stood until they were decided one way or another.

"Is Beth up yet?" Amelia asked.

"Elizabeth is not feeling well. I'm afraid you'll have to go without her."

"Oh, well." Amelia shrugged. "Do you think Nicholas could be persuaded to come with us?" she asked Mr. Villines.

"Nicholas?" he said doubtfully. "I am unable to answer your question, Miss Willard. I rather think not."

"What a pity. Well, Amelia," said Mrs. Willard. "Shall we go?"

"Yes, Mother. Good day, Mr. Villines, Father."

When they were gone, Havoc dropped his fork on his plate and sighed loudly.

"Mr. Willard?" Mr. Villines had refilled his own cup and was holding the coffeepot tilted over Havoc's empty one.

"Yes, thank you."

"I regret to say, I feel somewhat responsible for my nephew's lack of control, Mr. Willard. Nicholas is like a son to me, and it grieves me no end to learn he has handled things so badly. I ought to have told him from the very first that I would be proud to have Elizabeth as a relative."

"Thank you. Though to be perfectly honest,

Mr. Villines, I have been urging her to accept the offer of Mr. Beaufort Latchley."

"Beaufort Latchley?"

"He made the proposal to me nearly a month ago. I put him off because I knew how she felt about your nephew, and, at the time, I thought it possible he felt the same."

"I assure you, he did. I meant to speak to Nicholas about her, to let him know my wife and I think highly of Elizabeth. I did not, as I was under the impression they had come to an understanding the evening of Lord Lewesfield's ball."

"And it was my impression that they had not. Are you aware Ripton Rutherford proposed to her the very day after?"

"Indeed?" He smiled a little. "Then it's no wonder he was so impatient when he arrived here. Had my father not told him to invite you here, he'd have left for London that very afternoon. It is my own opinion that Nicholas has been in love with Elizabeth for quite some time, probably since the moment he saw her at Fitzroy Square. It simply took him time to get used to the idea."

"Mr. Willard?" Carsons came gliding into the room. "His Lordship wishes to inform you he is waiting in his study."

"Good morning, Mr. Villines." He threw his napkin on the table and stood up.

"Mr. Willard!" he called out when Havoc was at the door.

"Yes?"

"Let me be the first to welcome you to the family."

"Only let it be so, Mr. Villines."

CHAPTER
33
❧≫✕≪❧

ELIZABETH WAS IN HER ROOM WRITING A LETTER WHEN someone knocked on her door. "Come in," she called out. She put down her pen when she saw it was Nicholas. He leaned against the door frame instead of coming in. "I was writing to Jane Smithwayne," she said. "I would like to have her at the wedding. Do you think it would be all right?" His lazy smile made her breath catch in her throat.

"Anything you like. You may even invite Mr. Beaufort Latchley, so that I may have the pleasure of passionately kissing you in front of him."

"You could do it now," she said.

"An excellent idea." When he reached her, he pulled her to her feet, tipping up her chin to kiss her softly. She let herself relax into his arms. After a moment he said gruffly, "We had better get downstairs."

"What for?"

"My cousin Henry has arrived," he said.

"You don't sound happy about it."

Nicholas scowled. "He has already started drinking. It was the first thing he headed for when he arrived."

"Perhaps the trip here exhausted him," she suggested, "and he wanted only to relax."

Nicholas snorted in answer. "Will you come down to meet him?"

"Of course. Just let me finish this." She sat down to add a final sentence or two, then blotted the letter and directed it before slipping it into the pocket of her skirt.

"Give it to Carsons, he'll post it for you." Nicholas took her hand when they reached the door. "I've told Henry about us, and he wants to meet you."

"Ah, Miss Elizabeth," Lord Eversleigh said when she followed Nicholas into the drawing room.

She was surprised to see that Henry Villines was not handsome. He was tall, though not as tall as Nicholas. His hair was dark brown, like his eyes. His face was narrow with thin lips and high, hollow cheeks. He lacked the maturity that might have given his features strength. Her impression of him was not improved by the fact that he had obviously not had enough sleep during the past days. There were dark smudges under his eyes, which were slightly red, and his complexion was sallow. He did have a pleasant voice; in fact, it was his voice that made some women find him attractive. He had a rasping cough he declared he would shake in a day or two.

"Nicholas tells me you are to be married," Henry said after they were introduced. He examined her critically, just long enough and curiously enough to bring a blush to her cheeks. "Congratulations to you both."

"Thank you." She was glad to take a seat next to Nicholas.

"I'm sorry I couldn't get here sooner, Grandfather." Henry sat, sliding down on the chair and leaving his legs straight out in front of him. He grinned at Elizabeth before looking at his grandfather. "But I was detained in Bath."

"Well, you are here now," said Eversleigh. "And I am very glad of that."

"Where's Carsons with the damned brandy?" Henry made an impatient gesture.

"I told him it was too early for drink, Henry. And you will please refrain from such language while you are here. This is neither the time"— Lord Eversleigh indicated Elizabeth—"nor the place to be indelicate."

"Forgive me, will you, Miss Willard? May I call you Elizabeth?"

"Of course, Mr. Villines."

"And you shall call me Henry. You know, I've a da— A very troublesome headache. I wonder, Grandfather, if a glass of brandy shouldn't do me a world of good, just now."

"Perhaps you ought to lie down," Elizabeth

suggested. "It might improve your headache after such a long trip."

"Do you know, I think I shall do just that." Henry stood up. "Do you mind if I do?" He looked at Lord Eversleigh, who nodded his assent. "Well then. It was a pleasure to meet you, Elizabeth, and a damned shame I didn't meet you sooner. Though, come to think of it, I doubt if I could have gotten you away from Nicholas."

"Henry!"

"Sorry, Grandfather. It's this bloody headache of mine. Good afternoon."

"He's worse than I thought," said Lord Eversleigh when Henry was gone.

"Cut him off for a while," said Nicholas. "If that doesn't cure him of his bad habits, nothing will."

"I should keep him here for a month or two, until that cough clears up." He sighed, then looked at Elizabeth. "You, at least, will not disappoint both me and Nicholas?"

She smiled. "No, my lord."

Nicholas stood up. "Will you excuse us? I should like to take Elizabeth for a walk in the gardens."

They walked slowly, each watching their lengthening shadows on the ground. "I sent Chester to London last night," Nicholas said when he broke the silence. "To get this." He took something from his pocket and stopped walking. "This was my mother's." He took the necklace from its box and held it up. A single diamond suspended from the delicate chain sparkled in the fading afternoon light.

"It's beautiful, Nicholas."

"I want you to have it."

When he had fastened it around her neck, she turned to face him. "I keep thinking this is all a dream," she said. "And then I realize it is not—" She grasped one of his hands and held it so she could stroke his fingers. "I think how you have touched me, how even now I long to have you touch me, and it frightens me. I'm afraid something will happen to spoil my happiness. I wish we were married now, so nothing could take you away from me."

"Elizabeth, we were meant to be."

"Nothing is meant to be, Nicholas. Anything at all might happen. That's why we must take our happiness where we find it, and pray that we do not lose it too soon." She waited for the noise of a carriage rumbling over the courtyard flagstones to stop. "I've found my happiness, and now I'm afraid I will lose it."

"You aren't afraid of them, are you?"

She knew he meant Amelia and Mrs. Willard. "No." She looked at him. "I don't care what they think."

"Are you sure?" he asked teasingly. "I could always marry Amelia, just to make your aunt happy, you understand."

Her smile faded. "Don't joke. It might have been."

"But it isn't." He pulled her into his arms.

"This"—he stroked her cheek—"is what is. And, if you like, we can go hide in my room until supper."

"Someone will see us." She did not say it with much conviction.

"So? There's a back way. We must take our happiness where we find it, Elizabeth."

Elizabeth had just slipped into her room when Miss Lincoln came in with her freshly ironed dress. "There you are. I took the liberty of pressing this." She held up the rose gown for her approval. Elizabeth nodded. "Where have you been?" Miss Lincoln asked.

"In the garden."

"Mrs. Willard finally gave up looking for you." Miss Lincoln glanced at the dress and smiled. "Are you laced tight enough?"

"No." Elizabeth touched the necklace Nicholas had given her. "Was she very upset?"

"She thinks you're being ungrateful." Miss Lincoln began unbuttoning Elizabeth's dress and helped her to step out of it. "She's in a mood because of Amelia, I suppose."

"What do you mean?"

"She's worked herself up because Mr. Villines hasn't proposed to her yet." She yanked cruelly on the laces of the corset, and Elizabeth put a hand on the bedpost to steady herself. "This dress is such a lovely color for you, Miss Elizabeth."

"I shall die from this, I know it." She turned around when Miss Lincoln had tied the laces.

"I did not breathe a word, miss. About you and Mr. Villines, I mean," Miss Lincoln explained when Elizabeth said nothing. "All the servants know. Not that it came as any great surprise. Every time I saw him looking at you with those black eyes of his, I wondered why you didn't just faint at his feet."

"What!"

"Everyone talked about Mr. Villines and Miss Amelia, but I knew it was you he loved."

The party to celebrate the birthdays of Lord Eversleigh and Nicholas was not an elaborate one. Only the viscount's closest friends were invited. Lord and Lady Lewesfield had arrived from London just before dark and the rector, Mr. Franklin Conmarre, and his wife not long after. Henry was planted on a chair with a drink in one hand, listening with an abstracted expression to Mr. Joseph Eldon explain the perils of farming in Kent to Havoc and Mr. Villines.

When Elizabeth entered the drawing room, Nicholas was standing with Amelia and Mr. and Mrs. Conmarre. Amelia, looking radiant, was wearing the gown she and Mrs. Willard had picked up from the dressmaker in Dover that afternoon. She was watching Nicholas, and when he saw Elizabeth, Amelia followed his gaze.

"There you are!" Amelia exclaimed. "Why,

Beth, I do think we were beginning to despair of your ever coming down. Do come here. Mr. Conmarre, Mrs. Conmarre, this is my cousin, Miss Elizabeth Willard."

"A pleasure, Miss Willard," said Mr. Conmarre.

"Good evening," Elizabeth said.

"We thought perhaps you had disappeared. Amelia put a hand on Nicholas's arm. "Did we not?" she asked him. "Do tell us, what were you reading this time, Beth?"

"Actually, Elizabeth was keeping me amused most of the afternoon," Nicholas said. "Witchford Runs was rather dull without two of its guests."

"How very kind of you." Amelia smiled limply then glanced to where Henry was seated. "Nicholas, is that your cousin?"

Nicholas looked at Henry. "Yes, it is."

"Will you think me too forward if I ask you to introduce me now?"

"Not at all. If you will excuse us, Mr. Conmarre, Mrs. Conmarre."

Elizabeth was left to hear to Mr. Conmarre's description of his efforts to remodel the rectory. She listened politely but kept one eye on Nicholas and Amelia.

"Ah, Miss Amelia!" said Russell Villines. He frowned at Henry, who remained seated.

"Good evening, sir."

"I'd like you to meet my nephew, the Honorable Henry Villines. You were not here when he arrived his afternoon."

Henry finished his appraisal of Amelia, then rose at last. "I see the Miss Willards are equally beautiful." He bent over Amelia's hand.

"Why, thank you, Mr. Villines. I'm sure Beth will be pleased when I repeat the compliment to her."

"Beth?" He looked puzzled.

"She means Elizabeth, Henry," Nicholas said.

"Well, you must be very happy for her, Miss Willard."

It was Amelia's turn to look puzzled. "Happy for her?"

"Henry means you must be happy that Elizabeth is feeling better now."

"I didn't know she was unwell, Nicholas," Henry cried with a look of alarm. "She looked fine this afternoon. In the bloody bloom of health. I would never have guessed she was feeling unwell."

"Elizabeth was recovered by the time you were introduced."

"Well, thank God for that. Tell me, Miss Willard, where have you been hiding yourself? Why didn't you come to meet me this afternoon?"

"I've not been hiding anywhere, Mr. Villines. My mother and I went to Dover for the day."

"Just got back from Bath myself. The trip gave me a blasted awful headache. So, I suppose you might as well have been hiding from me, eh?"

"Why, Nicholas, where are you going?" Amelia tapped his chest with her fan when he started to leave. "You've been neglecting me most shamefully. I do hope Mr. Henry Villines is not as neglectful as you."

"I should say it was the other way round, Amelia. You were the one who left Witchford Runs today."

Amelia giggled and was about to answer when supper was announced. She turned to extend an arm to Nicholas.

"Perhaps Henry will do you the honor, Amelia."

"I'd be delighted."

Elizabeth was chagrined when Amelia was seated across from her. In all truthfulness, she had been hoping to be nowhere near either her aunt or her cousin. She dreaded what was to come. Fortunately, for the time being there were both Henry and Nicholas to keep Amelia entertained. Henry's interest in Amelia was all the reason she needed to sparkle, and in truth, at first he was rather entertaining. But he drank more than he ate, and before long the sound of his too loud laughter was heard often in the room.

Just as dessert was being served, Henry leaned over to Amelia. "Do you know, Miss 'melia," he said in a loud whisper, "I think you are almost as pretty as your cousin. I don't know how Nicholas made up his mind."

"Indeed, Mr. Villines?" Amelia leaned away from him and found herself looking at Elizabeth. She seized on the opportunity to turn away from Henry's increasingly unwelcome attentions. Her blue eyes settled on the diamond hanging from Elizabeth's neck. "Tell me, Beth, where did you get that lovely necklace?"

"Nicholas gave it to me."

"Nicholas?" She turned to look at Nicholas. "How very kind!"

Henry chuckled. "I see Nicholas and I have something in common."

"And what is that, Mr. Villines?" Amelia asked.

"Pray tell," put in Mrs. Conmarre, who had been listening avidly all the while.

"Henry, please remember yourself," Nicholas said in a low voice.

"I also give jewels to women afterward." He spoke loudly enough for everyone to hear.

"I'm afraid I don't understand, Mr. Villines," Amelia said.

"Henry!" Nicholas said.

"Oh, forgive me, Nicholas. Have I been indiscreet?"

"That will do, Henry," said Lord Eversleigh. He nodded to Carsons, and in a few moments the steward was ushering in several footmen who began to set up buckets of ice and champagne. The viscount rose and tapped his empty glass with a spoon. The conversation died as attention was fixed on him.

"Tonight," he began, "I have a very special announcement to make. One to which I believe my grandson Henry was just alluding. I have raided my wine cellar in honor of it, as you are about to see. It is a special occasion when Nicholas and I celebrate our birthdays, but tonight is even more special still." He waited until the last of the champagne glasses were filled. "In the twenty-seven years since Nicholas was born, he has given me many reasons to be proud. Now, I have reason to be prouder still. It is my great joy to announce the engagement of my grandson Nicholas to Miss Elizabeth Willard.

"I hope you will join me in this toast to their happiness." He had to raise his voice slightly to be heard over the murmurs of approval. "I am an old man . . ." He waited until everyone had sipped their champagne. "And I have long encouraged my grandson to marry so I may one day brag of my great-grandsons. When he informed me of his choice, I insisted that the wedding take place in the Whitchford Runs chapel, this December the thirty-first. It is my pleasure to invite you all to the wedding." He raised his glass again. There was silence while the guests followed suit, and then Mr. Villines stood and raised his glass.

"Like my father, it was with joy that I learned the attachment between Nicholas and Miss

Elizabeth Willard has finally been made public. Nicholas could not have chosen a better woman, and I salute him for his taste." He paused. "Likewise, I salute Elizabeth for hers." When the laughter subsided, he continued. "I hope you will all join me in welcoming her to this family."

When the ladies left the gentlemen at the table, Elizabeth was surrounded. "Why, Beth, dear," Mrs. Willard whispered in her ear, "this is so sudden, it quite takes my breath away. You might at least have told me the two of you were in love." She kissed her niece on the cheek. "The thirty-first! Why, there will hardly be time to get you a wedding gown."

"May I see the necklace?" Amelia asked. "She tells me Nicholas gave it to her, Mother." She reached for it. "Why, it's simply enormous."

"He told me it belonged to his mother."

"It ought to have been mine." She spoke in a voice low enough not to be overheard.

"Nicholas was never in love with you."

"After what Henry Villines said, I expect the truth is that he has to marry you. There's no other reason for it. Why, you aren't even pretty, Beth Willard."

Once Amelia would have silenced her with such a comment. No longer. She lifted her chin.

"Nicholas thinks I am, and that's all that matters to me. Now, excuse me, Amelia." Elizabeth walked away.

A few minutes later the gentlemen joined the women, and Henry continued his pursuit of Amelia as soon as he had a drink in his hand.

"Why, Nicholas," said Mrs. Willard when he approached them. "I was just telling Elizabeth how amazed we are at the news."

"We saw no reason to disappoint my grandfather once he expressed his wish for an early marriage." Nicholas took Elizabeth's hand. "I regret to say that I nearly lost her once. I won't take any chances now that she's agreed to marry me." He raised her hand to his lips.

"When were you in danger of losing her?" Mrs. Conmarre asked.

"I nearly lost her to my best friend."

"This sounds promising," Mrs. Conmarre said. "Please, do tell us. I adore a romantic tale."

"I have known Elizabeth since we were children. She has been a confidante and a dear friend in all that time. When she came to London this year, I had not seen her for nearly four years, though we wrote to each other constantly during that time."

"And when you saw her after all those years, you realized you were in love with her?"

"I believe I did. I did not admit I was in love until my best friend told me he had taken my advice and asked Elizabeth to marry him. That was just before I arrived at Witchford Runs, Mrs. Conmarre, and if my grandfather had not seen my state and told me to invite the Willards here, I would have returned to London the very same day."

"And you, Miss Elizabeth, would you have married Mr. Villines's best friend?"

"I think I might have."

"But," Nicholas interposed, "only to escape marriage to someone else. I soon learned that I was not the only man in love with Elizabeth Willard. You can understand why I want her safely married to me. Nothing will suit me better than to have these other gentlemen love her in vain."

CHAPTER
34

❋❯❮❋

"We must examine our evidence, Mr. Wells, logically and objectively." Percy stared at his outspread fingers on the table.

"What evidence? There isn't any." Mr. Wells scowled at Percy. "Sir, I don't see how your list making is doing any good at all. We're no closer to catching the man now than we were six months ago."

"On the contrary."

"Mr. Johns, it's been a month since Lady Lewesfield's emeralds were stolen, and we've still no idea who did it."

"But we do know how it was done. And how the thing was accomplished must necessarily give us a clue as to who might have accomplished it."

"Well then, who was it? Let's arrest the man and have done with it."

"If we move with haste, Mr. Wells, we will

only come to regret it. As I said, we must examine our evidence."

"And as I said, sir, what evidence?"

Percy sighed. "Very well, the evidence: we know the emeralds haven't been fenced in London. Assuming for the moment that he has not left the country"—he glanced at one of the lists before him—"they are, therefore, still in his possession."

"And what if he has left the country?"

Percy smiled. "I am confident he has not. No, he still has them. He is waiting us out."

Wells shrugged. "I don't see how this speculation tells us anything we did not know before."

"That is where you are mistaken. We know, Mr. Wells, a great deal more than it seems."

"Such as?"

"Such as, he is strong enough to subdue a man as tall as Arthur Brunswick. Mr. Brunswick is nearly six feet tall himself, you know. From my examination of the lump on the back of Mr. Brunswick's head, our thief must be over six feet, or else has abnormally long arms, a deformity that would not go unnoticed in London Society. Brunswick's impression was that of height and dark hair. Hair color may, of course, be easily disguised, but height is not so easy to hide. And that, Mr. Wells"—he held up one hand—"is as close to a description as we've ever been. Until now, that is." Percy took a sip of his ale. He took pleasure in saving critical information for the last. Mr. Wells was practically pop-eyed with excitement.

"What do you mean, 'until now'?" Mr. Wells leaned forward.

"Today, I learned that someone may actually have seen our thief at Lord Lewesfield's. Miss Lucy Benford-Smith saw a woman leaving the north wing of the house just after midnight."

"The thief is a woman?"

Percy shook his head disapprovingly. "Surely not, Mr. Wells."

"Then you think this woman, whoever she is, may have seen something?"

Percy nodded. "It took Brunswick somewhat longer than a quarter of an hour to free himself—from approximately eighteen or nineteen minutes before the hour until midnight. By the time he was free, the north wing was empty of persons, male or female. The young woman seen by Miss Benford-Smith could only have gained entrance to that part of the house after Mr. Brunswick was unable to perform his duties, and we know she left before he had escaped his bonds. Indeed, Mr. Wells, she may well have seen the thief, though most likely without knowing the significance of what she saw."

"And whom do you think she saw, sir?"

Percy smiled. "If I am correct in my surmise, Mr. Wells, he is no stranger to her. No doubt she thought nothing of seeing him."

"You know who it is?"

"I've known his identity for some time. And Miss Elizabeth Willard will provide me with the proof I need."

"Miss Elizabeth Willard?" Mr. Wells seemed to go limp in his chair. "Well. That's that, then. It will be some time before you can talk to her, and by then the thief will have disposed of the jewels."

"Why do you say that?" Percy looked alarmed.

"Miss Elizabeth Willard was married to Mr. Nicholas Villines not two days ago. They're on a tour of Europe even as we speak."

"Nicholas Villines?" Percy set down his ale with a thump. He was normally a taciturn man, but even Alfred Wells could see the news had astonished him. "Mr. Wells," Percy said, "as I have often said, there is no such thing as a coincidence."

CHAPTER
35
❧❯❈❮❧

ELIZABETH WAS JUST ABOUT TO GET OUT OF HER BATH when Nicholas came in. Miss Lincoln blushed a deep red when he did not leave immediately but instead shrugged off his coat and wandered over to the dresser, where he sat down.

"You may go, Miss Lincoln," Elizabeth said.

Nicholas waited until she had shut the door after herself, then he grinned and stood up. "You seem to have been abandoned. Do you need any help?" he asked.

"You might soap my back."

"With pleasure." He unfastened his shirt-sleeves and rolled them up to his elbows before bending down to take the soap from her out-stretched hand.

As always, Elizabeth felt a shiver of pleasure when Nicholas touched her. He dutifully began to wash her back, but eventually his hands began to move a little more slowly, sliding up and over her shoulders, then down to capture her wet breasts. She leaned her head against his shoulder and reached up to pull his mouth to hers. He nuzzled the side of her neck when she finally released him.

"Do you still love me, Elizabeth?" he whispered in her ear.

"I might," she said.

"You might!" He started to rinse the last of the soap from her. "What can I do to make you sure?"

"Hand me that towel," she said.

He held it up while she stepped out of the tub, then wrapped it around her. "Well?" he prompted.

"Since Miss Lincoln has gone, you'll have to take her place." Elizabeth stood still while he carefully and gently toweled her off.

"What else?" he asked when he was done.

"This." She reached around him for the cream she used. After removing the top, she handed him the bottle.

"And where am I to apply this?" he asked.

"Hmm?" she said. The moment his hands touched her, she shivered. He knew just how to touch her, where to be gentle, where to be firm. His fingers slipped over her, lingering over her waist and stomach before moving down to probe her. She clung to him, pressing herself against him.

"Do you remember now if you love me?" he asked huskily. He reached behind him to turn the dresser chair, then sat down, pulling her with him.

"I seem to remember that I do," she said. He was fumbling with the buttons of his trousers, and while she leaned to kiss him, she pushed his hand away to unfasten the buttons herself. His mouth under hers was hungry, and when her fingers found him, he held the back of her neck to bring her closer. She shifted, and when he was inside her, he slowly moved his fingers down her back, finally sliding his hands around her hips to hold her.

"How do you like Paris?" Nicholas murmured sometime later.

"Very much," she answered lazily. She stood and stretched, not taking her eyes off him. "What would Chester say if he saw the state of your clothes?" she admonished.

"He would think my wife is as wanton as they come." He rearranged his trousers, then rose. "Shall we go out for dinner?"

She nodded. "If you will help me dress."

"Well, if you must get dressed . . ." He watched her walk to the commode and pull out her underthings, taking them dutifully when she held them out. "Would you be too disappointed if we went back to London sooner than we planned?" He asked as he was tying the laces of her corset.

"Of course." She turned to face him. "Why do you ask?"

"I've had a letter from Grandfather. He wants me to try to make Henry into a decent gentleman. He can ask that of me now I'm a respectable married man."

"Must you begin right away?"

"It appears that Henry has managed to insult your cousin. Things had got to such a pass that your uncle felt it would be for the best if they left Witchford Runs before Henry mortally offended them all. Two of his friends arrived not long after your family left, and Grandfather says Henry's done nothing but drink since they arrived. He threw them all out, and now he wants me to go to London and keep an eye on Henry."

"Is it that serious?"

"Apparently so. He also wants me to talk him into seeing a specialist in London. That cough he had is only getting worse."

"Then we had better go."

"Next week."

"Should we wait?"

"I don't see why we should completely disrupt our travels just because my cousin is a sot."

"He's not well, Nicholas."

He sighed. "I know. But I'd rather not go back to England just now."

"We can always come back."

"I suppose so."

"Your grandfather's concern is reason enough."

"It's just that I would rather have you to myself, and when we get back to London, there'll be all manner of things coming between us."

"Nonsense, Nicholas. We ought to leave immediately."

He sighed. "Perhaps you're right."

CHAPTER
36
❋

"UNCLE HAVOC!" ELIZABETH THREW HER ARMS around him. "I've missed you," she said.

Havoc returned the hug. "I've missed you, too." He held her hand and looked at her. "Are you happy?" he asked softly.

"Yes, Uncle, I am." It seemed strange to be a visitor at Tavistock Square, and for a moment Elizabeth was homesick. She and Nicholas had only arrived from Paris the day before, and Cambridge Terrace simply wasn't home yet; every inch of it bore the stamp of Nicholas.

"Well! My dear Elizabeth!" Mrs. Willard held out her hands. "Come here and let me look at you."

"Good afternoon, Aunt Mary."

"Where is your husband?" Mrs. Willard smiled as though she had said something humorous.

"Nicholas had business to attend to this afternoon. Lord Eversleigh wanted him to check on Henry and get him to visit a doctor. I wanted so much to see you all again. I could not wait until he was free to come with me."

"A great deal happened while you were gone," Mrs. Willard said. "I don't imagine you've heard about Jane Smithwayne?"

"Why, Beth!" Amelia's entrance interrupted Mrs. Willard. "You're back terribly early. Did Paris not agree with you?"

"Oh, indeed it did, Amelia. But Nicholas had business that brought him back sooner than either of us expected."

"What a pity. Only a two-month tour of Europe. Imagine that." Amelia turned to her mother. "Have you told her yet?"

"Told me what?" Elizabeth inquired.

"Why, only that Mr. Latchley and I are engaged to be married."

"Engaged? Well! You must be very happy, Amelia."

"I am." She held out a hand to display a large diamond. "He gave this to me. Isn't it simply enormous? We plan a five-month tour of Europe, at least, so you will have to tell me what places to see."

"It's very beautiful," Elizabeth said after she had dutifully examined the ring. "Now, what were you going to tell me about Jane?" she asked her aunt.

"Only that she and Mr. Rutherford are practically engaged."

Elizabeth smiled broadly. "Jane and Ripton? Why, that's wonderful news."

Amelia sat down. "Quite a lot happened while you were gone," she said, dismissing the subject of Jane with a wave of her hand.

"Oh?"

"The police have been questioning simply everyone about the Mayfair Thief. They even asked us questions again."

"Why?"

"They wanted to know if we'd seen anything unusual at Lord Lewesfield's ball. And I said, other than one or two gentlemen who'd had too much champagne, I saw nothing unusual at all. Do you know, they even questioned Beaufort."

"Mr. Johns was quite anxious to talk with you, Elizabeth," Mrs. Willard put in.

"Was he?"

"Yes, so you mustn't be surprised if he is one of the first to call on you."

"Enough about Mr. Johns and this thief nonsense." Havoc stood up. "Something else happened while you were away, Elizabeth."

"What is that, Uncle Havoc?"

"Come with me, and I'll show you."

Nicholas stood up when he heard Mr. Baker walking down the hall to the front door. He went to the sitting room door in time to see Elizabeth hand something to Mr. Baker.

"Will you take this upstairs to our room?"

she said. "Put it on the table by the window, would you please?"

"Yes, ma'am." Mr. Baker cleared his throat. "Mr. Villines is in the sitting room, madam. He would like you to join them as soon as you can."

"Oh? Who is he with?"

"A Mr. Percy Johns." Mr. Baker paused. "Of the Metropolitan Police."

"Thank you, Baker," she said slowly.

Nicholas kissed Elizabeth on the cheek when she came in. "Here she is at last," he said to Mr. Johns, who was standing before the window, hands clasped behind his back, staring intently at the view of Regent's Park.

"Good afternoon, Mr. Johns," she said.

He turned abruptly at her greeting. She sat on a chair before the table and indicated he should do the same. Johns inclined his head but did not sit down. "I am very sorry to disturb you and your husband, Mrs. Villines, but I need to take a moment of your time."

"Of course."

Nicholas smiled encouragingly when she gave him a concerned look. "He wants to show you some letters, that's all, Elizabeth."

Johns looked apologetic. "I'm afraid police investigations are tedious for everyone involved." He took two sheets of paper from his pocket and unfolded them carefully. "Your husband has already told me he does not recognize the hand, but—" he shrugged "—I shouldn't like to be accused of not being thorough." When he had given them to her, he took a seat across from her then said, "Have you any comment to make on them, Mrs. Villines?"

She looked at Johns when she had finished reading. "Both of them seem to have been written by a philanthropist."

"Do they suggest anything to you?"

"They suggest there is at least one person in London who helps those less fortunate than himself." She let go of the letter she held, letting it fall to the table, then glanced at Nicholas. "I admire and respect whoever wrote these."

"You do not recognize them as being in your husband's hand?" The question was sharp.

Her eyes widened. "No. I'm sure if Nicholas were responsible for them, he would own up to it. Why don't you ask him for a writing sample, if you are so eager to establish him as the author."

"He already has, Elizabeth," Nicholas replied. "But he seems dissatisfied with the result."

She nudged the letters with one finger. "Is it important to prove to you Nicholas did not write these?"

"Is it possible to do so?" Johns asked.

"I've been corresponding with him since I was a girl, and I know his writing like my own. I'd be happy to show you one of his letters to me if you would care to see one."

"Very much so."

Alone in the sitting room, neither man spoke until Elizabeth returned and handed a letter to Mr. Johns. He placed it on the table next to the two he'd brought. The writing was in no way similar.

"Are you satisfied now, Mr. Johns?" Nicholas asked when the policeman had compared Elizabeth's letter with the ones he had brought.

Johns merely grunted in response. He turned away from the table without picking up the letters, though he remained seated. "No doubt you know about the theft of Lady Lewesfield's emeralds," he said to Elizabeth.

"The papers were full of the story. I understand they have not yet been recovered."

"Unfortunately, that is so." He tapped his knee with a forefinger. "Would you mind if I ask you a few questions about the evening of Lord Lewesfield's ball?"

"No." She sat down again and he swung around on the chair to face her.

"Do you recall our meeting that night?" Johns did not give her a chance to reply. "I cannot seem to forget it. You wore a most spectacular gown, Mrs. Villines." He gave Nicholas a sideways glance. "What struck me was how little jewelry you wore compared to the other ladies."

Elizabeth smiled wryly. "I did not then own much, Mr. Johns."

"You were wearing a necklace with a gold ring on it."

"Mr. Johns," Nicholas said abruptly, made apprehensive by the direction his questions had taken. "I fail to see the relevance—"

"It's all right, Nicholas, I don't mind." She folded her hands in her lap. "I'm flattered that you remember me so well, Mr. Johns. You are correct. The ring is my mother's wedding band."

"When I saw you later in the evening, Mrs. Villines, you were not wearing the necklace." He fell silent, waiting for Elizabeth to respond. "Are you reluctant to tell me how you lost it?" he prompted, with another quick glance at Nicholas.

Elizabeth's cool response was a surprise. "What possible difference could it make, Mr. Johns?"

"It might make all the difference in the world, Mrs. Villines." He leaned forward. "Did you see anything unusual that night?"

"What do you mean by unusual?" She shrugged to indicate she did not think she had.

"Anything at all." He watched her unblinkingly.

"I saw nothing. Or, rather, I saw nothing that struck me as unusual."

"Mrs. Villines, I believe you did see something."

Nicholas did not like the almost predatory expression on Johns's face. He started to interrupt, but Johns silenced him with a sharp gesture.

"I can't imagine what you mean, Mr. Johns."

"I mean, you were seen leaving a hallway which you should not have been able to enter under normal circumstances. *I* call that unusual."

Her eyes narrowed. "What are you suggesting?"

"It was at . . ." He paused to take a notebook from his coat pocket. After flipping through it, he stopped, perused the page, and then looked up. "Around midnight, Mrs. Villines. Most of the guests were either dancing or still partaking of the meal provided by His Lordship. You, however, were doing neither." He stabbed at the page with his index finger. "You were just leaving a portion of the house, the north wing, to be precise, that was forbidden to the guests. I am curious about why you were there, Mrs. Villines, and I am curious about what you may have seen."

Nicholas spoke up. "Mr. Johns, she has already told you she saw nothing."

He turned to Nicholas. "Nevertheless, I would like to hear your wife's answer."

"My husband is correct, I saw nothing." She lifted her hands, palm upward. "Nothing worth remarking, at any rate, or I should be able to tell you something more to your satisfaction."

"Forgive me for persisting, Mrs. Villines. But it is important for me to know why you were there."

Her expression hardened. "I was upset, and I wanted to be alone."

"About what were you upset?"

"Something which I consider to be of an exceedingly personal nature." She looked down at her lap.

"Such as?"

"Is it necessary for you to know?"

"The subject fascinates me, Mrs. Villines." His voice was suddenly kind, cajoling even. "There were men posted to keep the guests from that part of the house."

"Very well. I was upset because my cousin, Miss Amelia Willard, had led me to believe that Nicholas, my husband, was in love with her. I believed her lies. I thought he was going to marry her, in spite of—" She bit her lip and looked at Johns from under her eyelashes.

"In spite of what, Mrs. Villines?"

"Mr. Johns, I was, I am, deeply attached to my husband, and that night, I let him kiss me." Johns frowned. "Rather passionately, I'm afraid. Later, Amelia let me think he had also kissed her. He hadn't, not really, but how was I to know? I wanted to be alone after what Amelia told me, and to be honest, I hardly knew where I was going."

"And where did you go?"

She looked directly into John's eyes. "According to you, I went to the north wing of the house. Wherever it was, I stayed in the hallway." Nicholas suppressed a start at the unexpected statement. "It would have been rather forward of me to go into one of the earl's private rooms."

Nicholas took a seat near Elizabeth, leaning one arm along the top rail of the chair and rubbing a finger nervously against the smooth wood. It was not like her to dissemble this way. He studied her, wondering.

"I sat on a small settee at the end of the hall, quite alone and quite undisturbed," she continued, "until I was certain I could face Nicholas and Amelia if I saw them."

"How long were you there?"

"I don't know. It seemed like a long time, more than that I cannot tell you."

"And you saw no one? It is vital that I know, Mrs. Villines."

"No one." She shook her head. "Mr. Johns . . ." She pressed her hands flat on the table. "The last thing I wanted was to see anyone. If, as you say, that wing was restricted, then I can only respond such was not the case when I was there. Whoever was guarding the hallway was not doing his job."

"Indeed, he was at the moment unable to do so, seeing as how someone had garroted him." Johns smiled at Elizabeth's horrified reaction. "Garroting, when skillfully done, is a quiet and efficient method of rendering a man unconscious. Among certain elements in London, it is considered an art. When performed clumsily, or with the intention of causing death, the result can be an unpleasant thing to see."

Elizabeth became pale. "Do you mean to say someone was killed?"

"Fortunately, no. Whoever it was, was skillful. My man was quickly made insensible. He was also skillfully bound. It took him close to—"he glanced at his notebook"—twenty minutes to free himself. During those twenty-some minutes, almost anyone might have had access to that part of the house. You, Mrs. Villines, are one person known positively to have been there."

"Surely you don't think I stole Lady Lewesfield's necklace?"

"No." He smiled. "You are not tall enough to have conveniently garroted my officer. And, if you will forgive an indelicacy, my man would have noticed being in close contact with a woman while he was being attacked. For that reason, and others not important at the moment, I have concluded it was a man who assaulted my officer." He put away his notebook.

She leaned back, color slowly returning to her cheeks. "Have you finished asking me questions, Mr. Johns?"

"I have just a few more, if you don't mind."

"Of course not."

"What did you do when you left the hall?"

"I returned to the ballroom."

"Do you recall what time this was?"

She thought about it. "Well, on my way

back, I recall hearing a clock chiming midnight, which surprised me because I thought it was much later. I knew that Nicholas had asked Amelia for a dance after supper, and I was hoping to avoid seeing them together." She smiled ruefully.

Johns reached for his letters and folded them. "Are you quite sure you saw no one? Think before you answer. Perhaps you saw someone you know?" He replaced them in his pocket.

"I saw no one," she said apologetically.

"You are sure you did not see your husband, for example?"

"I most certainly did see Nicholas. I shall never forget it."

Johns did not take his eyes off Nicholas. "Where was he when you saw him?" A triumphant smile was on his lips.

"He was about to claim his dance with Amelia."

The policeman scowled. "You have no doubt of this?"

"None at all." Elizabeth was indignant. "You seem astonished, Mr. Johns," she said. "I'm sure if you ask my cousin, Amelia, she'll confirm that she and Nicholas danced after supper."

"I have," he said. "She did indeed tell me much the same thing, but according to her it was later than midnight."

She smiled. "Well, of course it was. I told you I saw him about to claim his dance. He was

369

waiting for Amelia to finish dancing with the partner she had."

"You are certain of the time?"

"Yes." She drew her eyebrows together. "Mr. Johns, I don't understand why you keep asking me the same questions. Do you hope to get a different answer if only you ask it often enough?"

"Mrs. Villines, please." He lifted his hands as if to appease her anger. "I am satisfied with your explanation for being in the restricted part of the house." He scowled once more, then slowly let out a breath. "Is it not possible," he suggested in a calmer tone, "that your memory is merely. . . incomplete? There's no harm in admitting that. Perhaps you did go into one of the rooms, Mrs. Villines. Under the circumstances, I don't see how one could find fault with your wanting to be alone."

"I admit I was distraught."

"Is it not possible you went into one of the rooms and there were relieved of your necklace by the Mayfair Thief?"

Elizabeth burst into laughter. "Do you really think I could forget such a thing? I assure you I would have been frightened out of my mind if something like that had happened, and I would not be likely to forget it." Her smile faded. "I will tell you once more. I did not go into any of the private rooms and I did not see anyone while I was in the hallway."

Johns leapt to his feet. "How did you lose

your necklace, Mrs. Villines, can you tell me that?"

Elizabeth's composure was impressive. "I'm afraid not."

"Why is that?" he demanded.

"Because I did not lose it. The chain broke, and I took it off."

"Then you will be able to show it to me, won't you?"

"Yes."

"You needn't do any such thing, Elizabeth," Nicholas interjected. "Mr. Johns, your questions are becoming tiresome and harassing. I won't have you badgering my wife in this fashion."

"Please, both of you." Elizabeth rose and crossed the room to ring for Mr. Baker, telling him, when he arrived, to bring her jewelry box to the sitting room.

There was a moment of silence during which Nicholas stared at her, wondering what in God's name she meant to accomplish. She knew the truth, he realized. His life, their life together, was in her hands.

Johns drew himself up when he saw Nicholas suddenly lean back and smile. "Your wife has not exonerated you by any means, Mr. Villines."

"Exonerated?" Elizabeth repeated. "Do you mean to say you still suspect Nicholas of being the Mayfair Thief?"

"Mrs. Villines, it is my job to ask questions,

371

however unpleasant their implications may be."

"I know my husband, and I assure you he is not the Mayfair Thief. I would know it if he were. Why should Nicholas steal anything at all? There were scores of people at Lord Lewesfield's ball, Mr. Johns, any one of whom probably had more reason than Nicholas to steal the silver, let alone Lady Lewesfield's emeralds. It's not as though he's in need of money, for he has plenty of it, as I'm sure his banker will attest. And if he were in debt, his uncle or his grandfather the viscount would not hesitate to pay it off."

"I do not believe the emeralds were stolen simply for their value in pounds."

"Why else would someone take such a risk?"

Johns shrugged. "For the challenge. To taunt the police, perhaps."

"That is quite enough," Nicholas said heatedly. "I won't have you trying to poison my wife against me."

Mr. Baker's return with the jewelry box silenced both men. Nicholas put a hand on Elizabeth's arm when she started to open it. "Don't, Elizabeth."

"Why not, Mr. Villines?" Johns asked.

"Because it isn't necessary." He returned Johns's gaze. "I'm not the Mayfair Thief, but if I were, the necklace, whether in there or not, proves nothing."

"I think not, Mr. Villines. Its absence will

prove your wife has told me a falsehood. In that case, one must wonder why she would lie." He looked at Elizabeth, a quizzical expression coming over his face. "Is it possible you know?" he asked incredulously. Johns reached across the table and pulled the box toward him.

Elizabeth prevented Nicholas from taking the box from Johns. "The time for secrets is past," she said softly.

Fascinated, he watched the detective open the jewelry box and begin searching the contents. Johns made an involuntary exclamation, then held up a delicate chain with a plain gold band suspended from it. "Did you not say this was broken, Mrs. Villines?"

"The chain is new. The ring, however, is not. If you look, you will see it is engraved with my mother's name."

He placed the necklace on the table, and sat silently, his gaze moving from Nicholas, to Elizabeth, to the necklace. Lifting his hands in a gesture that might have been one of defeat, he sighed, then rose. "I bid you good day, Mr. Villines, Mrs. Villines."

"Baker will see you out," Elizabeth said.

Nicholas said nothing until Elizabeth had put the necklace back. "I thought I'd lost it." He stepped toward her.

"I found it that night at Witchford Runs." She avoided his embrace, instead sitting down on the sofa and staring at him.

"What is it?" he asked, suddenly fearful because of what he saw in her gray eyes.

She spoke in a subdued voice. "I've wondered since then what other things you haven't told me."

"What do you mean, Elizabeth?"

"Have you lied about loving me?" She glanced down. "Did you marry me to keep me from telling what I know about the ball?"

"I married you because I love you, you must know that."

Her hands clutched the edges of the sofa. "How am I to be sure?" she asked bitterly.

He was momentarily at a loss. "Because I told you so at the ball," he said. "In Lady Lewesfield's room."

"So you did."

"And a hundred times since then." He went to her, pulling her up and into his arms. "You are my life. I should have trusted you with it long before this." He put his hands on either side of her face, staring into her eyes. "You were right, Elizabeth, there should be no secrets between us. But I was afraid you would leave me if you knew."

"Never, Nicholas."

"Can you forgive me for being such a fool?"

"There is nothing to forgive," she murmured. She melted against him. After a long while, she pushed him gently away. "Nicholas, there's something I must know."

"What is it?"

"Who wrote the letters, if it wasn't you?"

He smiled a little. "Chester." He pulled her into his arms again.

She put her hands on his chest. "What of the emeralds?"

"Disposed of long ago."

"And the Mayfair Thief?" she asked, resisting his embrace. "What's to become of him?"

"There's no such person anymore, Elizabeth. He's ceased to exist."

"Are you sure?"

He stroked her cheek with the back of his hand. "Very."

"Then I think my life must be perfect." She smiled her most bewitching smile. "Come with me, Nicholas." She led him to their bedroom, closing the door gently after her. "I went to Tavistock Square this afternoon, and brought this back." She pointed to the table where *vanda cerulea* sat, one blue flower arching slightly toward the window.

Carolyn Jewel earned a degree in political science from the University of California at Berkeley where she currently resides. She is the author of one previous novel, *Passion's Song*.